D0096959

After completing a psychology degree, Alice Hunter became an interventions facilitator in a prison. There, she was part of a team offering rehabilitation programmes to men serving sentences for a wide range of offences, often working with prisoners who'd committed serious violent crimes. Previously, Alice had been a nurse, working in the NHS. She now puts her experiences to good use in fiction. *The Serial Killer's Wife* draws heavily on her knowledge of psychology and the criminal mind.

THE
SERIAL KILLER'S WIFE

ALICE HUNTER

avon.

Published by AVON
A division of HarperCollins*Publishers* Ltd
1 London Bridge Street
London SE1 9GF

www.harpercollins.co.uk

HarperCollins*Publishers*
1st Floor, Watermarque Building, Ringsend Road
Dublin 4, Ireland

A Paperback Original 2021

7

First published in Great Britain by HarperCollins*Publishers* 2021

ISBN: 978-0-00-841407-8

Typeset in Sabon LT Std by Palimpsest Book Production Limited, Falkirk, Stirlingshire
Printed and Bound in the UK using 100% Renewable Electricity at CPI Group (UK) Ltd

MIX
Paper from
responsible sources
FSC **FSC™ C007454**
www.fsc.org

For Katie Loughnane
an inspiring editor and friend, thank you.

Chapter 1

BETH

Now

I'm half relieved, half annoyed when I hear the insistent knocking on the front door. Poppy has only just settled after the third reading of *The Wonky Donkey*. I've promised her repeatedly that Daddy will definitely be home to give her a goodnight kiss. It's gone eight, two hours past her usual bedtime.

'Daddy's here,' she says, her aquamarine eyes springing back open, all sleepiness evaporating.

'And it seems he can't be bothered to use his key,' I sigh, rising up from the Disney Princess bed. 'You close your eyes again, my Poppy poppet, and I'll send him up in a minute.' I run my index finger from the bridge of her tiny button nose to the tip.

I dash down the stairs, unconsciously bobbing under the low oak beam, ready to fling the door open and shout at Tom for his lateness and lack of consideration. But at the same time, I want to throw my arms around him: he's never late back from work and I've been winding myself up thinking something bad must've happened to him. I've tried convincing myself his train was delayed, or he's been caught up in traffic on the way back from Banbury station – having to commute from Lower Tew to central London and back every day isn't the quickest of journeys – but if that'd been the case, he'd have called to let me know he was running late. He wouldn't let his little Poppy down – he loves hearing her delighted squeals when he does the daft voices. It's something I clearly haven't mastered, given the number of times she made me 'try again' to get it right.

I unlock the solid wooden door and take a steadying breath. There's no need for me to be mad at him. He's late, that's all. Doesn't matter if he's woken Poppy up; he'll happily settle her while I reheat his dinner. *Don't shout at him.*

I swing the door open. 'Why haven't you got your key?' The scolding words are out of my mouth before I even realise.

It's not Tom.

'Oh, erm . . . sorry, I was expecting . . .' My sentence trails off. My heart tumbles in my chest.

'Good evening. Mrs Hardcastle, is it?' one of the two men says. They stand shoulder-to-shoulder at my small doorway, obscuring the view outside. I can't see the vehicle they've arrived in but given their smart, suited appearance and the fact they know my name, I instinctively know they're police.

'Y–yes,' I stutter.

My limbs tremble. I was right. Tom's had an accident.

I grasp hold of the edge of the door frame, closing my eyes tight. My breaths are coming fast and shallow as I wait for the inevitable.

'We need to speak with Mr Thomas Hardcastle, please.' The man, who looks to be in his early fifties, with hair greying at the temples and thinning on the top, opens a leather wallet and flashes a badge at me. 'I'm Detective Inspector Manning from the Metropolitan Police and this is a colleague from Thames Valley, Detective Sergeant Walters.'

His words fly over my head as relief floods through me. If they're asking to see him, they're not here to tell me he's been killed.

'He's not here. He's late back from work. I thought you were him, actually,' I say, my voice now more controlled. 'What's it in connection with?' I frown, suddenly aware DI Manning is encroaching on the threshold of my cottage. The other detective, whose name I've already forgotten, has stepped back and is now strolling around my front garden.

Manning doesn't respond.

'Can *I* help?' Irritation is creeping in now. What do they want?

'We'll come in and wait,' he says. He turns to the detective, who's now back by his side. 'Walters – check the back first,' he demands, in his gruff voice. I log his name in my memory this time. I don't feel I have a choice about letting them in to wait, despite my apprehension at allowing two men inside my home at this hour when I'm on my own. As if sensing my unease, DI Manning asks if I want to call the station to confirm they're official. I give a nervous laugh, say it's fine, and open the door wider.

I hear Poppy calling from her bedroom and shout 'I'll be up in a minute, sweetie,' up the stairs. 'Go on in there,' I point towards the kitchen and follow behind DI Manning as he walks. His stride is long, purposeful. I check my mobile. No missed calls. No texts from Tom.

Where the hell are you?

I slip the phone into my trouser pocket. 'Can I offer you a cup of coffee, or tea?'

'Yes, thank you. Tea. Black, no sugar.'

My mind works overtime as I put the kettle on and take two mugs from the kitchen dresser hooks. 'You didn't answer me. What is this about?' I attempt to keep my voice light – a curious tone, not a demanding one.

'Just a few questions at this stage,' he says, sitting heavily at my large oak farmhouse table. It was one of my favourite buys when we first moved here two years ago. I'd wanted to embrace the change, so we'd gone from modern, London furniture to the rustic Cotswold cottage look.

My pulse quickens at DI Manning's choice of words. *At this stage.*

'Oh? Questions relating to . . .?'

Before he can answer me, the back door into the kitchen rattles. I open the upper part of the barn-style door. DS Walters is there. He's obviously been checking the perimeter of the cottage.

Do they think Tom is hiding? *That I'm hiding him?* Something close to panic rises inside me as my imagination begins to run wild. I swallow hard, trying to push it back down.

I let Walters in and ask if he wants a drink. He doesn't

4

speak, just shakes his head – a piece of sandy-brown hair flopping over his forehead with the motion, which he silently brushes aside with his forefinger. If they're trying to put me on edge, they're doing a great job.

'You say your husband is late home from work. Do you have any idea where he is?'

'He commutes to London Monday to Friday. He works in banking . . . for Moore & Wells.' I can't think of what else to say, so I stop talking.

'Have you tried calling him?'

'I did earlier, just before putting our daughter to bed. But not since, no.'

'Could you try again now, please?'

My fingertips shake as I attempt to press Tom's name on the 'last numbers dialled' display. I accidentally press Lucy's instead and have to quickly cancel the call. On the second try, I hit the right contact. It rings twice, then goes to voicemail. Christ, he must've diverted it. I'm about to try again when I hear the front door.

It's Tom. Thank God. Now whatever this is can be sorted out.

'Tom! Where've you been?' I rush up to him, pulling him towards me tightly, taking in a slightly sour smell. He isn't wearing his suit jacket; he must've left it in the car. I whisper in his ear. 'Some detectives are here and they want to talk to you.'

I pull away from him in time to see his face go pale. His peacock-blue eyes flicker – with what looks to me like fear.

Anxiety gnaws at my stomach.

'Mr Thomas Hardcastle?' DI Manning is standing now as we walk back into the kitchen, his badge outstretched

5

as he approaches Tom. 'Detective Inspector Manning, Metropolitan Police.'

I see Tom's Adam's apple bob as he swallows.

'Yes. How can I help?' Tom says, glancing at me before returning his attention to the detective. Did I catch a tremor in his voice?

'We believe you might be able to assist us with a murder enquiry.'

Chapter 2

BETH

Earlier

The Nespresso coffee machine whirs noisily as I dash around the kitchen trying to do three tasks at once. It's not just because it's a Monday; every weekday morning begins like this. Frantic, loud, rushed . . . and very early. Poppy was awake by five, and for about ten minutes I could hear her pottering about in her bedroom, talking to her most-prized stuffed animals – a lion, a tiger and a sloth that Tom bought her – before she came in to me, not a hint of bleariness in her pretty eyes.

Unlike in mine. I never seem to sleep for more than four hours, meaning my eyes are *always* bleary.

Tom was already up, showered and dressed in one of his many suits – dark grey, his colour of choice for the majority of his clothes – sitting at the farmhouse kitchen table, his nose stuck in his iPad, awaiting his coffee, and for me to cook up a quick breakfast. It's the usual morning routine before he heads off, driving the twenty minutes to Banbury station where he'll catch the 7.04 a.m. train to Marylebone. He has no clue what my routine is after this, but I often tell him when I kiss the top of his head, as he sits calmly sipping his coffee and eating his scrambled eggs, that it's chaotic.

And he always smiles, looks up into my eyes, winks and says: 'But you wouldn't have it any other way.'

He's right, of course. Life is great. We both get to do what we love – him a finance portfolio manager and me, finally my own boss running a ceramics café – and then we come home to each other and our little Poppy. We are the envy of our neighbours and friends. Well, I suppose I have one or two friends, anyway – Tom is rarely inclined to socialise and hasn't really got involved in village life at all since we moved here. That's what living in London for too long will do to you – he's become *de-skilled* in the art of making friends. When I first met him, seven years ago, he'd been the life and soul, oozing charm, wit and intellect. But the London scene doesn't require effort like he'd need to put in here, in a small village. I must try and organise a dinner party; push him along a bit. It would help me, too – I work such a lot at the café I've been rubbish at 'putting myself out there'. But I'm hoping to change that with my new book club.

After Tom finishes his eggs and pops his plate and mug in the dishwasher, he kisses Poppy goodbye first, then comes to me, wrapping his arms around my waist, pulling me in close as he plants his lips on mine. His deliciously soft, full lips. As rushed as our mornings are, I savour this moment. Drink him in. He grabs my bottom and squeezes hard, immediately stirring up my excitement.

'I could take you right now, against the worktop,' he breathes heavily into my neck, peppering it with more sensual kisses.

'You could. But I think our daughter might have something to say about that,' I whisper, breathlessly.

Poppy is too engrossed in moving her breakfast items from one segment of her plastic plate to the other, mixing the toast soldiers with the banana slices, then stacking the halved strawberries on top, to notice what we're doing. But he pulls away anyway, and takes a deep breath.

'God, what you do to me, Mrs *Hard*castle.' He laughs at his usual joke, causing the corners of his piercing blue eyes to crease. 'Fancy sending me off to work in this state,' he says, taking my hand and pressing it against his crotch. 'You really should finish what you've started. What am I meant to do with this?'

I laugh. 'Oh, behave! You'll cope.' I go to remove my hand, but he holds it tight against him for a moment longer.

'Right. Well, clearly I'm going to have to. I'll be on my way, then. Maybe we can pick it up from here when I get home.' And he's gone, leaving me slightly breathless, my back against the worktop. Poppy makes a grab for Tom's iPad, which he's left in the middle of the table.

'Watch CBeebies?' she says, her hands outstretched.

'Ooh, hang on.' I snatch a wet wipe and quickly dab her hands with it. 'Don't think Daddy would want sticky little fingers on his screen.' In actual fact, Daddy wouldn't want her to use it at all. He's very protective over his iPad, but it's so convenient for keeping Poppy entertained, and I've been using it myself a bit more recently too when he's not around. I hand it to her to use while I get ready.

* * *

9

Just over an hour later, Poppy is dressed, her little *In the Night Garden* rucksack packed, and she's waiting patiently at the front door for me to gather my things. She wiggles side to side, singing something to herself that I can't make out. Bless her. She doesn't love going to nursery, but she's okay once she gets there. She hasn't particularly warmed to any of the other children; at least, she never seems to mention any by name. I think she takes after me at that age – slow to trust. Maybe I still am. I grab my keys and the pile of posters from the hallway table.

'Oh, wait a moment. Where did you put Daddy's iPad, sweetie?' I glance around the hallway and then quickly peer into the kitchen, but don't spot it.

'Er . . . I put it in . . . er.' Poppy gives a shrug.

'Never mind, I'll find it later.' I haven't got time to search now. 'Okey-dokey my little Poppy poppet, let's go!'

When we step outside, I take her hand. 'They're very pretty, Mummy, aren't they?' she says, pointing at the flowers in the garden with her free hand. I'm unsure what any of them are, but she's right – they are beautiful: purples, blues and pretty pinks. Trailing white flowers frame the doorway, giving it a homely and happy feel. It was what drew us to this large cottage when we decided to move to Lower Tew from London. Immediate kerb appeal. With its picture-postcard thatched roof and striking red bricks, we fell in love with it almost as quickly as we'd fallen in love with each other.

I first set eyes on Tom at the Sager + Wilde bar in Bethnal Green on the night of my twenty-fifth birthday. I felt a spark of energy as he moved through the people sitting at the outside terrace to get to my table. Another at his confidence when he ignored my friends and spoke just to me, taking my hand and kissing it. There was a spark when we saw this cottage, too. It was meant to be.

I believe in sparks.

'They are lovely, Poppy,' I say, bringing my attention back to the moment. 'I must find out what they are.' *It's only been two years*, I add to myself. Two years, almost to the day, since we moved in, and not long afterwards that I began my pottery café business – a dream I would never have thought possible when I was working as a recruitment consultant in the heart of London. I can't believe how everything has aligned so we can have this life. It's very nearly perfect.

But there's always something more, isn't there? Something else to strive for. Perfection is a state which is always at least one step ahead of where you already are. A completeness that's not really achievable. Flawlessness rarely is.

'Morning, Lucy,' I call as I walk into Poppy's Place half an hour later. I'd wanted to call it 'Poppy's Pottery Place', but Tom said it was alliteration overkill.

I hear a distant, muffled 'morning' from out the back. Lucy must be taking out the now-cooled glazed items from yesterday's painting session from the kiln.

After dumping my stuff in the break room, I take one of the posters I made up at home and pin it on the noticeboard. I'm excited about starting up the book club here again, but nerves aren't far beneath the surface. I'm not entirely sure how it'll go down; I don't want people to think I'm trying to jump into Camilla's shoes. A shiver runs down my back. It's been nearly a year, though – I've given it a respectful amount of time after her passing, haven't I? She was such a hugely popular member of the village, among the mums especially. There might be some who think it's inappropriate

11

I'm taking over something she started. The effects of her sudden death are still felt – the aftershock rippled through the community, because she left a two-year-old without a mother. Little Jess is almost three now, the same age as my Poppy – I can't even *think* about leaving her; it's too heart-breaking. Camilla's husband, Adam, must have gone through unimaginable pain. Probably still is doing.

I shake my head; I don't want to dwell on the tragedy.

'We all set?' Lucy's voice makes me jump. I spin around to see her, apron on, all ready to open up. Her long, auburn corkscrew curls are bundled up in a loose bun, a blue, flower-print bandana headband fixing the rest in place. She's only twenty-three, but she is confident, hard-working and trustworthy – and the kids (and adults) love her bright, cheery demeanour and the way she sings while they paint. Mainly it's songs from Disney films, but she pops in the occasional show song for the adults. She was a great choice when the café got popular enough for me to need someone else to help. She prepares the café and ensures all the machines are on and the fresh pastries and cakes are displayed, while I drop Poppy to nursery. Then she holds the fort while I leave to pick her up. She even opens up from nine until midday on Saturday mornings to serve hot drinks and snacks – my weekends are always reserved for family time; I was adamant about that right from the start. Lucy basically does all the hard work – something she jokingly tells me on a daily basis. Then I tell her she's paid well, and we laugh and carry on.

'We are indeed. Let today's fun commence,' I say, rubbing my hands together.

If only I'd known the day would end on such a serious note.

Chapter 3

BETH

Now

My hands tremble as I pour a glass of Pinot Grigio. DI Manning and DS Walters have taken Tom with them to the police station in Banbury.

'Does he need a solicitor?' I'd asked, cautiously, as they led him out.

Manning had used the same phrase, 'It's just a few questions at this stage', before thanking me for the tea and turning his back. It was surreal – my mind was two steps behind. I'd watched helplessly as Tom had left, only moments after he'd returned home. I'd had no chance to talk to him; ask how his day had been; ask why he was late. His shocked expression is imprinted on my mind.

But was it something more than shock I saw fleeting across his face?

I push the thought aside.

Oh, God. Poppy.

Poor little mite – I'd said I'd be up in a minute when the detectives first arrived, and that was over half an hour ago. Leaving my glass on the worktop, I run upstairs to check on her. Through the crack in the open door, I can see her, sound asleep, her hands lying over her chest. My heart melts. So innocent. *The closest thing to perfection we've ever achieved*, I think, as I gently close the door. *My sleeping beauty.*

All I want is the best for her; the best I can ever give.

I won't abandon her the same way I was as a child. I'm still haunted by the memories of my father not loving me enough to want to stay. My mother sank into depression and later, alcoholism, leaving my nanna to practically bring me up. She did her best, but the damage was done. It still affects so many of my decisions.

Poppy won't have a bad childhood; I refuse to let that happen to her. She has to have a happy, secure home with loving parents who will never let her down.

I drain the glass, then open the fridge, grab the wine bottle and refill. As I take another large mouthful, an image of my mother flashes across my mind.

Don't be like her.

I pour the remaining liquid down the sink and put the glass in the dishwasher. I need to stay clear-headed. It's only been half an hour since they took Tom; they've probably only just got to the station. He could be hours yet. Maybe I should try and settle in front of the telly – or even go to bed. Although I'm fairly certain that'll be pointless; I can't quell the tumultuous thoughts racing around in my head now, let alone if I lie down in a quiet room.

A murder enquiry, Manning had said.

Whose? Where? When? How?

And what makes them think my Tom will know anything about it?

Chapter 4

TOM

Now

I call my solicitor, Maxwell Fielding, en route to Banbury police station. I don't believe there's any such thing as an 'informal chat' where police interviews are concerned, and although I'm not being arrested or detained, according to DI Manning, I'm not taking any chances. Whatever this is about, I'm assuming they think I'm connected to the murder victim, so until I find out more, I want someone present who can advise me.

The fluttering in my chest intensifies as we reach the station.

A chill wind whips across the open space as the three of us walk from where DS Walters has parked his vehicle to the entrance of the police station. I shiver, cursing myself for not grabbing a coat before leaving the cottage – I had to leave my suit jacket in the car. I cross my arms firmly as I stride, stopping when I realise I'm too far ahead of the detectives. I'm not *that* eager to get inside. If I think I'm chilly now, I imagine it'll only get worse once they start on me.

Don't jump to conclusions: you've not been arrested.

My mind flits around as I attempt to predict the who, what and where. I'm shown into a small room inside the station and told to sit and wait. These kinds of delaying tactics are employed to make you nervous. Edgy. Cause adrenaline to pump around your body while you sweat about what's to come.

Maybe I'm overthinking it. I hope against all hope they really are just asking a few questions about someone who I've not seen forever – or even better, have never actually met. Maybe I don't even know the person. *The victim.* It could all be some tenuous link, like we went to the same gym, or they're an old banking client of mine. Yes, that'll be it.

I take a slow, long breath in, trying to compose myself.

I don't want to appear guilty before I've even opened my mouth.

My mind wanders to Beth's face as I left with the detectives. Her mouth agape, all colour drained from her pretty heart-shaped face.

She looked afraid. Like she had reason to be.

This isn't the first time I've been in a police station, but it is the first time I've been interviewed in relation to a *murder*.

I clench my fists under the rectangular table. My wedding ring digs into the flesh of the neighbouring fingers. I will my hands to relax again, pulling my arms from beneath the table and resting them loosely in front of me. I'll come across as less stressed if I do that. I close my eyes lightly, blocking out the dull yellow, windowless walls. The room is claustrophobic, airless, and that's without other bodies in here. Why couldn't they ask their questions in the comfort of my own home for God's sake?

Because it's bad, the voice in my head answers.

Oh, God. What's coming?

My eyes spring open at the sound of the door.

I guess I'm about to find out.

Chapter 5

BETH

Now

The mattress dips, shifting my body only slightly, but enough to wake me; I'd only been in a light sleep.

'Tom? What time is it?' I sit up, blinking rapidly.

'Shhh. Don't worry, go back to sleep, love,' he says. He swings his legs in under the duvet and cuddles up to me. His skin feels cold against mine and I shiver. 'Sorry, Beth,' he breathes into my neck.

'Sorry for being cold?'

'No. You know what I mean. I'm sorry for tonight – for being late, then . . . well, the rest.'

'Is everything sorted now?' Tiredness has drained me; my voice is a whisper.

'We'll talk in the morning.'

'But we never have time for that,' I say, groggily.

'Well, never mind – don't worry about it now.'

Being told not to worry about something tends to have the opposite effect.

'We'll talk now,' I say, pushing myself up on my elbow and looking at Tom. The moonlight creeps in through a gap in the curtains, but it's not enough to see any of his features. I flip over and turn on the bedside lamp.

'Oh, Beth! Not now.' He shields his eyes.

'It has to be now. There's too much going on tomorrow – I've got to prepare for a birthday party and then collect Poppy from nursery and take her back with me as the party starts at four—'

'It *is* tomorrow,' he groans, cutting me off. 'There'll be time in the evening. Now try and settle back down.' He begins to turn away from me.

'No, Tom. Sit up, please. I need to know what happened at the station,' I plead. 'Were you able to help them with their enquiries? Who is it they were asking about? Someone you know? Please tell me it's nothing bad.'

He relents, huffing as he stacks his pillows up against the headboard and leans back into them. I hear a long puff of air expelling from his nostrils. My pulse bangs in my neck as I wait for the answers.

'It was about Katie,' he says, simply.

'Shit.' He doesn't need to say more than her first name. I know who she is. Katie Williams was Tom's girlfriend just prior to meeting me. As far as anyone knew, she went off to travel the world, or something like that. I knew she'd broken Tom's heart – he'd told me on our first date. But we'd only ever spoken about her once since then. Tom doesn't dwell on the past. *You have to keep looking forward*, he always says.

'Yes. Shit.' He lowers his head, his chin almost touching his chest. I move close to him, laying one arm over his stomach, my fingertips circling the hair around his belly button.

'Right. That's a shock. When did they find her?'

'Oh, no,' Tom says, shaking his head. 'They haven't. They only *suspect* she's come to harm.'

'Well, that's good, then,' I say, optimism filling my voice.

'Maybe.'

'They only wanted to talk to you because you're an ex-boyfriend, then. Did they ask if you'd spoken to her recently?'

'That sort of thing, yes.'

'Which means you couldn't really help them, then. Seeing as you haven't.'

'Exactly. So, nothing to worry about. I've done my bit. Now, go to sleep, Beth. You'll be knackered when the alarm goes off.'

'I'm always knackered – it's my default setting,' I say, attempting a smile.

'I'll fill you in properly tomorrow.'

For the moment, I'm satisfied. I switch the light off, wriggle down the bed and lay my arm across Tom's waist. I want to let him know I'm there; the supportive wife. My mind doesn't want to settle, though, and it goes into overdrive, thinking about everything I know about Katie – which isn't a whole lot. She'd been on the scene not long before me and had been besotted with Tom. She'd spent all her free time with him.

I think about how charming Tom was; how easily I fell

under his spell. And how I remained under that spell, too. Katie only lasted six months. He'd been burned by her, he'd said – she'd changed, wanted different things.

I got to marry him. Have his baby.

I always considered myself the chosen one.

Chapter 6

BETH

Now

I hear the jets of water hitting the shower screen and lazily turn over to face the en-suite. Tom's left the door open, as he always does, and I can see him through the glass, gel lathered all over his torso, shampoo running down from his head. I watch intently, all the while wondering exactly what DI Manning asked him last night and how Tom responded. He appeared calm when he got into bed, so maybe that's the end of it. I tear my gaze away from him and rather than attempt to fall back to sleep, I get up.

He was right: I am knackered. I catch the dark circles beneath my eyes as I look towards the mirrored wardrobe. I'm going to need a trowel and heavy-duty concealer and foundation to cover those up this morning, plus a vat of coffee to perk me up. I've a busy day ahead and a child's party to get through. It's not until four p.m. and it's only for ten people – a handful of three- and four-year-olds and their parents – but it'll still take time to set up and I know the hour-long session will feel double that. I wasn't sure it was a good idea agreeing when Sally, the mum, had asked to book. Younger children are generally more difficult to cater for: their attention spans aren't quite long enough; they aren't so keen on sitting down for longer than five minutes. I was about to say no – but she mentioned Jess would be coming with Adam, and a twinge of guilt turned my no into a 'yes, of course'. How could I say no once I knew they would be coming?

Poppy's footsteps pad across the landing.

'Morning, my little one,' I say, sweeping her up. She squeezes me with her chubby little arms. 'And how did you sleep?'

'I had a long sleep, Mummy.' She beams at me, then suddenly scowls. 'But Daddy was naughty.'

'Oh, was he now?' I know what's coming.

'Yep.' She pouts. 'He didn't kiss me goodnight.'

The shower screen creaks, and within moments, Tom is out, his lower half wrapped in a towel. 'I'm so sorry, Poppy poppet! Daddy is a silly man, isn't he?' he says, grinning and reaching for her, his arms outstretched.

She giggles as he splashes her with droplets of water.

'Daddeeee!' she squeals as she dives behind me.

'Just let me get dried and dressed, then I'll give you the biggest bear hug ever to make up for it. Okay?'

'O-kaay,' she says, running out of the room. 'I going for my bekfast now, Mummy.'

'I'll be down in a second,' I call after her. 'Just wait at the table.'

'I know you're going to start on me straight away, Beth,

but we really don't have the time now. Look, I'll give you all the details when I get back later, okay?'

'I'm not Poppy. Don't speak to me as though I'm a bloody kid, Tom.'

'Darling,' he sits on the bed beside me, taking my hand in his. 'I'm not. We will talk about it, but you know our mornings are hectic. There's honestly not much to say. And definitely nothing to worry about.'

'Really? Nothing?' I hear the incredulousness in my tone. Tom straightens, moving away from me.

'Nothing for *you* to worry about,' he repeats, his eyes cold and serious. 'Like Manning said, it was just some questions.'

'Fine.' I let a long, slow breath out. But I can't shake my unease. Or the uncomfortable feeling that I don't believe him.

The walk to nursery is slow, with Poppy stopping every few steps to admire something she's spotted: a tabby cat; some flowers in a garden; a snail on a wall. We bump into Shirley Irish from the pub, who asks me about the book club.

'I was surprised to see your poster when I popped in for my order yesterday afternoon,' she says, her pointed nose wrinkling as though she's caught a waft of something unpleasant.

'Oh, really? I wouldn't have thought a book club was much of a surprise in a community such as ours, Mrs Irish,' I say, lightly. I always call her Mrs Irish to her face for some reason, despite her telling me to call her Shirley.

'Well, no. But you do remember it was Camilla Knight's book club before, don't you?'

I bite the inside of my lip to prevent myself saying *I don't think she'll mind, now. It's not as though she'll know*. Instead, I smile and tell her I thought it would be a nice nod to Camilla, and that she'd have loved to know the villagers were continuing something she'd started. Shirley bobs her head several times, her sheer, silky black hair swinging each side of her face in what I assume to be agreement, and I escape while I can. Is everyone going to be against me starting it up again?

'I didn't think I was ever going to get here this morning,' I say when I finally make it into the café.

'I was beginning to wonder if something was wrong,' Lucy says.

'Oh, no. Nothing wrong,' I say quickly. Too quickly. 'Just that Poppy was on a go-slow and then I ran into Shirley, from the pub.'

'You were lucky to get away, then. She doesn't half go on, doesn't she?'

I laugh at Lucy's comment. She's not wrong. As I go to take my things into the back room, my eyes fall on the book club poster. I take it down. Not because of what Shirley said – I'm determined to go ahead with it regardless of what she thinks – but because I would hate for Adam to see it later and think badly of me for taking over Camilla's club. She started it and she'd been running it for a number of years. When we first moved here and I opened Poppy's Place she'd swept in one day, her golden hair flowing over her shoulders like glossy honey, her slim figure encased in black, skin-tight leggings and a leopard print tee, and asked if she could use the place once a month on a Wednesday evening for her book club to meet.

She usually had it at her house, she'd said, but the group had become larger and their rowdiness had reached a level where it disturbed her one-year-old's sleep.

I'd always kind of hoped she'd invite me to read their chosen book; sit with the other yummy mummies and discuss what they thought about it. Instead, I was on the periphery for two hours each month, serving drinks and cakes. But I got to know their names and who their children were. I heard their gossip and what was going on in each of their lives. It was an eye-opener; I had no idea so much went on in such a small place.

And still, Camilla didn't accept me into her inner circle. The only time we'd bonded was over my cookie recipes, as she liked to bake too. Seems a lifetime ago now.

'Are you giving them the choice of any of the bisques?' Lucy asks.

'Oh, er . . . no.' I pop the poster under the counter. 'I think just the medium-sized animal ones, thanks, Lucy.'

'Righto,' she says. As she goes into the back, I hear her break into song. I smile, but then a cloud descends. Yesterday had been so normal: happy, carefree. Today, things are different. A heavy weight is squatting inside me, waiting. A sense that something bad is on its way.

Four o'clock comes around quickly and I'm glad we did the majority of the prep in the morning, as it's been really busy and I've been out over half an hour collecting Poppy, making a quick detour home to collect more cakes. I couldn't be more proud that Poppy's Place has taken off so well here. Bearing in mind I was a newcomer to a close-knit community, people have been keen to support me and the café. I glance over at the freshly baked cakes,

27

muffins and cookies arranged in the glass display case next to the counter. They look and smell delicious. Some of them are from suppliers but I bake a lot of them myself at home – it's my passion, and it's a huge positive being able to fit my baking around Poppy and even involving her too. I've enjoyed experimenting with new recipes, and Poppy loves being my official taster. The feedback has been great – I even overheard someone saying I make the best cookies she's ever had. Tom laughed when I told him. He said he'd never imagined me to be the homely, wifely type when we first met. I never decided if it was a compliment or a dig – but either way, being here, and running the café, has made me the happiest and most content I've felt in my life so far.

Poppy has been a little angel waiting for the kids to arrive, patiently sitting at the table nearest the counter, playing with the table-top café set I bought her because she wanted to be like Mummy. Luckily, Sally's invited her to Molly's party so at least I haven't had to worry about finding a babysitter.

The bisque animals are lined up ready to be chosen by the kids and their parents; the eight tables are all prepped with different colour paints. There are brightly coloured balloons dotted around the café, and 'Happy Birthday' banners on the walls. I look over to Lucy, who's tied her bandana in place and donned her apron. I feel like we're about to be invaded.

'We're all set,' Lucy declares.

'Great. And thanks so much for all your help – as ever. Just think, in an hour or so it'll all be over, and you can have a relaxing evening with Oscar,' I say.

'Oh, I love it, you know that. I'm in my element with

the kids. Besides, Oscar is working late tonight – something about having to complete a car service and deliver another car somewhere and get a train back,' Lucy says, waving her hand dismissively. 'God knows what time he'll rock up.' Lucy isn't a car person. She's never owned one: she prefers to tear around the village on her trusty, rusty bike or take public transport. Mechanics are a mystery to her, and she often tells me she goes to sleep listening to her boyfriend rattling on about it. I think it's pretty funny, although Oscar might feel differently.

'Ah, the joys of owning your own business, eh? I can relate,' I say. 'He's done so well taking over the garage from his dad, Lucy. Can't have been easy for him.'

'No, he misses him a lot. But you know, he's worked hard without much help. His dad would've been proud.'

'I'm sure he would, hun,' I say, reassuringly, and then I plaster on a warm smile and open the door to greet the birthday girl.

The calm quiet of the café explodes – a noise bomb of deafening toddlers and parents competing to be heard. It sounds like a party of twenty, not half that. It takes about fifteen minutes to get everyone sitting down at a table with their animals. I do a quick headcount: one child down. Adam and Jess aren't here yet – perhaps they cancelled. I ask Sally if everyone is here.

'Oh, er . . . no, actually. One more to come – Jess and her dad aren't here yet,' she says, her eyes flitting around the café. She flings her arm up and waves suddenly at something behind me, and I turn to see Adam walking in with Jess. She looks tiny – smaller than the other kids her age – which makes it even easier for her to maintain position, hiding behind her dad's legs, gripping tightly. He tries to pry her off so he can walk to a table, but she holds on desperately. Sally jumps out of her chair and bends down to her level to coax her away from him, without success. As Sally returns to her seat next to Molly, I notice a toy white cat is grasped in the crook of Jess's arm, which gives me an opening.

'I see your favourite animal is a cat, Jess,' I say. 'There's an incredibly special cat waiting for you over here – would you like to see her?'

Jess peeks around from behind Adam and cranes her neck to where I'm pointing. I hold my hand out to her and she tentatively takes it. Adam smiles at me as I lead her to the bisque pieces, and Jess chooses her cat.

'Thank you, you were great with her,' Adam says when they're sitting at the table ready to start. I draw up a chair and sit beside him.

'It must be such a challenging time for you both – it can't be easy to adapt.'

'No, it's not,' he lowers his gaze, but not before I see the tears in his eyes. 'You'd be amazed how many people think that because it's been a year, we should be over it and getting on with life. To be fair, I suppose we *are* getting on with it, to a degree. I'm back at the office part-time – I can do a fair bit from home to be around Jess more. But honestly,' he pauses, as if contemplating whether to confide in me, 'I need to be with other adults sometimes, you know? It's what keeps me sane. Whatever I choose, I feel like I'm doing everything wrong . . .' His voice breaks, and he coughs as though he's clearing his throat to cover it up. I really want to pop my hand on his or something, to show I empathise – but this is the first time I've properly spoken to him, so it doesn't seem appropriate.

Instead, I ask him about Jess: how she's getting on at nursery; what she enjoys; how he manages with working and looking after her. Somehow I end up offering to have her for tea next week.

'Really? Yes, that would be great. She needs to mix more with children her age outside of nursery. She's quite shy.'

'Oh, Poppy is the same. You'd be doing *me* a favour!' I grin. 'I've spent so much time here, trying to make a good go of the business, I fear I've neglected her a bit.'

'Ah, I'm sure you haven't. You'll be an inspiration to her. And no doubt you spend lots of quality time with her when you're away from here.'

I wonder if he's just being kind, but then he stares right into my eyes and gives me a genuine-looking smile.

'I love being with her. Being a mother is the best job in the world.' As I say it, my heart drops. Oh, God – why did I say that? I didn't think. 'I – I mean . . .'

'It's fine, Beth. Really. Being a parent *is* the best job – no need to feel bad on my account.'

'I don't think before I open my mouth sometimes,' I say, my face hot.

He laughs. 'Do you know most people avoid me like the plague? Even now, they don't know what to say. They feel awkward, so they give me a pleasant *good morning*, or a *how's things?* But then they panic if I give more than a one-sentence answer.' He brings his head closer to mine and whispers conspiratorially, 'I'm surprised we were invited to this party, actually. Honestly, I'm thankful you're talking to me! Please don't worry about saying the wrong thing. I can assure you I won't take any offence.'

'Okay, that's good,' I grin, relieved, as I get up from

the table. 'Right, I'll leave you and Jess to paint – looks like your cat is going to be the most colourful one I've ever seen!' I smile at Jess. 'Best check up on the others.'

I do the rounds, glad I've spoken with Adam. It must be so lonely for him. Maybe getting Poppy and Jess together will be of benefit to both of us.

As five o'clock approaches, a nervous knot starts tying itself tightly in my gut as I think about getting home. Now the party is almost over, I can allow myself to think about the murder enquiry. I'll finally be able to talk to Tom soon. I don't know how these things work, given they don't have a body, but if they're treating it as murder, they must have sufficient evidence pointing them in that direction.

Poor Katie.

I can't imagine why they thought Tom could help, though. Despite him seeming fine this morning, it must've unsettled him to have the police turn up.

'Thanks so much for letting us have the party here,' Sally says, squeezing my arm. 'Molly's really enjoyed it. So have I. I'd love to come in on my own soon, actually, and make something a bit more . . . adult!'

'Well, you're very welcome, of course. And I'm glad Molly liked her party – it's been fun!' And I mean it, even if I hadn't expected to. I'm utterly exhausted, but admittedly, it wasn't as stressful as I'd imagined.

The stress is yet to come.

Chapter 7

BETH

Now

Tom's car is parked in the lane outside the cottage. It invokes mixed emotions in me. I'm thankful he's home on time, but a wave of nauseous anticipation still surges through me. I take several deep breaths and open the front door.

I immediately sense a problem. The house is silent.

Tom isn't here.

'Daddy?' Poppy calls, running into the lounge, out again, then into the kitchen, looking for him. For a moment, I stand stock still, my mind in disarray. His car is here. He is not. I check my mobile. If Tom was going to go out, surely he'd have texted? There's a missed call from an unknown number, but zero new messages.

'Maybe he's gone for a run,' I suggest to Poppy as she toddles back to me. It *is* possible. As we weren't home,

33

rather than waste his time sitting on his own, he could've taken the rare opportunity to run. He used to regularly, but with our busy days, he prefers to spend his time with Poppy before she goes to bed.

'He back in a mimmit,' she says with a shrug.

'Yes, I expect so, sweetheart. Let's get tea, shall we?'

As I pop my bag on the hallway table, I see the flashing red light on the answerphone. I press play.

'I don't want you to panic, Beth . . .' Tom's voice fills the hallway, so loud it's distorted, the echo bouncing off the walls. I quickly tap the volume down button, blood whooshing in my ears. 'Sorry. I've been brought into the station again. I might be a bit longer this time. Don't worry, I've got my solicitor here with me. I'll call again when I can,' he says. I think he's finished, but then I hear a sigh. Followed by the whispered words: 'I love you, Beth.' The line goes dead.

My arms and legs are leaden. I can't move. What am I supposed to do? I wonder if I should call the station. Or Tom's solicitor. Although if he's with Tom he won't be able to shed any light yet either.

Jesus Christ.

The detectives obviously came to the cottage to get him, because Tom's car is here. Did the neighbours see?

A shiver tracks down my spine.

I feel light-headed.

I need to call *someone*. Do *something*. But apart from Tom, I have no one I can turn to or lean on. How did I let that happen? Too busy setting up the café. Too busy with Poppy. Too busy being a wife. Tom has always said friends are over-rated and they'd distract us from each other. I've kept Lucy and the nursery group mums at arm's

34

length, and so I'm not comfortable turning to them now. Tom's voice fills my mind:

We only need each other, Beth. No one else matters.

But Tom isn't here. And suddenly, I realise he was wrong – I *do* need other people.

Only now, there is no one. I'm in this alone.

Chapter 8

TOM

Now

I knew I'd made the right decision calling Maxwell from the off – even though DI Manning and DS Walters only wanted to 'ask a couple of questions'. At least he's up to speed, knows the situation now they've brought me in again. I didn't go down the *no comment* route in the first interview as there was no need. A few simple enquiries 'to gain a picture of Katie' – that's all they were after, they said. Why would anyone choose to give a no comment interview in that situation? In my mind, it immediately points to guilt. I've seen the real-crime police documentaries, and God, that gets my goat when the person interviewed mutters no comment every five seconds. It's all I can do to stop myself hurling the controls through the telly screen. Surely it looks better for me if I answer their questions openly.

If I'm seen to be cooperating maybe they'll begin to look elsewhere.

That said, now this is my second interview, and they look far more serious than before, I'm considering taking the 'remain silent' approach. No doubt Maxwell will advise this course too, because what if I say something wrong? Implicate myself somehow? At least if I don't engage, they can't trap me. Because that's what this feels like. A carefully laid trap. Draw me in with the soft questions, lull me into a false sense of security by making me think I've done my bit to help, then, *wham!* – hit me with the heavy stuff.

What do they think they know?

They can't know anything. There's nothing to know.

If I repeat this enough times in my head, there's a possibility I'll believe it.

I was so stupid not to talk to Beth when she wanted to. Leaving it until tonight was clearly a huge mistake – and now it's too late to rectify; I was only able to leave a short message on the home phone. I bet they speak to her before I can.

'Are you charging my client with an offence, Detective Manning?' Maxwell asks. He's sitting beside me, casual yet authoritative in his precision-tailored bespoke silver-grey suit, his copper-red hair neatly gelled. His voice is calm, steady, assured. He's the no-nonsense, give-it-to-me-straight kind. And he's worth every penny I'm going to be paying. With luck, this will be the last time I need to call on his services.

'As you know, your client admits he was in a relationship with Katie Williams of Bethnal Green, London, immediately prior to her disappearance. We also have evidence suggesting he may have been involved in that disappearance. This makes Mr Hardcastle a person of interest.'

37

My confidence evaporates.

It's the first time DI Manning has mentioned this, and my gut reacts badly. I'm aware of voices continuing, Maxwell asking something about disclosure, the detective giving some kind of response, but the words are slow, distorting as they mix together in a blurry mess; I can't decipher the meaning of any of them. The sudden sensation of being on a boat in rough seas causes saliva to flood my mouth.

'I'm going to need a toilet break. Now,' I say, before dry-retching.

Maxwell stops talking and jumps back as I push past him; then Manning scoots his chair back, gets up and leads me towards the toilets. He opens the door and lets me go in.

'I'll be outside,' he says, as though he imagines I'll do a runner. I give a quick nod, then dash to the cubicle where I add the contents of my stomach to the putrid-smelling, yellowing liquid in the toilet bowl.

A suspect.

After all these years.

Chapter 9

KATIE

Eight years ago

She noticed him the second she walked into Energies. Tall, muscular, dark hair and the bluest eyes, which rooted her to the spot from across the room. Katie even heard herself take a sharp intake of breath. God, he was gorgeous. A new instructor? This was a different time for her; she usually chose the early morning sessions before work, but every so often she left it until later. It had been a stressful day – although every day as a new freelancer was stressful – trying to win a big PR job she'd had on her radar for months, and she wanted to unwind with a yoga class before settling down for the evening. Maybe he always came in at this time and this was just the first time their paths had crossed.

Peeling her eyes away, she composed herself and carried on walking. But should she ignore such an instant connection? What if she never saw him again?

Turning on her heel, Katie strode quickly towards him. She had nothing to lose. He was bound to be in a relationship – she would probably be humiliated – but she wasn't one to think things through. Her motto was 'grasp every opportunity'.

'Hi, I'm Katie,' she said, thrusting out her hand and offering a wide smile. 'Are you an instructor?'

'Well, hello, Katie,' he said. His eyes were hypnotic close up. They sparkled. *A man who is clearly used to attention,* she thought. His voice was deep; sexy. Katie felt a fluttering in her chest. He took her hand and held it firmly. Lingered. Warmth flowed through her. 'It's lovely to meet you. And no, I'm not an instructor – this is just my regular gym. I'm Tom.'

Their eyes locked and Katie was lost. Now she'd spoken to him, she couldn't think of a clever, witty, or even slightly conversational follow-up. She stuttered, lowered her eyes, then looked back at him from under her long lashes. Her dad called it her Princess Diana look. Katie hated the royals.

'What are you here for?' Tom asked, saving her from further embarrassment.

'Yoga. I find it very spiritual. I'm planning on becoming an instructor eventually.' She wasn't sure why she added that; she had only ever told her friends this ambition – never a total stranger. Tom nodded and smiled. He had perfectly straight teeth – one of the attributes on Katie's dating tick list, along with gorgeous eyes and a fit body. Tom was doing well here; he might even hit the perfect score.

That had never happened to Katie before.

At twenty-four, she'd begun to think she was only ever

destined to date losers. Her dad had become so disillusioned with her choice of boyfriends as a teenager, he'd refused to even let them inside the house. But then, her dad had become disillusioned with Katie, too, it seemed. He'd run off with some over-baked woman he met in Spain after her mother passed and Katie hadn't seen him since – she'd just get the odd email letting her know he was still alive and living it up with Little Miss Sunshine. Anyway, Katie was getting ahead of herself – it was unlikely she'd be lucky enough to get past this first meeting with Tom. Certainly wouldn't be asked on a date. Maybe she should ask him.

'I'm sure you'd make a great instructor.' He beamed. 'Look, I'll probably still be around after your yoga session.'

Oh, my God. He was actually interested. She *knew* it was the right move to introduce herself.

'Yeah? Well, if you're in need of refreshment afterwards, perhaps we could grab a drink.' She was pleased with her boldness. It made her come across as confident. Men liked confident women.

'Excellent.' Tom grinned, took a towel and wiped the sheen from his upper arms. Katie's eyes followed, watching as he slowly rubbed it over his biceps. 'I'll be waiting,' he said with a wink.

* * *

TOM

I'd seen her go into Energies Fitness Centre several weeks earlier, a yoga mat tucked under her arm. I'd happened to be across the street, glancing in a shop window, and her reflection caught my attention. It was meant to be. I knew immediately that I wanted her. As luck would have it, the woman who ran the yoga classes was a friend of a mate of mine and I managed to tap her up for info when I went for my regular evening workout. It wasn't hard to find out Katie's usual patterns; I watched from afar, waiting for the right time to approach her. She'd caught me off-guard today. At first, I'd felt put-out, but then I realised she'd just done the work for me.

And that excited me.

Chapter 10

BETH

Now

As I reach down to scoop up the morning newspaper from the hallway floor, my eyes focus on the headline and my insides turn to liquid. LOCAL MAN UNDER SUSPICION OF MURDER. Jesus, how did they get hold of this story so quickly? Tom hasn't even been arrested or charged with anything and yet here they are, splashing lies across their pages. This has to be libel. I slam the paper onto the kitchen worktop and stab my mobile keypad with my finger.

'Maxwell, it's Beth Hardcastle,' I say and before waiting for his response, carry straight on. 'Listen, the newspapers are circulating vicious lies – they're not even bothered about the truth. Tom is *helping* the police! This kind of misinformation is going to ruin us. They can't get away with it!' I can't keep the panic from my voice, even though Poppy is staring wide-eyed at me from the kitchen table.

I take a steadying breath and walk into the hall, the phone hot against my ear. I attempt to keep my voice low and even. 'Seriously, Maxwell – how am I meant to protect myself and Poppy from the fallout from this?' Possible repercussions fly through my mind, adding fuel to my rising anxiety. I hadn't given any thought to what would happen if the press got hold of this until now. 'There must be something you can do.' Out of breath, I finally stop speaking and wait for him to tell me he'll sue them for libel or defamation of character or something. But he's worryingly quiet.

'Beth, I'm sorry,' he says, slowly. 'There's nothing we can do, I'm afraid. It's a different situation—'

'Innocent until proven guilty is what's *meant* to happen, isn't it?' I snap. 'But these days, bloody gutter journalists want to sell papers, spread their vile lies online, just to increase readership. It's disgusting. It might be just the local press covering this now, but that'll change! Tom is innocent! He's only assisting with their enquiries for God's sake. He's not even been arrested, let alone charged—'

'Actually, Beth – you might want to sit down.'

I freeze. Try to swallow but can't. 'What? What is it?'

'They've arrested Tom. He's in custody.'

I ranted at Maxwell – how it's utter madness that Tom is now in custody, that they think he's killed Katie Williams. Tom. *A murderer.* Maxwell was adamant that what little evidence they had wouldn't be enough to charge him, otherwise they'd have done it immediately. He was positive. But then, that's his job. He's telling me what I want to hear. That's what he's being paid several hundred pounds an hour for: to make sure Tom gets out and comes home to me and Poppy. I reminded him of that at least six times before the end of the call.

How am I meant to work all day in the café knowing this? Everyone will be looking at me. Judging. Oh, my God. Poor little Poppy. How could this be happening? A few days ago, everything was great. We were living the dream.

Being afraid to leave my home is not a feeling I've ever experienced before. But now, hovering at the end of the path with Poppy's tiny hand gripped in mine, my pulse leaps and judders, like a car engine on an icy morning. I poke my head out from the gateway, giving a cautionary glance up and down the road before we step out. 'Are you playing, Mummy?' Poppy giggles.

All of a sudden, hot anger burns inside me. We are meant to protect her: ensure she's safe, loved and cared for. I wish Tom were here now so I could yell at him. I'm furious with him for putting us in this situation; and keeping it bottled up is unbearable. I have to speak to Tom; there's so much I need to ask him. But when will I get that opportunity? *Will* I? I breathe in so deeply, I'm aware of my nostrils flaring. Poppy laughs again, thinking it's all part of the game. 'Are you a dragon?' she says.

I do *feel* as though fire could erupt from my nose and mouth at any second; I'm certainly irate enough.

'Yes, I'm an angry dragon and I want my BREAKFAST!' I force myself to joke, and I crouch down and tickle her under her ribs. She squeals in delight.

We walk on, towards nursery, my head lowered so as not to catch anyone's eye. I have to get this part over with.

45

Chapter 11

TOM

Now

There's a different person sitting with DI Manning now as I am shown into a larger interview room and seated near the back wall opposite them at a square table. I'm on edge – the new person is glaring at me, her steel-grey eyes unblinking. I look away first, and immediately I know I've failed her test. *Dammit!* I can sense her smiling without needing to look.

Why is she here? Where did DS Walters go? I'd been prepared for him, not this young, smug-looking woman who thinks she's something special.

'Morning, Tom. Comfortable night?' DI Manning says without looking up from the open folder in front of him.

I snort, but don't respond verbally. Maxwell isn't here yet and I'm not uttering a word until he's beside me. Manning shifts his attention to me, relaxes back in his chair and interlocks his fingers, resting his clasped hands on his paunch.

'This is Detective Constable Cooper,' he says, nodding to his left. 'She's my colleague from Homicide and Major Crime Command.'

My heart flutters violently. Two detectives from the London homicide squad now. They must think they've got something significant, then? I try not to stress about it because Maxwell said that during disclosure they didn't share the nature of *all* the evidence they held against me, which in his experience pointed to the fact it was weak and they were just 'playing the game'.

Say no comment.

Should I trust in Maxwell's experience? That is the reason I asked him here, so I should, I guess. But my mind is split.

DC Cooper offers what I can only assume is meant to be a smile – her thin lips stretch into a straight line, but none of her other facial features move. Maybe she's had Botox, which seems to be common in women these days even before a wrinkle appears, and her muscles are frozen so she can only manage that weird grimace. I force myself to keep eye contact with her now. She's about my age. I don't feel comfortable with that. She's attractive, in a common kind of way – not *pretty* – there's nothing particularly striking about her. Clear, pale skin, no make-up, a smattering of freckles over her nose. Poker-straight, strawberry-blonde hair that sits on her shoulders. Her face doesn't give much away; I can't read what she's thinking. I shift in my seat and look to the closed door. Where *is* Maxwell?

'How was your night?' DC Cooper says.

Now I've been asked twice, I suppose I ought to respond. 'I've had better accommodation,' I say. 'I'm afraid I'm going to be giving a rather low rating on TripAdvisor. I won't be staying again.'

'We'll see about that,' she says, without taking her eyes from mine. I'm determined to hold her gaze.

Now probably isn't the time to come across as cocky; I must keep that in check.

Finally, the door opens, and Maxwell enters.

'Good. Let's get going then, shall we?' DI Manning says, straightening himself up in his chair and shuffling the papers in the file on the table.

'You holding up?' Maxwell asks me as he takes his jacket off and hangs it on the back of his chair. I shrug. I'm not, but I don't want to say as much. Being arrested and having my DNA samples taken along with my finger-prints was a shock last night. Made all of this very real. I didn't sleep – not just because of the uncomfortable bed and the bleak surroundings, but because my mind wouldn't settle. Images of Katie's face when I last saw her, muddled with Beth's. I haven't been able to speak with Beth, but Maxwell told me he'd go and see her later today – we've come to an agreement about how much he should tell her; the detectives aren't the only ones who can hold back information. I hope she's all right.

And my little Poppy. What will Beth have told her?

I've never been away from them this long. What if I'm taken away from them for good? How will they cope? I'm all they've got.

I'm losing control of my breathing. I must focus on this moment; this room. Breathe slowly. I've gone over and over the questions I think they'll ask. Dredged my memories from eight years ago and rehearsed the story I need to tell.

Don't let them rush you, get you flustered.

Stay calm. Give considered answers.

Or say *no comment*.

That option is still one I want to avoid taking, though, despite Maxwell's advice. Guilty people stay silent.

The innocent – and the clever – answer with confidence.

The recording starts. Introductions are made.

The questioning begins.

Chapter 12

KATIE

Eight years ago

'Come on, Katie. We've talked about this,' Tom said.

Katie wanted to point out that no, *they* hadn't. *He* had spoken about it, told her his feelings about it. Said what they were going to do and what they weren't. None of it had been a discussion in which Katie had been an active participant.

As had become usual.

They'd been together almost four months, and everything had been perfect to begin with. Tom was infatuated with her, and she revelled in the attention. Couldn't believe her luck that she, Katie Williams, got to be the girlfriend of drop-dead gorgeous Tom Hardcastle. The shiny new relationship was beginning to lose its sheen, though. Lately, he'd become quite the bore – always wanting her to himself; not wanting Katie to socialise with her friends.

'Tom, babe – if you remember, I didn't agree to your

plan. It's a tradition that I go out with my friends to celebrate May Day—'

'Oh, come on – we all know no one cares about May Day. They just want an excuse to meet up and get hammered like they used to. You've got me now. Wouldn't you rather spend your bank holiday in my company than with your old uni mates? I've got it all planned: a picnic in the park – with champagne no less – a romantic stroll along Regent's Canal . . . and a special surprise . . .' He took Katie's hand and swirled her around, laughing. 'Really, babe, you're going to *love* it. I can't wait to give it to you.'

Katie relinquished.

'All right, all right,' she said. 'I'll text and explain that my amazing boyfriend has sprung a surprise on me and that we'll arrange to meet up another time.'

'That's my girl,' he smiled.

Katie pulled her mobile from her handbag and began messaging. Tom sat beside her, watching intently. She turned slightly, uncomfortable that he was looking over her shoulder as though he didn't trust her to text the right thing. She hit 'send', popped her phone in her pocket and Tom moved away. Katie's shoulders slumped. She'd been looking forward to catching up with her mates.

'Coffee?' he asked.

'Sure.' She watched him disappear into the kitchen before slipping her phone back out and sending another quick text to Isaac, apologising for dropping out of their usual plans. Before Tom, he'd been the one person she always confided in. But apparently she didn't need him any longer.

According to Tom, he was all she'd ever need again.

***

TOM

I'd been longing to spend some quality time with Katie. Just her and me; not her immature friends. Why she still wanted to spend time with them was beyond me. I'd taken such a long time organising the perfect, romantic day for her. Not some rowdy, drunken party like some idiotic teenagers. They weren't at uni any more – how long were they going to act like it?

I wasn't lying when I told her I had a surprise. I was going to show her friends just how things were going to be from here on in.

52

Chapter 13

BETH

Now

They can't hide the whispers behind their hands. We might be in a nursery, but we're adults; I know they're talking about me. About Tom. I must decide right now how I'm going to play this. I could pretend it's not happening – that would be preferable. And this whole thing could blow over really soon. Maxwell said the police can hold Tom without charge for a twenty-four-hour period, which is up at eight tonight, but Maxwell thinks they'll apply to have it extended. He wasn't forthcoming on the finer details, I noted, and my mind was too numb to question him. My only knowledge of these things comes from watching *24 Hours in Police Custody*. I know that, if it's a serious crime, they can hold people for longer if they've got good grounds. The upshot from my one-sided conversation with Maxwell – and the only snippet of hope – was that even if the police manage to get the maximum ninety-six hours window to charge Tom, if they don't have enough evidence at the end of that, then they have to release him.

As much as Maxwell is hopeful this will be the outcome, what if he's wrong and Tom isn't released? I need to ensure I protect myself and Poppy here and now. I'm not naïve enough to think I can sweep this entire situation under the carpet – I know it wouldn't be smart *or* beneficial to ignore it. I need to face the other mums.

After kissing Poppy goodbye and handing her over to the teaching assistant, I head towards the gossiping parents. Their faces freeze as I approach; they all look in different directions so as not to catch my gaze.

'Morning,' I say, in a quiet voice. I offer a sad smile then, without warning, I lose my control and throw my hands to my face as it crumples and the tears fall.

'Oh, God, Beth.' One woman, whose name I can't recall, rushes up to me and places her hand on my shoulder. 'Are you okay? We couldn't help but hear . . .'

I feel other hands on me, rubbing my back and arms as I'm gently guided outside. Several reassuring voices compete to be heard.

'It's so terrible, I can't . . .' A sob prevents other words forming.

'Are you going to Poppy's Place now?' It's Julia, mum of the triplets, who asks. 'We'll walk with you. Come on.' And I'm bundled away from nursery towards the café. I'm in the middle of a gang of local mothers: protected for the moment.

Once inside the café, the five mums sit at the larger circular table near the back and I busy myself preparing lattes. Lucy looks at me, her right eyebrow arched.

'Have I missed something?' she says.

'If you're asking that, then yes, you have.'

'Are you all right? You look a bit peaky.' Concern twists her delicate features. 'Is Poppy okay?'

The hissing of the milk heating wand prevents more conversation for a few minutes. When we've made the drinks, I pop my hand on Lucy's wrist and tell her I'll fill her in properly after the mums have left, but that Tom has been taken to Banbury police station to help police with their enquiries. Her mouth falls into an 'O' shape, but she quickly recovers and gives me a curt nod and a sympathetic smile.

'Here you go, ladies. On the house.' I place the tray of lattes on the table and give a wavering smile as I sit down.

'So, Beth, how are you doing?' Ellie gushes. 'Must be an awful shock. I mean . . . *Tom*? Do they really think he's capable of harming that poor girl?'

'The papers have it all wrong,' I say, emphatically. 'I have no idea how they think they can get away with it. Honestly, I didn't even want to leave the cottage this morning.' Tears cloud my vision. I feel sympathetic hands on me again as I bury my head in my arms on the table and allow a sob to escape.

'Oh, my lovely – we're all here for you; try not to worry. They've not *charged* him, have they?' Julia asks.

'No. And once they realise that he has nothing to do with her disappearance, they'll release him, I'm sure. But everyone will always say there's no smoke without fire. He's in the *newspaper*. His name is tarnished and so is mine now. Low-life journalists. This could ruin our lives.' Another sob wracks my body.

'Look, whatever happens, everyone loves this café –

you've done such a fabulous job and people will continue to come here. Of course there will be gossip, that's inevitable. But the truth will prevail,' Julia declares dramatically, as though she's giving a speech in court. 'It won't stop customers coming through these doors, and you and Poppy will be supported, I promise.'

It's the most interaction I've had with the yummy mummy club for the entire two years I've lived here. But it's all well and good them being supportive and lovely while they think Tom's innocent. They could turn on me just as quickly if the worst happens and he *is* charged.

He won't be, the voice in my head tells me.

Thankfully, for now at least, it seems my fear of leaving the cottage this morning was unfounded. Poppy and me – we're okay for the time being. And if Maxwell does his job, Tom will be released shortly, and this whole situation will diffuse into nothing more than village gossip. Village gossip that will soon be replaced with something else. And actually, I'm finally interesting enough to have been brought into the circle of friends I've wanted to infiltrate since moving to Lower Tew. Tom's shock arrest has brought something positive after all.

The day drags, my mind replaying the chat with the nursery mums on a loop. I try to busy myself clearing tables, wiping down the counter and stacking cups, but I'm counting down the minutes until it's time to leave and pick Poppy up. My mobile vibrates in my apron pocket. I reach in to get it, but pull my hand back. It's irresponsible to ignore it, but the thought of what news the call might bring fills me with dread. I'm sure they'll call back. I'll face it later.

I fill Lucy in on what happened. Not in any great detail – the same as I didn't with Julia and the others. The bare minimum to feed their curiosity, that was all.

Lucy goes very quiet afterwards and hardly speaks for the rest of the afternoon. Absolutely no singing – so unlike her. Initially, I thought it was politeness – she didn't want to appear overly happy or jolly following my news. But I begin to sense there is more to it.

Just as I'm about to leave, I say, 'You've been uncharacteristically quiet, Lucy. You okay?'

She doesn't look me in the eye when she answers with a brief, 'Yeah, I'm fine.' I don't want to push her. A niggling worm of worry burrows inside me. She seems concerned. Why?

I don't have time to delve deeper into it now. I put on my coat and she gives me a weak smile and says she'll see me in the morning. I'm uneasy when I leave, and I can't ignore the repeating thought in my mind: *Lucy doesn't believe Tom is innocent.*

I have a feeling she's not alone.

Chapter 14

BETH

Now

While I walk, I finally look at my phone. It was Maxwell who'd called – several times by the look of it. Texts, too, asking me to contact him. There's also a missed call from a withheld number. Could that be from Tom? I don't know that he's able to make calls, or what I'd want to say to him if he could. That's if I even *want* to talk to him – whatever is going on, the police must have *something* on him to have made the arrest in the first place. If I do speak to him, no doubt my words will be those of anger, upset, hurt – not support. But then, if I don't do it now, I have no clue when I'll get the opportunity.

Although I'm tempted to walk to nursery with my head bowed, I don't. I force myself to keep looking up, glancing around me as I walk briskly. The short journey will take me past home and I wonder if I should pop in first to return Maxwell's call, in private. No. I'll continue on; keep reality at bay for just a little longer – I'll have to listen to what he has to say soon enough. The strong breeze whips up fallen leaves, and cool air pushes into my face. Long, auburn strands of hair blow across my eyes and as I brush them away, I see what's up ahead.

I stop short.

In the lane outside my cottage, I see numerous vehicles all haphazardly parked, doors flung open, as if abandoned in haste.

Police cars.

My body shakes as I stand frozen to the spot, gawping at the scene. I force my weak legs to move towards them.

What the hell's going on?

A car comes screeching up behind me. I turn sharply, almost hoping it might plough into me, but it comes to an abrupt halt. I chastise myself for even allowing that kind of thinking. Poppy needs me.

Maxwell bursts from the driver's door, his face beetroot red. 'I've been calling non-stop.' His voice is stern. At first, I'm affronted that he's telling me off and I want to tell him that I have had a lot of things to deal with today and was just about to phone him, but the situation is clearly grave and I refrain. He slams the door, swoops past me and heads to the uniformed police officers at the entrance to my home. A few words are exchanged, then I see a smartly dressed, stiff-postured woman with strawberry-blonde hair approach him. She shows him a piece of paper, which he rips from her hand, studies for a few seconds, then gives back to her.

He heads towards me. I've barely moved. My pulse

thuds as he informs me they have a search warrant to seize and retain anything in the property which could relate to the murder charge. I'm numb as I hand over my key.

What are they expecting to find?

Chapter 15

TOM

Now

'I'll ask again,' DI Manning says, his ruddy face displaying his exasperation. 'Where were you? We know you didn't show up to work.'

'No comment.' I can't believe I've uttered that phrase. I want to hang my head, slap myself. The word 'guilty' screams repeatedly in my mind. God, if I were watching this interview on the TV in the safety of my lounge, I'd be about ready to launch the remote at the screen. At my stupid face. I don't think I have any other choice though; Maxwell is adamant I should shut up from here on in, and although I've gone against his earlier advice, now it seems my best, and only, recourse. I mustn't give them anything further that they can use against me.

'CCTV footage didn't show you at your usual train station and your work colleagues had no knowledge of your whereabouts. You aren't being forthcoming as to whether you had any other appointments,' DC Cooper runs through the list. 'It isn't looking good for you, Tom – all this secrecy the day after you were questioned about Katie Williams just adds fuel to the fire. If you cooperate now, it'll be looked upon more favourably than if you refuse to speak. This no comment nonsense makes you seem guilty as charged.' Her cold eyes are boring deep into mine. I wonder if she has a partner. She doesn't wear a wedding band. Wouldn't surprise me if she were single, living alone with just a cat for company – if she ever actually leaves this place. Lonely. Bitter and twisted. In need of a good seeing to. I turn away from her.

'The evidence against you is mounting, Tom. My officers have been to your home and searched through your belongings. What's the betting they're now in possession of more evidence to add to our file?' Manning taps the fat cardboard folder in front of him. It's probably filled with blank sheets of paper – another game they're playing to make me talk – but his words do cause a burning sensation in my gut. Coppers raiding through my stuff. Traipsing through my rooms, trawling through items of Beth's and Poppy's and bagging them up for no reason? My nostrils flare as I attempt to control my breathing. I make fists under the table, push them into my thighs until it hurts.

'Hit a nerve?' DC Cooper says. 'Worried about what we've secured? Because it's my guess you hadn't thought about Katie Williams in quite some time before DI Manning here came knocking on your door. It's my guess you thought you'd got away with it. Got complacent in your idyllic life with your pretty wife and daughter. You certainly weren't expecting something you'd escaped justice for eight years ago to rear its head and cause you problems now, were you? Which means you've not been as meticulous as you should've been – you got lulled into a false sense of security. So, I'm betting you've left vital clues. Things you assumed were irrelevant, things you thought only *you* would know the meaning of, for us to pick up and piece together now. It's surprising how inconspicuous, *innocuous*, something can look until you have something else to add. Then the picture begins to take shape.'

Shut up, shut up, shut up! I have to bite the inside of my cheek, hard, to stop the words leaving. The sanctimonious bitch. Why is Manning letting her take the lead here? He's the superior. My stomach twists at her words. I dumped my work laptop, but I couldn't find my iPad – I'd rushed out of the house Tuesday morning and assumed I'd be able to find it later on, only they'd got to me before I could. *Shit.*

If Beth had been home when I'd called from the station that evening, I might've been able to get her to agree to get rid of it for me. Although that in itself would've caused various issues.

'What are our tech guys going to retrieve from your phone or from your home computer, I wonder? When did you last communicate with Katie? Will your emails back up your claim she went travelling?'

I open my mouth to launch into a rant, but Maxwell's hand shoots in front of me – a warning. I hiss the words through my gritted teeth: '*No. Comment.*' A bead of sweat trickles down my face, and I try to wipe it away without them noticing. The bitch, Cooper – she does though. She smirks and I have the urge to punch her. I look past her, focusing on the wall behind. I visualise Beth, Poppy and me as a family in our perfect cottage. I will have that again. If I keep level-headed.

If they don't find anything on my iPad.

If they don't uncover the truth about where I was on Tuesday.

Chapter 16

BETH

Now

The woman I saw earlier is standing stiffly outside my front door as I walk down the path. Poppy is grasping my hand tightly. Or I might be the one holding hers tight.

'Mrs Hardcastle,' she says. 'I'm Detective Constable Imogen Cooper. I'm from Major Investigation Team 8 in the Homicide and Major Crime Command, working with DI Manning. Here's your key back.' She stretches out her arm. 'I locked up – I was going to come and find you,' she says, dropping the key into my palm. Imogen Cooper is petite, but her stance is assured and I'd bet she's tougher than she appears. She must have to be in her line of work.

'Well, no need now.' I clasp the key in my hand and make to move past the detective.

'I'm sorry.' She steps in front of me so that I can't rush inside. 'I realise this feels like an intrusion. Has to be done, I'm afraid.'

'Sure,' I say. I don't want to talk about this in front of Poppy really. 'How . . . er . . . is it, in there?' I nod towards the cottage.

'Oh, we've taken what we need at this time. Tried not to make it look as though a herd of elephants has stampeded through. But you know . . .' She smiles awkwardly.

Great. So, it's a total mess, then. And the words 'at this time' sound ominous.

I shake my head and sigh loudly.

'Has Maxwell Fielding spoken to you?'

'No, not yet. I was in a rush to get Poppy.'

'Right.' DC Cooper puts her hands in her trouser pockets and lowers her gaze to Poppy. 'We've had a little game inside your house,' she says, attempting a smile. 'I'm sorry we might have made a bit of a mess that your mummy will need to clear up. Grown-ups aren't always great at putting things away; they can be a bit clumsy.'

DC Cooper's face tilts up, her eyes meeting mine. My pulse skips. She side-steps me and I take my opportunity to shoot inside.

I hear her say, 'I'll see you soon,' as I close the door. For a moment, I stand with my back against it, taking stock. Shaking.

From the way she was acting, from what she said, I'm guessing they found what they were looking for.

Chapter 17

BETH

Now

It feels such a violation knowing that police officers have been in my cottage, in my bedroom, touching my things. I didn't have time to hang around to witness them filing out with plastic bags full of Tom's things, maybe even my things. I'd had to leave to get Poppy from nursery. It was probably better not to watch anyway. I'd only have been fretting about what they were looking for; what they'd find.

I can't immediately tell what they've taken – each room is in varying degrees of disarray. Rushing around the cottage, all I can tell is that it seems as though they've been thorough. Hopefully that means they won't be back, despite Cooper's words. Thankfully, they've been less careless in Poppy's room, I notice. I flit around, straightening the toys on her bed, closing drawers and cupboards. I gather some of her discarded clothes and bundle them quickly into the wardrobe. It'll do for now.

Our bedroom is in a greater state of chaos, as is the kitchen. The main computer has gone, and I can't see Tom's iPad – those are the obvious items, the ones I fully expected them to seize. Nonetheless, a violent shudder runs through me. This situation is going to get worse, and I'm afraid of being taken down along with Tom: dragged into a spiralling vortex. I need to think about what I can do to prevent the total destruction of my family. As far as I know, they still don't have Katie Williams' body, so I can't see how they've enough evidence to link Tom to her and keep him in custody. Maxwell clearly isn't telling me everything, but according to him what they have so far is shaky. It must be enough to keep them investigating, though. Enough for a jury to condemn Tom to life in prison? I can't see it. Unless they *have* found Katie – and in some way linked Tom to her, although God knows how – then surely they won't have a case. I must research similar cases, see what the outcome has been for those accused of murder in the absence of a body.

After a quick meal for Poppy, and a microwave dinner-for-one for me, I put Poppy to bed and go back downstairs to continue tidying the kitchen. I managed the lounge and hallway within half an hour of getting home; the utility and the rest of upstairs are next on the list. As I slide paperwork back into the drawer set aside for utility bills and other important post, I realise some bank statements are missing. We have a joint account, but Tom also has another separate one. He's always had it, and although I closed mine when we married, we kept his to use for emergencies. As far as I am aware, the last time it was used was when I bought the kiln for Poppy's Place, as I'd run out of money thanks to some unexpected rewiring. I don't see how recent statements, which probably don't even show any transactions, would be of any help to the police for something that happened eight years ago.

A knocking at the door jolts me out of my thoughts.

Chapter 18

BETH

Now

Maxwell is sitting opposite me, elbows resting on the kitchen table, his large, amber-coloured eyes trained on mine. My hands are gripped together in front of me, my fingers turning red as I squeeze them while I wait for him to 'bring me up to speed'.

'The police have been granted an extension, I'm afraid, Beth. I warned you this might be the case, and of course I fought against it, but after the search warrant, I was expecting it.'

'I don't understand, Maxwell.' I shake my head, then lower my chin into my cupped hands. He's not giving me the full picture, I know it. What isn't he telling me? 'I thought after tonight, they'd release him, and he'd be back home.'

'Yes, I know, I'm sorry.' He looks weary; it's been a long day for him too, no doubt. 'It's not ideal. It'll be reviewed

70

in the morning then, if they want it, a further extension for the full ninety-six hours will have to be sought from the magistrate. Anyway, DI Manning and DC Cooper will want to question you, Beth. So you should be prepared.' He's using a gentle voice – no doubt reserved for distressed relatives and distraught spouses. People like me.

My mouth dries and my tongue sticks to its roof. I take a sip from my glass of water. I've made Maxwell a coffee, but I couldn't face one myself. Even though the caffeine hit might be welcome after this impossibly long day, it would mean I'd be awake all night. 'Right,' I say, recovering from the initial bad news. 'That's fine. Although, I'm not sure what they think I can add. Surely he's given them everything?'

'They'll ask what you know about Katie Williams: things Tom has told you.' Maxwell sweeps over my question and I wonder just what Tom *has* told them. 'They'll also want to get a feel for what Tom is like as a person. Answer their questions with as little detail as possible.'

'As little? Why? Wouldn't it be better to be as detailed as I can be?'

'No. The more info you give them, the more rope they'll have to hang him.'

I sit back hard against my chair, my mouth slack.

'Oh, sorry,' he says quickly. 'Poor choice of words. You know what I mean. Just give them yes and no answers where possible and keep any description succinct. If you waffle on, it's more likely you'll say something that could possibly incriminate him.'

'Really? Like what? I don't get this, Maxwell. If he's innocent, nothing I say will land him in it.'

'That's not necessarily true. They believe Tom is involved

71

in Katie's disappearance – and suspected murder – so the things you thought were inconsequential will suddenly be looked at under a microscope. In retrospect, something unimportant can look like the most significant fact. It all depends on the angle the investigating team want to put on it. Do you understand?'

'I suppose,' I say, not really understanding at all.

'Think of this. In a recent criminal case a couple were suspected of killing their baby, which they both strenuously denied. They said they'd found him in his cot in the morning and were unable to rouse him. During the police interview, the mother talked and talked, and in trying to give a full account, she said too much. Things she thought were usual actions, like the fact she regularly gave the baby Calpol for teething pain. The detectives – and later the newspapers and social media – started to suspect she'd overdosed him. She was accused of accidentally killing her baby and trying to cover it up.' He pauses for breath. 'You see? She gave a long-winded story, believing she was being helpful, and that's what happened. Something entirely innocent on its own was taken apart by police. They made her statement fit the angle they wanted to take – that she was guilty of manslaughter. In your case, it could mean Tom being charged with murder. Don't elaborate, Beth. Answer with brevity and clarity. It's easier to remember what you've said, too.'

I shoot him a confused look. 'You're making it sound like I'd be lying.'

'I'm not implying that,' he shakes his head. 'But you have to be careful. If you want Tom out and back at home with you and Poppy after their time is up, you need to think about what you're telling the police.'

'Do you believe Tom had something to do with it, Maxwell? Is that what you're trying to tell me?'

'Of course not. Although it's not my job to believe or disbelieve. Tom has instructed my firm to act on his behalf. If this gets to court—'

My heart pumps furiously. 'You said they didn't have enough evidence to even charge him, and now you're talking about court,' I say, pushing myself up from the chair, my hands flat on the table as I lean across it towards Maxwell. 'And how can we be sure that Katie *is* dead? Aren't they still looking for her?'

'All the evidence, or lack of, points to Katie no longer being alive, Beth. She's just completely disappeared. At first her friends accepted she had just gone travelling, but it seems her only communication with them was via email, and they began to suspect they weren't even from her. She never used a credit card to buy anything abroad. There's no trace. So, with no proof of life, I'm afraid they're searching for a body.'

'Tom had nothing to do with her disappearance, or her supposed death, Maxwell,' I say. 'You said you'd get him released.'

'I know what I said, Beth,' he sighs. 'Surprisingly, given that DI Manning is such an experienced officer, he's playing silly buggers, not disclosing all the evidence to me. I'm afraid to say I think the investigating officers are looking pretty smug with themselves. I've a bad feeling they might have enough for the CPS to allow them to bring charges: they're holding *something* back and at first I thought it was because what they had was weak, but now I'm not so certain.'

It takes several seconds for this information to sink in,

and when it does, I feel my legs give. I sit back down heavily, shaking my head vehemently. 'No, no, no.'

'I'm sorry, Beth. It's just a *might*, but I wanted to prepare you for it. We'll do everything we can to ensure we get him back home to you and Poppy.'

I'm worried about Tom, but I can't stop thinking about what this means for me. It dawns on me that if Tom is charged, I'm going to be the most looked-at person in Lower Tew.

The wife of a suspected murderer.

Chapter 19

BETH

Now

Maxwell was right. After he left, the police were on the phone within the hour, asking when a convenient time to chat would be. I've managed to put them off and said tomorrow after lunch would suit me. They asked me to go to the station, but after I explained I didn't have anyone to pick Poppy up from nursery, they agreed to come to the cottage. Leaving it until tomorrow gives me time to think about everything Maxwell talked about and consider how to frame my answers, too. Clearly I'm going to need it.

Earlier, Maxwell rattled off the types of questions he thought would come up and, despite everything he kept telling me, I said too much every time I tried to answer one. 'Too much waffle,' he said. Waffle which, if he is to be believed, could make things worse for Tom.

Pushing them to wait also allows the hours to tick away. The less time they have to gather evidence, the more likely the ninety-six hours Maxwell said they'd push for will elapse and they'll have to release him.

I've tidied the kitchen, put Poppy's toys away and now, as I'm about to crash on the sofa and put my feet up, there's another knock on the door. I attempt to quiet the panicked voice inside my head telling me it's the police trying to catch me out by turning up early.

But it could be.

Shit.

I take a deep, juddering breath in and open the door, leaving the chain across. I expect to see two stern-faced detectives as I had on Monday night, but it's just one person standing there. I'm relieved it's not police, but somewhat shocked to see Adam instead.

'Hi,' he says, a hesitant smile playing on his lips. 'I realise this is an uninvited intrusion, but I . . . well, I heard about Tom's arrest.' He squints, as though he's afraid he'll get shouted at. 'If you want me to mind my own bloody business, then please, just tell me to do one. But, in case no one has asked you how you are, or whether you need any support, I thought I'd be that person. I know what it's like to be avoided, remember?' His smile now is wide, reaching his eyes. His kind eyes. He radiates warmth. So much so, I burst into tears.

'Oh, no. I'm so sorry.' He raises both hands in front of him, palms up, and takes a step back as though he's physically caused me harm. 'I really didn't mean to upset you, Beth . . .' He looks mortified.

'No. No. It's fine – it's just been a very long day. You've not upset me.' I close the door a bit so I can unlatch the chain, then open it wide and step aside to let him in. 'Thank you. I'm sorry for crying.'

'Don't be. I cry all the time,' he says. I laugh through my tears. Then I fret as I realise he's not joking.

'Oh, you're serious. I – I didn't mean to laugh. You've every right to cry.'

Now Adam laughs.

'Let's start again,' he says. 'I'm popping over to offer my shoulder to cry on, if you so wish. Or to chat, share a moan, listen while you freak out – or whatever might be helpful to you at this point.'

'All of the above, I think.'

He nods. 'Good. Then I'm glad I didn't bottle it at the top of your path.'

'You were thinking about it?'

'Oh, God, yes! I don't know you very well. I mean, you seem lovely. You were amazing with Jess yesterday and you offered to have her over here, which was so kind of you. But still, you could've bitten my head off for all I know.'

'Yes, that was a distinct possibility, I guess. Now, can I offer you a drink? Where is Jess?'

'I have a wonderful neighbour called Constance, who likes to help me out sometimes. She's at mine looking after her. I very rarely call upon her of an evening, but thought this was an occasion when I should. And yes – I'd love a drink. Do you have hot chocolate?'

'I was personally going for something with high-volume alcohol content, but if you'd like an "Options" drinking choc . . . that's all I've got?' I put my head on one side.

'God.' He shakes his head. 'You must think me a real bore for even suggesting hot chocolate. But it's Jess's favourite and I've taken to drinking it with her now. Better than opening a bottle of whiskey, which is a slippery slope when you're on your own and responsible for a three-year-old.'

'Of course. I feel like a terrible parent now! Hot chocolate it is,' I say. I don't think he's a bore at all. I think it's commendable he refrains from drinking and puts Jess first all the time. He's clearly a thoughtful and responsible dad.

'I wasn't implying you were a bad parent because you wanted a drink,' he says, his eyes wide. 'Oh, dear. I've certainly got off on the wrong foot.' He's flustered; flashes of red track up his throat. He rubs his face.

'Hey, Adam. Stop,' I say, walking into the kitchen. Adam follows. 'You're here. Do you see anyone else?' I wave my hand around. 'The police have invaded my home today, searching for evidence to condemn my husband.' I hear the catch in my voice and cough to cover it up. Adam's eyes widen but I carry on speaking so he doesn't ask about it. I don't want to cry again. 'Having company right now is probably the best thing for me and I don't have anyone else to lean on. Don't worry about what you say – I'm no better than you at this stuff, trust me. Remember at the café when I said things I immediately regretted? You said you didn't mind.'

Adam nods and takes a deep breath, appearing to compose himself following my shock revelation. 'No, I didn't mind, you're right. It's not about what people say is it? It's their actions. It's someone taking time to talk, offer their ear. That's what matters.'

'Exactly. And I feel the same. I'm grateful you made the decision to pop over.' I find the sachets of hot chocolate and grab two mugs. It's good that Adam's here – I'd have hit the bottle and had at least two glasses by now if I'd been left to my own devices.

'Good – then I'm glad I made it to the door.'

'Me too. You being here will help take my mind off the fact the detectives want to speak with me tomorrow.'

'Oh, wow.' He raises his eyebrows. 'Heavy. You must be so anxious, especially after today's search. Look, I'm not here after the inside scoop – you don't have to tell me anything.'

'I know. Thank you, Adam. I trust you.'

Probably more than I trust my husband right now.

Chapter 20

BETH

Now

Last night helped. Adam was every bit the good listener he promised, and although I didn't divulge all my current feelings – or the horror I felt at having my home ransacked by so many people – it felt good to share some of my fears; vocalise them to someone other than a solicitor. We ended up talking more about Camilla than Tom. He's clearly been devastated by losing her, especially the way it happened – a severe anaphylaxis reaction. He said she'd become complacent about her nut allergy, having not had any issues for years, and she didn't religiously check labelling. She carried an EpiPen, so there'd never been any real worry about something so tragic happening.

He said he talks about her all the time with Jess, but he can't open up to anyone about how he feels deep down; how it's impacted his life; how lonely he is. He told me how he misses adult company and conversation, but he doesn't want to put his needs ahead of Jess's. Poor Adam. As it turned out I think he needed me more than I needed him. Although at least he took my mind off my own situation. He's going to bring Jess into the café again, make it more of a regular thing so she can have fun, but also so he can interact with adults. I think it's the perfect solution for him.

I wonder what my perfect solution is.

Poppy was reluctant for me to leave her at nursery this morning. Maybe she can sense my growing anxiety. I saw the group of mums from yesterday and had a quick chat, careful to avoid any mention of the police search or Tom's arrest. They didn't speak about it either even though I bet they know about both events and are dying to find out more. After my chat with DS Manning and DC Cooper in a few hours, I should have a clearer picture of where all this is heading. Then I'll prepare for the next stage.

If it all goes well, perhaps Tom will be home later. We'll go back to our regular lives. It's so weird to think that a few days ago everything seemed happy, easy and carefree. How quickly things can change. In an instant, your path can take a sharp turn and lead you somewhere you never anticipated.

I'll be glad once this police chat is over. At least they've agreed to carry it out at home, rather than the station. I couldn't face the added humiliation of that – although it does mean the neighbours might spot them coming to the cottage. Again.

'Morning,' I say as I step inside the café. Two tables are taken: people enjoying drinks and cakes. No one is doing any pottery painting. The customers, none of whom I immediately recognise as locals, return polite greetings and watch me as I walk through. The hairs on the back of my neck prickle.

'Hey, Lucy. Everything all right here this morning?' I ask as I pop on an apron. Lucy stands behind the counter, refreshing the plates with new pastries and baked goodies.

'Yeah. Although, it's a bit odd.'

'Oh? Odd how?' I have a feeling I know where this is going.

'The customers were queuing! Waiting for me to open. Just seemed a bit eager to me. And they aren't from Lower Tew.' Lucy narrows her eyes.

As I thought. Already news is travelling; curiosity is building. Sightseers. And I don't think they're here for the views or the pottery. Nausea catches me off-guard and I hold my stomach. 'Well, any custom is money in my pocket,' I say, giving a forced laugh.

'Yes, well. Let's hope it doesn't become a circus around here. This is a lovely, small community – the locals wouldn't want it becoming known for anything other than its picturesque cottages and fabulous pub,' she says, before adding with a strained smile, 'And pottery café, of course.'

'Look, Lucy – it's the last thing I want too, you know.' I can't keep the hurt from my tone. Lucy has worked for me for over a year and we've always got on well. I'd hate for this to affect our working relationship; I need her. 'I'm certain it'll all blow over. I'm talking to the police later, I'm hoping that will help clear some things up. Tom is a good man,' I say, quickly wiping a rogue tear with my sleeve.

'I'm sorry, Beth. I don't mean to be unsympathetic, especially after you've had such bad news.'

'So, you've heard the latest then?'

Lucy puts her arm around me and lays her head on my shoulder. 'It's a village, Beth,' she says as way of explanation. I sigh, and she continues. 'I love working here, and I love living in Lower Tew. I get a little over-protective of the place sometimes.'

'I know, hun. And it's lovely that you care about your community so much; I love your passion. It's why I hired you, after all. It'll all be okay, I promise.'

It's a promise I instantly regret making. How do I know it'll all turn out okay? There's no guarantee Tom will be released at the end of the detention period. Nothing is certain.

I give myself a shake and a good talking to.

It *is* certain. Of course everything will be fine.

The police can't have enough evidence to charge him – they just can't. Be positive. Unless something to contradict it comes up, I have to show the world that everything will be all right. For now, for my own sake and Poppy's, I am working on the assumption Tom is completely innocent, and there's no chance he could possibly be charged with such a terrible crime.

The truth will prevail.

Chapter 21

BETH

Now

I've been sitting twiddling my thumbs, literally, for the past half an hour. Clock-watching. Waiting. Why are they so late? Is it because they've been tied up with getting permission from a magistrate to extend Tom's custody time? He's not home and their thirty-six hours was up earlier, so I'm guessing they've succeeded. Maybe they're just late on purpose to put me on the back foot.

Breathe.

This morning's breakfast is still churning in my stomach; my digestion has gone all to pot. If they don't hurry, I'll be late picking Poppy up from nursery, too. I already feel guilty enough leaving Lucy on her own for longer than usual; I don't need the extra stress of worrying about letting Poppy down on top.

Christ's sake – hurry up.

The heavy knock makes me freeze. This is it.

Come on, Beth. You've got this.

I clench and unclench my fists a few times, jiggle my shoulders to loosen them, take some deep breaths, then calmly walk to the door.

'Mrs Hardcastle,' DC Cooper says, tilting her chin up. I swallow hard, then invite her in. Just as I think I'm getting away with it being just one detective, the large figure of DI Manning sweeps around the corner and strides up my path. He gives a curt hello and follows Cooper inside.

'We met briefly yesterday, as you might recall,' she says. As if I'm likely to have forgotten that experience. 'I'm Detective Constable Imogen Cooper, working with DI Manning. Thank you for seeing us today.'

I note Cooper's eyes darting all over the room, taking in every minute detail. Didn't she already do that yesterday? Is this for show now? Her demeanour is doing nothing for my nerves.

'If you'd like to come into the kitchen, I've got fresh coffee brewing and I've baked cookies.' The smell of my lemon, ginger and white chocolate chip cookies is wafting through the cottage. They usually go down a storm with the customers so I'm hoping it'll soften the detectives up a bit.

'Thanks,' she says. I think I catch a hint of a smile, but I could be wrong. It's hard to tell – her expression hasn't really altered since she walked in the door. I have the feeling I'm in for a rough ride. I look to DI Manning and smile. Thankfully, he reciprocates, and I allow my racing mind to slow a little.

They take a seat side by side at the farmhouse table and get notebooks and pens out. I try to focus on pouring the coffee. My hands are trembling but there's nothing I can do about that. Surely nerves are common – and expected – in a situation such as this? They won't think it's unusual, or a sign that I'm worried, will they? As much as I would like to stretch this moment out, put off the inevitable questions, I know I can't afford to play for time.

'There you go. The best cookies from Poppy's Place,' I say, brightly, as I place two plates in front of the detectives and turn back to fetch the tray of drinks.

'So, this Poppy's Place is your café?' DC Cooper asks.

'Yes, it's a ceramics café – you can paint pre-made bisque pieces, like plates, mugs, animals and things, and have a coffee and cake while you do it. Then it'll be popped in the kiln and I fire them overnight and the pieces are collected the next day, or I can deliver them. I opened it not long after we moved here, and it's been amazing. It's so well supported . . .' I tail off as I realise I'm already doing it: chattering away, when really I could just have said, 'Yes, I own the café.'

It's fine. Now I've got my jitteriness out the way, maybe I'll be able to answer their proper questions with more brevity.

'Sounds . . . interesting,' DI Manning says, giving his colleague a sideways glance. I want to add that it's not everyone's cup of tea, but I bite my tongue.

'How are you doing, Mrs Hardcastle – given your husband is in custody?' Imogen Cooper asks, before taking a sip of coffee. I feel it's a trick question. She's asking it nonchalantly, no pen in hand, all to make me think this is breezy and conversational. Trying to put me at ease, perhaps. Or that's what she wants me to believe.

I wish Maxwell hadn't come here yesterday now. He's

86

managed to get me so worked up I'm overthinking the simplest questions. I force my shoulders down, and consciously relax my muscles. I'm going to do this my way.

'Not great, really. As you can imagine this has come out of the blue. A lightning bolt, if you will. I just can't understand it if I'm honest. How can you think Tom is involved in this woman's disappearance?'

'I'm sorry this has all come about so suddenly, Mrs Hardcastle—'

'Please call me Beth, DC Cooper. Such a mouthful to always refer to me as that,' I say with a smile.

'Beth, I understand you're shocked by your husband being taken into custody. We have reason to believe he was the last person to see Katie Williams, so of course, he is of interest. Often it's been the case that the last person to see the missing individual was the one to have a hand in the disappearance.' Now Cooper takes her notebook and poises her pen. She looks to DI Manning and he leans forward, placing his mobile phone in between us, ready to begin his questions.

I lick my lips, trying to lubricate them, but there's little available moisture. I take a quick gulp of coffee.

'For the benefit of the recording, DI David Manning and DC Imogen Cooper are interviewing Bethany Hardcastle at her home address . . .'

I feel myself zoning out as he continues to talk 'for the recording'. There's a rushing noise in my ears: a high-pitched squealing which is about to tip me into panic mode. I wasn't expecting this. The pens and notebooks were already enough to make my nerves multiply.

He starts talking to me, rather than the phone. His

voice brings me back from the edge, and I pull myself together.

'You lived in London prior to moving here?' he asks, looking directly into my eyes.

'Yes, that's right. We had a flat in Bethnal Green. Well, it was Tom's flat – I moved in with him then we got married. When I fell pregnant, we realised we'd need to move at some point as it wasn't big enough for a growing family. But once I had Poppy it wasn't the right time, then when I returned to work from maternity leave, I got a promotion. So, we stayed a while longer. I knew within months it wasn't what I wanted, though.' I stop talking. One, to take a breath, and two because I know I'm doing the dead opposite of what I've been instructed to do.

Brief answers. For God's sake.

I lay my hands in my lap, grasping them together and squeezing my fingers until it hurts. I purse my lips together to prevent more word vomit.

'Where and when did you meet?' he asks. He sits back in the chair, and it crosses my mind he's settling in for another novel-length answer.

'It was seven years ago. I remember it clearly, because it was my twenty-fifth birthday: Saturday April the fifth. It was outside Sager + Wilde. I was sitting on the terrace with my friends,' I smile at the memory and stop speaking. Manning raises his eyebrows and sits forward to scribble something. I wonder why he's bothering to take notes if it's being recorded. To convey the seriousness of the visit? To ensure I'm as fully on-edge as possible?

'Did he tell you about his previous relationship with Katie Williams?'

'He did – that night, in actual fact. I remember him

saying how his heart had recently been broken and he wasn't expecting to meet anyone and get such an instant connection as he had with me. He said it in a jokey way in that moment, really. But when we were going out together and things were getting serious, he did confide in me that he'd been pretty gutted about Katie's sudden departure. He'd not expected her to up sticks and go abroad like she did.'

'Gutted enough to try and prevent her leaving?' Cooper says.

I turn to look directly at her. 'No. Tom was honestly heartbroken *because* she left. She'd gone. He didn't stop her. And you know, after you told him the other night about your suspicions something had happened to her, he was devastated. All the years he'd assumed she was living her dream life abroad and you destroyed that belief. He might've been the last to see her in *this* country, that you know of, but surely someone saw her afterwards?'

Both detectives look down at their notepads, neither responding. I'm guessing they haven't found anyone else who says they saw her. They still have Tom as the last person. Which is why they're still holding him. But if that's all they've got, that proves nothing. They aren't going to be able to charge him, there's no way.

'In the seven years you've known Tom, have there been any times he's shown aggressive behaviour towards you? To your daughter?'

I shake my head and sigh. Maxwell had said this would be an angle they'd take, but I'm appalled now that they're actually asking. 'No. Absolutely not. He's the most gentle, kind and loving man, and he loves Poppy more than life itself,' I say. 'Ask anyone,' I add.

'A good, family man,' Manning mutters.

'Yes, exactly. Which is why this is all such madness. You're wasting your time looking at Tom. Wherever Katie is, Tom doesn't know. She could be living off the grid?' It's a hopeful suggestion. I want to ask why they've suddenly decided she's come to harm almost eight years after she left the country, but they aren't going to tell me. Let them ask the questions; no point riling them while they have my husband locked up.

'We'll be the ones to formulate the theories, if you don't mind,' DI Manning says, flatly. I mumble an apology.

'How would you describe your relationship?' he asks.

'Great, thank you,' I say, a little too abruptly. 'We're very happy. We've carved out the perfect life for ourselves here.'

'You both appear to work very hard, Beth. Must be difficult to find time for each other, especially with a toddler. Relationships often struggle to stay on the straight and narrow when there are demands placed on them from every angle.' It's Cooper who says this, and it's clear she's digging. I'm not having that. As she hasn't directly asked a question, I remain silent. Maxwell would be proud. She seems to realise this is what I'm doing, and asks, 'With you immersing yourself in your new business as well as looking after Poppy, and with Tom spending a lot of his time at work, or commuting, how has that impacted on you both?'

I'm careful to take my time in answering, drinking some coffee while I think. I am aware of their eyes looking expectantly at me.

'Of course it's inevitable you move through different stages in a healthy relationship, and Poppy coming along took some adjustment. But she's the best thing ever to have happened to us and we both adore her. Tom is besotted,' I say, smiling. 'We've learned to adapt, and we've managed to keep our marriage fresh. Tom always ensures we have some "us" time in the evenings and we have wonderful weekends together.' I think that's a fair assessment, give or take.

'Tom gets home from work at what time?'

'Around six p.m. – earlier if he can leave work promptly. He likes to spend some time with Poppy and read her a bedtime story. He arranged slightly different working hours with the bank so he could do that.'

'Right,' DC Cooper says, looking down and flipping through her notebook pages. She lifts her head and for a moment says nothing as she keeps my eye contact, her lips tightly pursed. I push down on my bobbing leg underneath the table. 'As you have a "great" relationship,' Cooper does annoying air quotes with her fingers, 'I assume you share everything? You know, as in, there are no secrets between you?'

It's a trick question. *Every* couple has at least some secrets, surely? But if I say that, she's going to twist it and make out I've lied about how good our relationship is.

Play it safe.

'We share everything, yes.' I keep it brief. My counselling from Maxwell is paying off.

'So, you know why he was late home on Monday evening then?' Her gaze doesn't waver from mine.

Shit. I don't. I never got the chance to ask him. I've fallen into her trap with this. Now's the time to simply state the truth.

'No, I never got the opportunity because DI Manning dragged him away the moment he got home.' I shoot Manning a caustic smile.

'He came home again later that evening, though. Did you not discuss it then?'

'I was in bed, and then he left for work early, as usual.'

Cooper nods, slowly. 'Really?' she says.

My heart rate picks up. 'Yes, really,' I say. I hear the quiver in my tone. No doubt they caught it too. Cooper sits forward, her face close enough now that I can smell the coffee on her breath and see the intensity of her eyes: the flecks of blue against the steel grey.

'Would it surprise you to know he didn't *go* to work the following morning?' she says.

I unconsciously gasp. *What? Tom didn't go to work on Tuesday?*

I've no way of coming back from the shocked reaction I've just displayed. And I can't think of anything to say in response.

'I'll take that as a yes, then.' Cooper's eyebrows shoot up and her lips form a line as she scribbles. The noise of the pen scratching over the paper is the only sound in the room.

Chapter 22

BETH

Now

My chest is tight as I walk towards the nursery; each shallow breath seems to catch in my lungs. I have to make an official statement at the police station in Banbury as soon as I can. The seriousness of the situation has finally penetrated my brain and I'm going into self-preservation mode.

Tom has lied to me.

Manning and Cooper left me with little doubt about that. *They* can't be lying about Tom not going to work. Under certain circumstances I'm sure they must play around with how they put information to people they interview, but this doesn't appear to be one of those instances. They said they'd checked CCTV footage and Tom wasn't seen getting a train to London, and he never showed at the bank. The fact I didn't know will go against Tom. But I'm guessing the *cause* for his absence from work is going against him far more. Do the detectives already know the reason why? Although I can't see how it would link to something that happened eight years ago anyway.

The question needles at my brain: what *was* he doing, if not working? He left at his usual time; he was wearing a suit; he took his briefcase as normal.

He wasn't wearing his suit jacket when he came home on Monday evening. I recall it now, and I also remember the sour smell when I hugged him. I hadn't given it much thought, as everything had got away from me once the detectives took him. But what was that? Sweat? Tom isn't a particularly sweaty person unless he's been on a long run.

Why couldn't he trust me enough to tell me why he was late, and where he really was on the Tuesday? Perhaps he was more worried about having been pulled in for questioning than he was willing to let on to me. Or perhaps past memories being dragged up had upset him. I wonder if he's given a thought to how upset *I* am about all of this. How sad his daughter will be when he's away for yet another night. If I get the opportunity to talk to him on the phone, will all the questions flood out? Or will an angry tirade erupt from me instead? After the latest revelation, I don't think I even want to hear his voice. Hear more lies.

'How are you, sweetie?' The voice, though quiet, makes me jump. I look up sharply. I'm at the entrance gate to the nursery.

'Sorry, mind was elsewhere,' I say to Julia, attempting a smile but failing.

'I hope things haven't got worse?' she says, one perfectly

neat brow arched. I think they're microbladed. Unsure what to say, I merely let out a long stream of breath.

'Oh. Dear. Well, look – if you need to talk, please give me a call, won't you?'

'I don't have your number,' I say, instantly.

Julia gives a nervous little laugh. Maybe she's just realising she's never really given me much time before Tom and I became the focus of juicy village gossip. She pulls a card out of the side pocket of her Gucci handbag and hands it to me.

'Anytime, day or night,' she says. She sounds genuine. I turn the card over in my hand. Gold-embossed script adorns the front – *Julia Bennington, Beauty Therapist*. Ah, that explains it – I can't believe I missed what she did for a living. I wonder how she does it all with triplets; she is basically Supermum.

'Thank you,' I say. My voice breaks, tears springing to my eyes.

'It'll be all right, sweetie,' she says, rubbing my arm as we head inside. Poppy's face lights up as she sees me, and for a moment my anxiety melts away. She runs over awkwardly, a painting in her hands.

'Mummy! I made it for you,' she says, thrusting the still-damp picture towards me.

'Oh, that's wonderful, darling.' I hold back more tears as I see three different-sized blobs with stick-like arms and legs. 'Me, you and Daddy,' she points.

My heart breaks a little.

Oh, Tom. What have you done to us?

Chapter 23

BETH

Now

Friday mornings are when I usually deliver any fired pottery items to those unable to pick up from Poppy's Place. I've arranged for Lucy to do it – it'll take her several trips on her bike, so she can open the café later as a one-off. A shiver runs through me as I think about it – opening late will no doubt cause tongues to wag. I dropped Poppy to nursery without bumping into Julia, which was a relief as I was too nervous to stand and chat. I have to be at Banbury station by ten – I've had even less sleep than normal, because my mind wouldn't stop going over and over the statement I'm about to make.

Now, as I park at the back of the police station, I realise I can't recall a single thing about the journey here. I used to think I dealt with stress well – I have always been in control of it, not the other way around. Today, the gnawing pain in my lower abdomen, the searing white-hot headache, the trembling hands, are all signs I've lost the fight with it this time. This stress is different, though. So much hangs in the balance.

Checking my appearance in the visor mirror, I make a silent deal with myself, then get out of the car and walk confidently to the entrance.

I have given my official statement, but surprisingly, not to DI Manning or DC Cooper, as I'd assumed. Maybe that's because they got what they wanted yesterday, and the paperwork gets left to the lower ranks. Or perhaps it's because I'm not important enough. Admittedly, it helped me a bit to have less pressure. But I'm still not confident I came across well – since being told that Tom didn't go to work on Tuesday, my mind has been all over the place, and my unease must've shown, despite all my overnight rehearsals.

I glance around the station before I leave, wondering where exactly Tom is. DS Walters, the detective who came to the cottage on Monday night, catches my eye and walks towards me. My immediate instinct is to leave quickly before he reaches me, but my feet refuse to move.

'You know your husband has been moved, don't you?' He narrows his eyes.

'No? What do you mean *moved*?'

'I'm sorry, I thought you'd been informed by his solicitor. Because it's a Metropolitan Police case, Detective Inspector Manning and Detective Constable Cooper are continuing questioning at their command unit in London.' He smiles sympathetically as he delivers this new information.

'Right,' I say, dropping my gaze to the floor. I don't

want him to catch the look in my eyes. 'Have they . . .' I cough to clear my throat, 'have they charged him, then?'

'No, not yet, Mrs Hardcastle. They've got until tomorrow evening and I think they wanted him on their turf to continue questioning.'

Walters' wording makes me think they might go to great lengths to ensure they charge Tom. I can't stop myself conjuring images of Tom being 'interrogated' like they do in some films. I imagine him being waterboarded, beaten until he admits guilt just to stop the pain. So that the copper can get his man, regardless.

Back in my car, I sit for what feels like an hour. I can't drive while I feel this nauseous. I didn't eat breakfast, which isn't helping. My stomach groans and lurches as I grip the steering wheel, taking deep breaths in through my nose and out of my mouth to overcome the sickness. I hadn't anticipated the fallout; hadn't allowed my mind to really *go there*. But now, I must begin to prepare for the strong possibility that Tom isn't coming home.

Chapter 24

TOM

Now

How many more hours left? It feels an eternity. I focus to work it out – they only have thirty-four hours left to hold me without charge. They've brought me to their unit in order to up the ante; to increase the pressure on me so I give something away and incriminate myself. I've never been great at being in enclosed spaces and this new eight-by-eight holding cell, despite its starkness, is closing in on me; the space is shrinking minute by minute. Soon, it'll be like being in a coffin. I wish there was fresh air instead of this recirculated, stale atmosphere containing the desperate breath of those in custody.

And if I think this is bad, I hate to imagine a prison cell.

I certainly don't want to have to *know* what it's like.

'Please, Maxwell – do a good job. Get me out of here,' I mutter as I pace. I can literally take three strides before

I have to turn and go back. After a few goes at this, I am dizzy, so plonk myself down on the hard camp-like bed. What will Beth have told my work? They'll be wondering why I've not been in contact by now – especially Celia. Christ, I hope the police haven't spoken to my colleagues; that would be awkward. A lump forms in my throat. No, no – it'll be fine, *don't panic*. I won't be here for much longer: I must sit this out, stay calm. It'll be over soon. I'll be back at home with Beth and Poppy and this will become a distant memory. A bad one. A near miss. But one we can overcome. Beth loves me. This won't alter that.

Although, I do have some explaining to do. And I'll have to be economical with the truth – or, come up with an entirely different version. One which doesn't involve me telling her I've been lying for months. Everything had been going well: not even a minor bump in the road all this time. We both got what we wanted. Needed.

And now, from beyond the grave, Katie might ruin it all.

Chapter 25

BETH

Now

Poppy's Place is relatively quiet when I finally walk through the door. I took the drive back slowly in case my light-headedness impeded my judgement.

'Oh, blimey, Beth,' Lucy says, looking up from the far table as I enter. She stops what she's doing and rushes to me, putting her arm around mine. 'Sit down quickly – you look terrible.'

'Thanks a lot,' I say, attempting to sound jokey. I let her pull me towards the nearest table and I thud down on the wooden chair. 'I didn't have breakfast.' I inhale deeply, prop my elbows on the table and rest my head in my hands. Lucy disappears from my side and returns with a large brownie and a hot chocolate.

'Here, this should help raise your blood sugar,' she says, her expression set. 'Apparently these delicious, gooey chocolate brownies are a speciality of the rather talented owner.' She smiles and watches as I take a bite.

'Yeah, I heard she was a pretty good baker,' I say, the chunk of brownie slowly and uncomfortably travelling down my throat. I help it down with a gulp of hot chocolate, ignoring the burning sensation. 'Thank you. What would I do without you?'

Lucy shrugs, the skin around her neck flushing pink. 'You'd manage, Beth – you're one of the most driven women I've met. You'd do this single-handedly if you had to.'

'Well, thank you for the vote of confidence, Lucy – but really, I need you. Now more than ever before, actually.'

'Oh, God,' she lowers her voice to a whisper. Her eyes widen and she clasps a hand to her chest. 'Has he been charged?'

'No, not yet. But I have such a dreadful feeling, Lucy. The Major Investigation Team have moved him to London now – they've still got until Saturday evening to question him. To gather evidence.' I swallow hard, take another sip of my drink, and look around me at the few remaining customers. Thankfully, they don't seem to be watching me or listening in to our conversation. I recognise all the faces today, which is reassuring. For now, anyway. If Tom is charged, all hell will likely break loose.

'Do you think there's any evidence to gather that will allow them to charge him?' Lucy asks. I hesitate. How should I answer? By defiantly stating there's nothing to find because Tom is one hundred per cent innocent? Or should I admit out loud that Tom has lied to me – that they *must've* found something during the house search otherwise they wouldn't have been able to extend the custody time? My thoughts are a mess.

'I honestly don't know, Lucy,' I say, deciding to be straight with her. I need to be upfront with *someone,* and I don't have many options.

She's silent for a while, staring straight ahead, out the front window and beyond. I wonder what she's thinking. Probably how on earth I can sit here and say I'm not certain whether I think my own husband is guilty or not. It's not exactly what I'm saying, but it is what I'm implying.

'What can I do to help, Beth?' she says, focusing back on me.

'There isn't anything you can do,' I shrug, tears making their way down my cheeks, tiny drops splashing on the table. I wipe them away. 'Unless you can tell me where Tom went on Tuesday because he didn't go to work like he told me!' A bitter laugh escapes my lips.

'Oh, erm . . .' Lucy's face slackens, her surprise clear to see. She shakes her head a little and blows out her cheeks. 'Wow. Okay, then you're right – I can't help. I don't ever see him really. The odd occasion at a weekend, maybe, and I've seen him at the garage a couple of times when I've popped in to see Oscar, but that's about it. He doesn't exactly mingle with the villagers, does he?'

'Nope. He doesn't. In fact, I'd say your boyfriend is the closest thing he has to a mate around here.'

'You've no clue why he didn't go to work?'

'Not one. I just can't get my head around it, Lucy. Day in, day out, week after week, we have the same routine,' I sigh. I'm surprised at myself for confiding in Lucy so readily, but speaking my thoughts out loud to another person has an immediate effect. The tension I've been holding seems to flow out of me. Opening up is

103

helping, so I continue. 'Maybe that's the problem – I was complacent. I wouldn't even have thought to look for any anomalies on Tuesday morning. I was still reeling from him being taken in for questioning the previous evening and I was trying to get him to tell me about it. I was so focused on that, I wouldn't have seen anything untoward in his actions, or spotted any differences in his behaviour.'

It hits me now that I wouldn't even know if Tuesday was the first time Tom had missed work. How am I to know if it was a regular occurrence? The fact he lied to me once means he could easily have lied before.

My confidence in him being released is waning. Not just because of evidence the police might have, but because I'm suddenly aware he might always have been holding things back from me. Has my trust in him for all these years been misplaced?

Chapter 26

KATIE

Eight years ago

Katie lay on her back, Tom next to her, the heat from their bodies mingling and their breathing rapid. Beneath her, the picnic rug was rumpled and uncomfortable, but she didn't move. Her mind wandered as she contemplated their relationship. Today had been a good day, just as he'd promised. He'd gone to a lot of effort with the picnic – brought all her favourite foods – and he'd lovingly held her hand as they'd chatted. His gift to her had been overwhelming – a total shock, but she'd recovered from it quickly enough. The sex that followed had been wild and abandoned; neither had cared if anyone saw. It was electric, like when they were first together. For those short moments, Katie had forgotten her concerns. Forgotten her cancelled plans with her friends.

Tom was a good boyfriend, wasn't he? The fact he only ever wanted her to spend time with him was natural in a new relationship, she told herself. Maybe it was her who was being unfair, expecting him to put up with her immature friends when quite clearly they were still caught up in their post-uni lifestyle. She and Tom had moved on – had reached a different stage in their lives. Tom wasn't afraid of commitment; today had proved that. Perhaps she was, which was why she had shied away. He could be so intense; but that was something she'd loved – craved, even – at the start. But now sometimes, just sometimes, that intensity frightened her.

She lifted herself up and, propping herself on one elbow, stared at Tom. She ran a finger over his slightly parted lips. So soft. His high cheekbones, beautifully chiselled; his intense eyes, large and the most amazing shade of blue she'd ever seen; his dark hair, wavy and dishevelled in a way that looked as though he'd styled it that way. Everything about him made her heart beat faster. Physically, he was perfect. But she couldn't help sensing that something *imperfect* lay beneath. Something tugged at her unconscious: a stubborn red flag; a warning voice that refused to be silenced.

But for now, she relished his touch; his smell; his love for her. She'd worry about the rest another day. And maybe it was too late now anyway, seeing as she'd accepted the engagement ring.

***

TOM

I knew the picnic and the present would win Katie over. How could she fail to be impressed? How could she say no? Judging by the sex, the way her body shuddered when

I made her climax, I'd definitely sealed the deal. It had been a perfect moment.

If only she hadn't gone and ruined it when we got back to the flat.

How dare she go behind my back like that? I trusted her. She knew how much I loved her; wanted her. I went out of my way for her all the time. I'd spent so much time and effort, and she repaid me by lying.

I read the texts over and over again.

She was mocking me, insinuating that I was forcing her to cancel her stupid plans – that she really couldn't do anything about it. Is she trying to make me out to be some control freak? It's like she *wants* to destroy our relationship. We've literally just committed to each other. Had she accepted the ring to placate me? So as not to cause a scene? Isaac can fuck right off – he's always trying to wheedle his way in. He clearly wants her; I won't have that. He must be stopped.

I'll have to bide my time. Reacting immediately when I'm this wound up won't be the best way. I'll sit on it. Work out how to ensure she stays with me.

Chapter 27

BETH

Now

Poppy keeps asking when Daddy is coming home. We're on our way to the café before we head back to the empty cottage. I've promised her she can choose a new animal to paint: anything to keep her little mind occupied and stop her getting upset that Daddy isn't going to read her a bedtime story again. Tomorrow will be even worse. Being a weekend, she'd usually play games with him, or we'd all set off for a walk, or maybe go to Westgate shopping centre in Oxford and have food out. None of this will be on the agenda this time. *Maybe next weekend, though?* the small voice in my head asks.

'Oh, thanks, Lucy,' I say, as I see she's set up a table for us already.

'You're welcome. Hey there, Poppy!' Lucy reaches a hand down and ruffles Poppy's hair affectionately. 'How's my favourite princess this afternoon? Good day at nursery?'

Poppy giggles. 'Good day, thanks, Luce.'

I grin. It's so great to hear Poppy laugh, and I love how she calls Lucy 'Luce' – it's adorable. I'm grateful to Lucy for being so upbeat – she's being her usual cheery self, despite what I divulged earlier. It's almost as though that conversation never happened. I wish I could paper over the last few days as easily.

'Excellent – glad to hear it. I've got some special animals waiting to be loved,' Lucy says, taking Poppy's hand and leading her to the selection she's put out.

I make myself a latte and pour orange juice for Poppy, put two chocolate chip muffins on plates and take them to the table. Poppy dons a pink flowery apron and begins painting. She's incredibly independent, especially for a three-year-old, and doesn't wait to be told what to do. This is good, in part, but I'm guessing it might be a tad challenging in the not-too-distant future. I sit, quietly watching Poppy as I eat. She glances over as she reaches for a new colour, says, 'I'll eat mine when I'm finished, Mummy,' then returns her expression to one of intense concentration, brows furrowed. She's so precious, so innocent. I can't bear to imagine her ever feeling upset. Hurt. *Abandoned.*

I push those thoughts away, and while she's busy painting, I quickly flit around the café picking up a used mug and neatening the table that's just been vacated. Anything to help stem the flow of negative thoughts. It's almost four; not long until closing time. How will I fill my evening once we get home to the cottage? Poppy will be in bed at six, and by six thirty I'll be sitting eating a microwave meal for one, as I haven't been bothered about cooking or shopping this week. The telly will have the usual crap on; nothing interests me at the moment. Maybe I'll just go to bed.

'Well, hello there.' The silky-smooth voice catapults me from my musings. Adam is standing just inside the doorway, Jess's face pecking out from behind his legs.

'Hi, Adam,' I say as I walk over, then, bending down to her level, 'and hello, Jess. Poppy will be so delighted to have a friend to sit with and paint animals. She's over there,' I point to the back of the café, to Poppy, who is deep in creative thought as she jabs the paintbrush, distributing green splodges all over the bear. A glowing sensation swells inside me as I see the tip of her tongue poking out of her bow-like mouth, her eyes screwed up in concentration. Jess comes out from behind Adam and walks over to Poppy. I'm pleased she appears less shy than last time.

'You okay?' Adam cocks his head, his eyes seeking mine. 'If you don't mind me saying, you look very tired.'

'Great. Roughly translated as "you look like shit", then?' I offer a tentative smile, afraid I'm about to cry and embarrass myself yet again.

'No, not at all. If I thought that, it's what I'd have said.' He smiles and laughs. 'You know me.'

Only, I don't know him. But currently he's the only person I feel fully at ease with. For some reason I trust him, and an overwhelming sense of calm comes over me when I'm in his company. Then I remember I used to have the exact same sense with Tom, and that's not working out well for me right now.

Still, there's no harm in chatting with Adam while the girls paint. They look good together: almost like siblings, they're so similar. My womb aches. Tom and I haven't

110

discussed having another baby since Poppy arrived. Beforehand, we often talked about having a family: Tom used to inform me he wanted two or four children. 'Definitely not an odd number,' he used to say. I was adamant that in that case I'd be happy with two. Now, I wonder if we'll even have that. I'm not desperate to have another yet, though. Up until recently I've been very happy with the way things are.

'Penny for them.' I hear Adam's voice and turn towards him.

'Sorry. I've been to the station today to give a statement and I found out the detectives from homicide command have taken Tom to London to continue questioning him. I'm a bit preoccupied.'

'I expect you are. I'm sorry, Beth. I can't imagine how stressful it is for you, waiting like this. How much longer can they hold him?'

'Until Saturday evening. They have until eight p.m. I believe.' I let out a juddering breath and look into Adam's eyes. 'What if they don't release him? What the hell will we do if they charge him, Adam?' Desperation clings to each word.

'Honestly? All you can do is cross that bridge if it comes to it, Beth. It's the only way to get through this. It's how I cope, anyway. Literally hour by hour, day by day. I don't tend to look forwards into the future, it's too scary. That's when I lose control. I was given some helpful advice: if you can't change it, let it go. Otherwise you'll be consumed by worry.'

'And if I *could* change something?'

Adam frowns. 'What do you mean?'

'Never mind,' I say. 'Right, you've been without a drink

111

for too long. Such dreadful service,' I say, brightening and finally moving into the shop. 'What can I get you?'

Adam regards me for several seconds before responding. 'A lemonade, please.' I turn and head to the counter, but I can feel the weight of his stare – he knows I was about to say something else. Knows I held back at the last moment.

Chapter 28

BETH

Now

'Is Daddy gone work *again*?' Poppy asks, the second she runs into my bedroom, launches herself at the bed and scrambles up. It's five a.m. It's Saturday. Sadly for my sleeping patterns, she can't differentiate between weekdays and weekends. Last night when I tucked her in I'd asked her – in a moment of desperation – to please give Mummy a lie in in the morning, and if she was awake before the light came through her curtains, to stay in her bedroom and play with her animals. It was a long shot, and one which has failed. Not that I was sleeping anyway, or even resting peacefully; my mind is far too busy working its way through every possibility, every path our lives might now take.

'Yes, Poppy – I'm sorry. He'll be . . .' I'm about to say, 'home soon', but I shouldn't lie even further to her. I can't make false promises. 'He'll be gone for a bit longer,' I say, the words sticking in my throat as I know even this might not be exactly true. If he's charged, it'll be a while before a trial, then if he's convicted . . .

A sharp pain shoots through my temple. I can't let my little girl grow up without her father like I did.

Fucking hell, Tom.

Nerves prevent me eating. I sit watching Poppy devour her breakfast, queasiness consuming me. Rain, or perhaps hail, pelts against the windows – I haven't even bothered to draw back the curtains to look. Hardly any light penetrates the heavy dark-green material: I'm hiding away from the world, tucked away in my cottage. A part of me wants to burrow even deeper into the depths of self-pity, but I have Poppy to think about. The relevance of today will no doubt overshadow everything, though.

Today is *the* day.

Eleven hours to go.

Maxwell calls to 'prepare me' for either outcome: Tom coming home, or Tom being charged with murder. Strangely, I'm equally scared for both eventualities. Maybe it's not so strange. I should give myself a break – these have been the most stressful and difficult days of my adult life; of *course* I'll be feeling uneasy, nervous – whether he's released without charge or not. Maxwell also says that, in theory, they could charge him and still release him on bail until his trial. This to me seems the worst option. How would we cope? How would we *be* as a couple if he's back home, but charged with Katie's murder? I can't even begin to imagine how our usual day-to-day routine would be upended, or what conversations we'd have. I ask Maxwell if, given the nature of the charge, they'd

114

even consider bail. Surely they'd detain him immediately? A man accused of murder would be deemed be a risk – to himself, if not to others?

'It could go either way, Beth,' he says. 'It's an historical crime and Tom has no criminal record: no previous convictions; nothing that's brought him to the police's attention prior to this. The man has never even had so much as a bloody parking ticket. He's squeaky clean.'

'Apparently he isn't, Maxwell, or we wouldn't be in this situation, would we.' My throat tightens. How can he be glossing over the facts that, one, Tom was arrested, therefore the police must have *some* form of evidence against him; and, two, that he lied about going to work. And about God knows what else.

'Well, I was about to add a caveat. As I mentioned before, Beth, the detectives are holding back certain evidence and it's possible that whatever that is *might* lead to bail being denied.' Maxwell's voice sounds strained. Why do I get the impression *he's* the one holding something back, not the police?

'Has Tom asked you not to tell me everything because he's worried I won't cope with the truth? Are you sure there's not something I need to know about him?'

'He's your husband, Beth. You should know him best.' I catch a hint of sarcasm, maybe even an accusation, buried within his words. He's right, of course. I should know him better than anyone else. The fact I'm not jumping up and down in protest – shouting about the travesty of his arrest, adamant about his innocence – doesn't look good. Doesn't show what a wonderful, supportive wife I am.

'I *do* know him, Maxwell. And he's a good husband

115

and father,' I say, firmly. 'I told the detectives that when they first spoke with me, and I'll tell anyone else who asks the same thing. Tom wouldn't have done anything to Katie.' My conviction seems a little too late; I hear a deep sigh from Maxwell on the other end of the line.

'Then trust in the justice system, Beth. If Tom is innocent the evidence can only be circumstantial at best.'

My heart dips. Alarm bells ring in my head. '*If* he is innocent? Don't *you* believe he is?'

'Of course, of course. I've known Tom a long time and he's given me excellent financial advice. He's never come across as someone capable of causing serious harm. But they're still investigating and judging by what they say they have on him, and what they're still looking into, I've no real way of telling which way this will go. But, rest assured, he'll be given the best legal counsel, whatever happens later.'

I hang up and pace, wringing my hands, which are unsettled and fidgety like my thoughts. I just want this evening to hurry up – I need this to be over. I wipe down the kitchen table and take Poppy upstairs to get her dressed. Then, while she's playing animal hospital with her toys, I slump down on the sofa in the lounge and put the radio on for background noise. The morning news is a welcome distraction. Other people's problems, not my own. Although, as the newsreader's voice becomes ever more serious, I think it's possibly not the best type of distraction. A walk around the outskirts of the village would be a better option and the fresh air would be good for me and Poppy. If, of course, we aren't stared at. Everyone in Lower Tew must be aware of Tom's arrest. It's humiliating.

I rarely give a thought to my previous life in London, but right now I have a craving for the anonymity being in the huge capital offered. Yes, I had friends and colleagues who knew me, and knew a bit about what was going on in my life, but there wasn't widespread interest in my business. Mostly, nobody was bothered about what I was or wasn't doing. Lower Tew is the opposite. Although, hearing about the regular deaths in the city – on the news bulletin now there are reports about the fatal stabbing of a teenager, the body of a sex worker being found, and yet another a hit-and-run – I do know I'm lucky to be here, in the relative safety of a village. I have to forgo anonymity for a safer environment for Poppy. We made the right decision moving here, regardless of my current 'celebrity' status.

I pray the focus is taken off me by the end of the day. But mud sticks, as they say. Is the fact Tom was arrested going to be forgotten, even if he's not charged? I imagine if they charge someone else, then it might. If not, the finger of suspicion may always point at my husband. Poppy's life here might always be blighted by this.

Will we have to move again?

Chapter 29

BETH

Now

Poppy walks with a comical wobble – the bright yellow anorak that matches my own is tight around her little body and her wellies reach to her knees; both constrict her movement. The rain has been falling heavily overnight so there's an abundance of decently sized puddles, and I've let her walk a little ahead of me so she can be first to reach them. The joy on her little face as she jumps and splashes in the water-filled dips in the lane brings tears to my eyes. I must protect her, no matter what.

She begs me to join in – and for a glorious moment, I forget the surrounding gloom and just enjoy being with our bright, beautiful three-year-old as we race to each puddle and scream when the water erupts around us.

Then the clouds in my mind descend once more, and the burning, knotted ball of anxiety lying dormant in my stomach awakens.

Six hours to go.

To anyone watching us, we would seem perfectly happy right now – and indeed, Poppy is – but for me, the knowledge of what might come holds this brief happiness hostage. I look up at the dark-grey clouds, heavy with rain, rolling across the sky, threatening to break at any moment. I can't help but think it symbolic.

'Time to go home, my Poppy poppet,' I say. She doesn't whinge; just holds up her hand for me to take in mine. I think she's tired. I certainly am. We turn around and head back through the village, thankfully seeing no one. I couldn't cope with polite conversation; or worse, people avoiding me altogether. The only person I wouldn't mind bumping into is Adam. At least I know he hasn't judged me over this mess. Yet.

Five hours to go.

Warm and cosy, back in the security of our home, Poppy and I snuggle on the sofa and watch *Twirlywoos*. It's about the only level of telly programme I can take right now. Poppy is enthralled by the brightly coloured bird-like characters, and while she is quiet, I find my eyelids closing under the weight of my exhaustion.

Four hours to go.

A ringing sound startles me out of my nap. Poppy is no longer beside me. I leap up, momentarily dazed and disorientated. I relax as I see her sitting cross-legged on the carpet, inches from the television screen, her face upturned. Was it my mobile? Or the house phone? It's stopped, anyway. I rub at my eyes, lick my dried lips and tell Poppy I'm getting us a drink. My body aches as I walk into the kitchen; everything feels stiff from falling asleep on the sofa. I glance at the kitchen clock. Five

119

fifteen – I nodded off for longer than I thought. I may as well start cooking something for dinner.

Less than three hours to go.

I try my best to read Poppy's story with the voices she loves Tom using. She laughs, and I know it's because I'm making a hash of it, but she doesn't tell me that this time. I tuck her in, leave a nightlight on and kiss her goodnight. My heart sinks as she asks again when her daddy is coming home. In a short while, I'll know myself. I'm counting down the minutes.

One hour to go.

My mobile rings. It's too early to hear from Maxwell, but adrenaline shoots through my veins nonetheless. The pounding in my chest begins to subside when I see the caller ID.

'Hey, Adam. Everything all right?'

'I rather think it's me who should be asking you that question. Have you heard anything yet?'

'I'm expecting a call at around eight. Their time is up then. But I guess they could charge or release him at any time, so—'

'Oh, gosh, yes. I should free up the line, sorry,' he says. 'I have such terrible timing.' I can sense his embarrassment and I feel bad for him.

'No, really, it's fine. If I'm honest, I could do with the distraction – today has dragged enough, but this last hour is going in reverse, I swear. It's killing me,' I say.

'I can imagine. Time has a habit of doing that when you are desperate for it to whizz by. Then, when you want to breathe and take stock, or enjoy a moment – keep it going for as long as possible – it ticks away at twice the speed of light.' His voice is soft, and I can tell he's talking about his experience with losing Camilla. 'I'm aware that doesn't make sense. I'm crap at analogies.'

'Oh, trust me, it makes perfect sense. What have you been up to today?' I ask, to change the subject and try to bring him, and me, out of the depths of misery.

We've been talking for what I think is about ten minutes, but as I wander into the kitchen to get a drink, I glance at the wall clock and panic grips me. 'Adam! I've got to go, sorry. It's gone eight!'

He gives a gasp, says a brief 'Good luck!' and hangs up.

Shit, have I missed the call? How could I have let that happen? I hastily check my mobile. No missed calls. I slam the phone on the kitchen worktop and steady myself. The taste of bile is strong in my mouth; I haven't eaten all day, there's nothing but acid in my stomach.

Please hurry up and get this over with.

Eight eleven.

My phone remains stubbornly silent. Unlike the whooshing noise in my ears. I'm afraid to think what my blood pressure might be. At this rate I'll have a heart attack or a stroke before I know about Tom.

'Ring already!' I tell my phone.

And then it does.

I want to cry – the tension is too great. For a few seconds I just stare at the screen. Maxwell's name fills me with fear.

I want to know, yet I don't.

Once I answer, everything will be different. Our lives will be altered whatever the outcome. We're cats in Schrodinger's box.

For the minute, Tom is both innocent and guilty. Am I ready for the reality of which it'll be?

With a deep breath, I stab the button to accept the call. 'Beth?'

The coward in me wants to immediately hang up. 'Ye–yeah, it's me,' I say, surprised at the weakness of my voice.

'Right,' he says. 'I have some news.'

The world stops spinning; dizziness overcomes me. I'm going to fall off.

'Breathe, Beth.' Maxwell's voice sounds distant. I do as he says.

'Go on,' I say, sitting down before I faint.

The next words out of Maxwell's mouth will determine my and Poppy's future.

Chapter 30

BETH

Now

'I'm so very sorry, Beth. Tom has been charged with the murder of Katie Williams.'

Everything else Maxwell says is drowned out by the frantic beating of my heart. Opposing thoughts collide in my mind; emotions crash together and splinter: I have no idea what to do; how to react; what to say. I catch the words 'denied bail' before a splitting pain in my head takes over everything, paralysing me, and I hang up without responding. Without asking Maxwell what happens next.

I couldn't even ask for an explanation or ask to speak to Tom.

I need to lie down in a darkened room.

'Mummy!' Little hands nudge my shoulder and I open my eyes.

Oh, no – how long have I been asleep? Disorientated, I slowly sit up. 'Poppy, darling, why aren't you in bed?' It can't be morning already. The striking pain in my head has dulled, but nausea hits me – the acid is churning, threatening to expel itself.

'You didn't come when I called,' she says. My bedside lamp illuminates her tear-stained face. I don't remember turning it on, don't remember climbing into bed even. I try to assimilate my last memories and the recollection of Maxwell's call comes crashing back.

Oh, God. What will I tell Poppy?

'I'm so sorry, sweetheart – did you have a bad dream?' I swipe my hand under Tom's pillow, take my mobile phone and check the time. It's not quite midnight. 'Do you want to jump in bed with me?' I pull back the duvet on Tom's side.

'Where's Daddy?' Poppy rubs at her eyes, her mouth formed into a pout.

This is it. This is where I need to tell her something more solid than 'away working'. But I'm not alert enough to think up anything better. Anything that's closer to the truth.

'He's not going to be home for a bit, Poppy. He's got important work to do,' I say, reaching out and lifting her into the bed. We snuggle down and I stroke the delicate skin on her cheek. 'Go back to sleep, my poppet.'

For now, she appears content with the brief explanation, but I know it won't last. I have no idea what she'll pick up on once she's outside of these four walls. Whether the news of Tom's charge, his possible conviction, might impact on her beyond his absence from home. Sleep will be impossible now; I can't silence my worries. When the sun rises, will everyone be waking to the news that Tom has been charged with murder? Will Julia and the mums, Lucy, *Adam*, be as supportive when they find out? I've been lucky to have started to make closer friendships in the village, but it's still early days and it might not be enough now. It's not as though they were the kind of deeply meaningful friendships that could take the strain of such a revelation.

They'll be kind for Poppy's sake, though, won't they?

Chapter 31

Smooth, unblemished hands grip her throat. Tighter and tighter, until she can draw no more breath. His weight begins to crush her; his straddled legs press in hard against her sides – but the air already in her lungs has nowhere to go. It remains trapped, burning inside her weakening body. She imagines her lungs bursting like overinflated balloons. The sensation, which at first she'd found almost pleasurable, is now painful. She wriggles harder beneath him; reaches a hand to push at his chest. His grasp doesn't loosen.

He's going to kill her.

Her bulging eyes stare at the damp spot on the ceiling. Will this be her last image? This isn't how it was meant to be.

The edges of the jagged mark above her blur. Darken. She drifts.

A gasp.

Light floods her vision as air is released, then is quickly

126

sucked back into her lungs – again and again, until she is able to speak.

'What the fuck was that?' she screams, rubbing at her throat.

He smiles.

'Seriously, don't ever do that again. Why didn't you stop?'

'Sometimes I don't know how to,' he says with a shrug, as he removes himself from her and sinks down on the bed. 'You enjoyed it though. Every bit as much as I did.'

As her breathing regulates, she thinks about his words.

No. There'd been no enjoyment for her.

For the first time, she'd been afraid.

A few more seconds and she might not have recovered.

He gets up and heads to the bathroom. She hears the shower start up.

This is the last time she should allow him to go that far.

She can no longer trust him.

Chapter 32

TOM

Now

This is a living nightmare. How the hell can they say they've enough evidence to bring charges? They haven't even found a body, it's fucking ridiculous. And Maxwell just sat there, taking it all in. Said nothing. Did nothing. *Pathetic.*

The duty officer's face looks as though a swarm of bees has stung it. I stare at him blankly as he reads the charges. The words, 'You will be remanded in police custody until you are taken for your court appearance,' go unprotested by Maxwell and, despite my shock and disbelief, by me. Their meaning slowly sinks in.

I'm not going home.

I'm not going to see Beth or Poppy.

Not making bail is partly my fault, I know. Maxwell did say that remaining silent about my whereabouts on Tuesday would go against me – that it added another strand for the police to investigate – but I had no choice. That's probably why bail was denied, not because of the evidence they have. Maybe they think I'm a flight risk.

Christ. I could go to prison for life.

Don't think that way.

Maxwell will build a solid case in my defence. Beth will help him. It will be all right in the end. This is a short-term predicament. I can't possibly be found guilty of murder. Placing me at Katie's last known location, linking me with some random emails, the word of her poxy friends and her dad – her dad, who had barely anything to do with her in life – might be enough for the CPS to allow the police to charge me, but it won't be enough for a jury. It won't stick. *Beyond reasonable doubt.* That's what they have to prove. They have to prove I actually committed the offence, and they won't have jack shit. And I have Beth; she'll throw me a lifeline.

But she can't provide an alibi.

They haven't got a body, though. They have no idea about time of death, so I don't *need* an alibi.

These thoughts consume me as panic rises. My chest tightens, my hands tingle.

'I don't feel well,' I say, doubling over. I'm probably having a heart attack.

'Come on, fella,' a voice says, as hands reach under my armpits and I'm pulled upright and dragged to a nearby chair. 'Put your head between your legs – you're faint is all. No need to panic.'

Easy for him to say. His entire life isn't unravelling in front of him like mine is.

Why the hell has this happened now?

Chapter 33

BETH

Now

'She must've known, surely?'

The whisper may as well have been a shout.

With Poppy's hand firmly grasped in mine, shoulders back, head held high, I stride past the group of mums standing outside the nursery entrance. Inwardly, my gut twists and I feel sick, but I won't let them see how concerned I am. I spent most of yesterday in a confused state, fretting about the repercussions of Tom being charged. Trying to second-guess how the yummy mummies would react. How the new development will affect Poppy. I'm glad I had Sunday to pull myself together but now, hearing the whispered accusation, panic begins to surface again.

I go inside and search out the friendly face of Wanda, one of the nursery assistants I know Poppy has a bond with.

'Good morning, Poppy,' Wanda beams as she heads towards us. I breathe a sigh of relief she's here. Poppy is reluctant to let go of me, and I wonder if she's sensing my anxiety.

'We've not had a great night,' I say, quietly. Wanda coaxes Poppy to let go of my hand and take hers instead.

'Give us a second, Mrs Hardcastle. I'll be back.' She offers a sympathetic smile, then takes Poppy to the book corner where the triplets are sitting, speaks in hushed tones to the teacher in charge, then returns to me.

'She'll be fine. No need to worry,' she says, knowingly.

'I'd be so grateful if you could keep a close eye on her today, though. And please call me if she doesn't want to stay.'

'Of course, of course. I had a very quick word with Zoey – she's a little busy right now, but she suggests you stay behind at pickup to have a chat?'

'Thank you, yes, that would be helpful.'

'Good,' Wanda says. 'We can work together to make sure Poppy isn't negatively impacted here at nursery.'

'I hope so,' I say, relieved. It's the strangest conversation – nothing is said, yet an understanding is reached, meaning she knows already. I imagine there will be a few of these types of conversations over the coming days. Weeks. Months even. With this realisation, my pulse stutters and I make a hasty retreat before my body reacts further.

The mums are still huddled together like a coven; they've moved outside the gate now and I won't be able to pass by without acknowledging them. The 'she must've known' comment echoes in my mind, and now, as I near them, another snippet carries through the air.

'You can't be married for that long and not know.'

For a split second, I speculate that they're talking about something entirely unrelated. Perhaps it's my own emotional instability making me certain that people will gossip, jump to conclusions and immediately believe the accusation. Maybe I'm paranoid. They could be talking about anyone – someone who's having an affair, maybe?

They aren't, of course. Nothing else interesting is happening in Lower Tew.

This *is* about me. And their faces confirm it when I reach them. A few have the decency to look embarrassed and turn away, but others make eye contact defiantly. Julia is among them. For a horrifying moment I think I've lost her support too, but then her face softens, and she steps away from the group.

'Oh, sweetie, I'm so sorry to hear the *awful* news,' she says, putting both hands on my shoulders then pulling me into a hug. It takes me a few uncomfortable seconds of this embrace before I move my arms away from my sides and reciprocate. Should I be crying? Will that make them feel differently, I wonder? But tears do not come. My tear ducts have run dry; there are no more in reserve even if I wanted to put on a show.

'Thanks, Julia,' I say, gently extricating myself from her arms. 'What a mess, eh?'

'Yes, yes. So shocking,' she says, turning back to the others. 'We were just saying that, weren't we ladies? What a terrible shock it must've been for you, poor thing.'

That's not what they were saying, but I have to go with it. Julia's disingenuous concern is what I expected, really. I'm still classed as a newcomer – I haven't immersed myself in village life beyond chatting to people at the café and offering limited support to local events – and they barely know Tom. For two years I've been focused on my family and business, and now that's going to come back to bite me. So, despite knowing their reasons aren't entirely genuine, I need these women. I need their support, however superficial. I can still build a real friendship if I try hard enough, even in these grim circumstances.

My mind wanders to Adam. He always drops Jess off at nursery early – mainly, he confided in me, to avoid 'Mumsgate'. I don't blame him one bit. Will he have heard about Tom by now too? He might be the only person I can turn to for genuine support. Part of me wants to call him, but I'm afraid of his response. I want to think he'd be okay; that he'd treat me as before. *I'm* not the one who's going to be on trial.

But maybe that's not true. Given the murmurings of the mums at the gate, it's possible I already am.

Chapter 34

BETH

Now

It feels wrong, somehow, to be at work today. I'm not firing on all cylinders – I've already messed up a customer's order and knocked into the kiln, causing an immediate bruise to form on my upper arm. Maybe I should shut up shop and go home to contemplate the future before I do any real damage. I need to contact Maxwell anyway to ask him what comes next.

What's the process when someone is charged with murder and held in custody until a court appearance? I should ask him what part I have to play in the aftermath: whether I'm going to be questioned again. After his phone call on Saturday night, I couldn't cope with the detail. I didn't feel I could call him yesterday – everyone needs a day off. That was the excuse I gave myself, anyway. But now, I know I must face it. I can't bury my head in the sand and pretend it hasn't happened.

I let out a huge sigh. Decision made. No one is currently painting any pottery, so when the few customers who are having a morning cuppa and a cookie finish, I'll call it a day. I'll pay Lucy for the full shift, regardless. She'll no doubt be relieved to be getting away from me: she's been noticeably awkward around me since I came in; her reaction to my news that Tom has been charged with murder was one of horror – although I'm not sure if it was entirely authentic or put on for my benefit. She'd already mentioned how she didn't want Lower Tew to become 'a circus' and now, with the official charge, I imagine she fears that it'll become just that. She's probably right. She's currently out back, brushing off the shelves in the kiln. I won't disturb her – she's obviously doing what she can to avoid me.

I start aimlessly wiping down clean tables to pass the time.

'Are you still planning to start the book club, then?' I leap at the voice behind me – I'd been so lost in thought I hadn't heard Shirley sneak up.

'Oh,' I say, my hand flying to my chest. 'Sorry, Mrs Irish, I didn't realise you were there.'

She furrows her brow and continues without waiting for me to answer. 'Only, given the current circumstances, I imagine you've enough on your plate?'

Heat rushes to my face. 'Er . . . I haven't given it much thought, to be truthful, Mrs Irish.'

'I really wish you'd call me Shirley – there's no need for such formality. I'm not a teacher.'

'Sorry,' I say, a snippet of annoyance taking the warmth from my cheeks. 'Habit, I suppose, as we don't know each other well. I only mean to be polite.'

She gives a humph and opens her eyes wider. 'So?'

'It's not due to begin for two weeks, *Shirley*, so I'll wait and see. Don't worry, I'll update the posters if there's any alteration,' I say, heading back to the counter. Thankfully she doesn't follow. I should expect some frostiness – maybe even straight-up rudeness – because of Tom's charge. I swallow painfully as the thought hits me: what if I receive more than that? There could be animosity, even hate, levelled at me. My husband has been charged with *murder*. The weight of this reality is beginning to sink in. People might well target their disgust, their abhorrence, at me. The words I overheard at the nursery gates play over in my head.

She must've known.

I press both hands to my stomach as the griping pain worsens. Word hasn't spread fast or wide enough yet, but it will. Even if I have some support right now, it may well disappear once this hits the national headlines, once tabloid press come looking for the story – the inside scoop. Nothing good ever comes from their soap-opera stories. The angle they'll all take will focus on the monster who killed a young woman. Tom's face will adorn papers and news programmes and there'll be no getting away from it . . . and then they'll turn their attention to me. How many of the people of Lower Tew will rush to give their opinions, their take on knowing the suspect? On knowing *me*. Will anyone take our side? Will anyone believe that Tom is innocent?

Poppy must be protected from all of this. She is my responsibility. And if Tom is sent to prison, I'll be the *only* one responsible for her. The thought horrifies me. I never imagined having to bring up our child alone. It wasn't in the plan. Leaning on the counter, I hang my head. I remember Tom's delight when I showed him the stick with the two blue lines. How he hugged me tightly, then panicked, pulling away, afraid he'd hurt the baby. I'd only been eight weeks pregnant then, but Tom's need to look after our baby had been so strong right from the off, that I knew he was going to be a good dad. His idea to move out of London was born from his need to protect; his desire to ensure his child grew up in a safe area.

His excitement in his flat the day we boxed up our old lives to start our life in our dream house was contagious, and we got lost in the giddy anticipation of family life – deciding which things to keep; which to bag up for charity; which to take to the tip. I'd found some of Tom's university stuff as we packed.

It was fate that we'd met. He'd gone to Leeds uni and studied Economics and Finance, while I'd studied English Literature at Southampton. It had seemed a lifetime ago, even then – that heady mix of experiencing independence and making an abundance of new friends. Learning almost took second place. I'd had a year out after graduation, gone to France to ski before securing my first recruitment job in London. I'd been there ever since. Meeting Tom that night in Bethnal Green, when I'd first felt that spark, was a moment of serendipity. I'd kept everything back then – receipts from Sager + Wilde as a keepsake of our first meeting, pressed roses he'd bought, silly gifts – even a plastic ring which he'd pretended was an engagement ring as a joke. Of course, I'd also had items from past relationships: a few photos, similar little keepsakes.

Tom isn't one to keep things. All that sentimentality annoys him – he didn't even have photos of his parents and he still doesn't carry around photos of me and Poppy.

He made a fuss about the things I had kept from my life before him. So it was uncharacteristic of him to have kept any of his uni stuff. He had insisted I pack a worn-looking sweatshirt that was clearly two sizes too small, and I had questioned his need for it. I was throwing away all of my old things – partly at his request, partly because I was keen to start afresh. I wasn't taking any ghosts with me.

'Hello – is anyone serving?' One of my regulars interrupts my memories. I drag my hands down my face.

'Yep, sorry, Amy.' I take her drink order, then go to the front door and turn the sign to closed. Once the remaining customers have left, so will I. I need to pick Poppy up and have 'the chat' with Zoey, the teacher in charge at nursery. But before that, I feel the need to see Adam. I'm surprised he hasn't called me to hear the outcome; it makes me think he already knows, and now, despite his initial support, he's backed off. He's probably changed his mind – who would want to be associated with the wife of a suspected murderer? Perhaps he had expected Tom to be released without charge, and now that isn't the case, he's not willing to put himself in the line of fire. The inevitable fire that'll come my way.

Does he think I must've known too? Or that I at least *should* have?

Knowing how he always puts Jess first, I'm betting he wants nothing else to do with me. But I need to know for sure.

Chapter 35

BETH

Now

I reach Adam's house and stand awkwardly as I wait for him to answer the door. I feel as though I'm opening myself up at my most vulnerable – if he turns me away, I can't say how I'll react. The door opens and Adam takes a step back when he sees it's me, but it's not to let me in. It's shock at seeing me standing here. He recovers – I see him inhale deeply, and I give a simultaneous smile and shrug. My eyes and nose tingle with the onset of tears. He jolts forwards, sticks his head outside, and gives a furtive look up and down the road. I follow his eyes as he checks whether anyone is around.

Silently, he takes my elbow and pulls me inside, closing the door quickly.

'Look, I'm sorry. I – I shouldn't . . . have come,' I say, my voice faltering. 'I understand if you feel too uncomfortable, allowing the wife of a suspected murderer inside

139

your home . . .' I turn to leave, hurt by his reaction, but knowing it was inevitable.

'No, no. You don't have to go, Beth. I'm just concerned what people will think.'

'Right. Course. But if you're that worried, I should go. I don't want to put you in an awkward position.'

'I'm worried how it will look because I'm single and I'm letting a woman whose husband is in custody into my house. It might look, you know . . . dodgy.'

I frown, not really following.

'People might think we're having an *affair*,' he says, whispering the last word like someone might hear him. I laugh.

'Really, Adam? Why on earth would people jump to that conclusion?'

'Well, I don't know. I always feel like Camilla's group of friends are particularly keen to keep tabs; whether that's because they're being protective of me, or of Camilla's memory, I don't know. And then there's the fact that it's a tiny village and people like to talk?'

'Oh, yes. I'm beginning to understand *that*.' We're still standing in the compact hallway. Adam's so close I can smell his aftershave – a spiced, woody scent. 'Really, I can go. I realise I've put you on the spot turning up like this.' I gaze down at the floor.

'Do you want a drink?' His voice is calmer now, and his posture is relaxing.

'If you're sure, then yes please. I haven't got anyone else—' my voice catches, '—to turn to. I'm sorry.'

Adam nods. 'I'm glad you felt you could come here.' He tentatively places his hand on my shoulder, then leads me down the hallway into his home.

140

Chapter 36

KATIE

Eight years ago

She twizzled the ring around on her finger, mesmerised by the light refracting off the diamond, and then she removed it, placing it back inside the red velvet box. She'd been overcome when Tom had flipped the lid open to reveal the shining, antique single diamond-set ring at the picnic. She had been torn between excitement and apprehension. But she'd been careful to only show Tom her excitement. He'd gone to a lot of trouble; she couldn't very well refuse it. Instead, she'd covered her shocked reaction with a display of affection.

'It's the beginning of our future together, Katie. I've got money saved; we could get married this year,' Tom had said, his words passionate, but also rushed, as though he'd consumed a dozen coffees. 'It's the best I could afford. That's all I want for you: the best. Always.'

Katie hugged her knees as she recalled his words. He

hadn't lied when he'd told her he had the best surprise for her, but she never imagined he'd be proposing. She'd been contemplating her relationship with Tom lately – where it was going; if he was right for her. This sudden move on his part should feel amazing: it should fill her with joy, not trepidation. Were they in the right place to make such a huge decision about their future? His love for her was obvious, but she couldn't be certain hers for him was enough.

But she'd said yes.

She could change her mind later. It wasn't as if the date had been agreed. People break off engagements all the time. And she might come around to the idea yet. She should give it some time to sink in. Maybe get her friends' opinions.

While he was at work, Katie sent a group text to her friends. Keen to make up for letting them down on their usual plans, she hammered out a message that she hoped would help justify her choice to spend the bank holiday with Tom, not them.

You'll never guess the surprise Tom sprung on me . . . only a bloody engagement ring! Squeee! Sorry for not spending the time with you guys, but he'd had it all planned. K xx

She tapped her mobile anxiously as she awaited some responses. Finally, several dings alerted her to messages.

Oh, that's really great, hun – so pleased for you. Had no idea you were that serious xx

Sammie's message made Katie squirm a bit, but it was Isaac's she was more concerned about.

Really? Wow, that is a shock. What did you say? Xx

Isaac's reply could be taken two ways. Katie thought it came across a bit sarcastic, but it was difficult to attain

142

meaning from text – intention and tone could be misinterpreted.

It was a surprise, most definitely. I didn't see it coming. I said yes. Xx

After a few more questions and a promise to get together for a proper chat they signed off, telling Katie to let them know when she and Tom were both free so they could begin organising an engagement party.

On the whole, they'd appeared happy for her, which she was relieved about. She wondered if they'd question her decision; talk about it behind her back. Discuss whether they thought she was rushing into it. No doubt it wouldn't be long before they called her individually to gain a fuller picture. It's what she'd do if one of them announced a sudden engagement.

Her mobile pinged and her shoulders slumped as she read a new text from Isaac. She had a feeling he'd be the first to comment privately.

Hey, babe. Hope you don't think I'm being negative, but . . . are you absolutely sure you want to do this? You don't think he's making false promises so you'll stay with him? I hope I'm wrong. But you know I only ever have your best interests at heart. You mean the world to me, you know that. And after the other night I thought things might have changed. XXX

* * *

TOM

And after the other night I thought things might have changed. XXX

Well, that's just perfect. I read the text over and over, getting angrier each time. I thought I might've been over-reacting when I checked her phone before; jumping to conclusions. But no. I'd been right. They're clearly at it behind my back. What other night? The one where Katie said she had to nip to the shop to get some more wine and she was gone for almost an hour? She'd told me she'd run into a friend and they'd chatted for ages.

The liar. She was seeing *him*.

Chapter 37

BETH

Now

I'm relieved I've spoken to Adam and that he didn't shun me. Now, though, as I walk through the village towards nursery, it's Zoey I'm worried about facing. I'm scared of what's to come: how much she already knows; how much explaining I'll need to do. I'll have to ask her to put extra support measures in place. None of this mess should impact on my daughter. It wouldn't be fair on her. I pull my coat hood up even though it's not raining, in the hope of a quiet journey. I'm late, so with luck I'll have missed the majority of parents. Unless they're hanging around, chatting to each other, gossiping, wondering why I've not shown up yet. Tension builds behind my eyes as I approach.

Julia is standing near the gate with her triplets running rings around her, but she's without her usual posse. That's strange. I nod as I reach her, say a quick hello, then walk through the gate.

'Beth, sweetie!' she calls after me.

I turn, slowly.

'I thought you might be feeling a bit, well . . . lonely. I wanted to ask if you'd be up for me popping over later?' she says, her head cocked. 'I'll bring wine?' She lifts her shoulders and smiles. I hesitate, about to decline her offer, but she sees that coming. 'Go on, Beth. I'm desperate for some adult company of an evening – I'm bored stiff of Matt.' She rolls her eyes and gives a forced giggle. I wonder if she really means that; I suspect it's an excuse she's plucked out of nowhere in the hope I'll give in.

It can't hurt.

'That would be really lovely, thank you,' I say.

Julia stands taller, her expression brightening. 'Oh, brilliant!' she says, beaming. 'I hate thinking of you rattling about in that cottage alone while all this . . . *stuff* . . . is happening to you.' She grabs hold of her brood and herds them across the road, calling 'I'll be at yours for seven!' as she goes.

I immediately begin to doubt Julia's intentions and I go to shout after her to withdraw my acceptance, but she's already disappeared around the corner. I could text her later saying I've got a migraine or something to get out of it. With the pulsating pain I'm experiencing in my head right now, that might not be a lie anyway. I rub at my temples and go inside.

Poppy is sitting on a chair, legs swinging, backpack on her lap. She looks tiny. A lump forms in my throat. I want to wrap my arms around her; protect her and keep her from whatever backlash Tom's arrest will cause. 'Hey, my little Poppy poppet,' I say, reaching out to her, pulling her from the chair into a tight cuddle. I feel her hands grip my arms. I can't stop the tears.

'Don't cry, Mummy,' she says. All the tension from the past week that I've been holding onto, keeping in check, threatens to leak out of me now, in this instant. I jam my teeth together, breathe in deeply through my nose and compose myself. I can't fall apart. I need to be strong for Poppy.

'I'm just so happy to see you,' I say. Her pale-blonde eyebrows lower, as though even she knows that's not why I'm crying.

'Okay, shall we take a moment to chat in the office, Beth?' Zoey says. 'Poppy, if you stay with Wanda for a little bit longer, I want to talk to your mummy.'

A flash of concern crosses Poppy's face, but it's quickly replaced with a smile as Wanda takes her hand and leads her to Pets Corner. They have a new giant African land snail which she finds fascinating.

Inside the office, Zoey tells me not to worry. But when I explain that Tom has now been charged, her relaxed expression tightens. I'm surprised this development is news to her; I'd have thought the gossip would've reached everyone by now. She shifts awkwardly in her seat, then clears her throat.

'Oh, I'm very sorry to hear that. This must be a very stressful time for you. Look, I'm not here to judge.' The very fact she's said this makes my tummy flip. She thinks Tom's guilty. Does she think that somehow I am, too? 'Our responsibility is to Poppy, to help ensure she's not adversely affected by anything while she's in our care.

Internal, and to some extent external factors, too. But I obviously have no control over what happens outside of this establishment, Beth.'

'No, no. I realise that. I was only going to ask that you keep a closer eye on her here; make sure no other children or staff treat her any differently.'

'The children are too young to understand. They are very unlikely to behave differently.'

'They might pick up things from their parents. I'm betting *they'll* have lots to say about my current situation.' I wring my hands together in my lap, the thought of it making me anxious.

'We will of course keep a closer watch on Poppy. We'll listen out for anything like that and nip it in the bud. We want nursery to be a safe haven for her, a place she can continue to develop and grow.' Zoey reaches across and puts her hands over mine, giving them a gentle squeeze. 'She'll be all right, Beth. Kids are amazingly resilient.'

The memory of my dad leaving me flashes through my mind's eye.

Are they?

Because that's not my experience.

Chapter 38

She's lying silent, motionless on her back, her bound wrists secured to the headboard, her legs spread, each ankle attached to a bed post. His breathing is becoming louder, quicker. The blindfold prevents her seeing him but she hears his movements; knows where in the room he is. Knows what he's about to do.

She used to get an adrenaline rush of anticipation. Now, she just wants it over. Wants to reach the other side without fear clouding her mind for the entire time it takes him to act out his fantasies. She hopes she made herself clear last time and that he won't strangle her to the point of passing out again.

'I need to teach you a lesson,' he says. Her hopes diminish as she feels hot palms on her chest, rising upwards, settling on her throat.

She takes a deep breath. Prepares herself for his game.

His weight suddenly shifts off her. She's confused. She tries desperately to sense where he's gone, what he's doing.

This is new. *She breathes steadily now; twists her head to listen, to figure out what he's up to. Then something smooth is slipped around her neck.* Is he using his tie?

She feels a strong tug as the material constricts her throat. Hears his moan of anticipation, his arousal building.

Here we go.

Chapter 39

BETH

Now

'Oh, God!' I start at the knock on the front door and quickly push the dishwasher drawer closed. It's seven o'clock; I'd forgotten all about Julia coming over and I never texted her an excuse. The urge to pretend I'm not in is strong, but as she'll know I am, it's not an acceptable get-out. I haven't even washed and changed – too busy tidying up the kitchen following dinner – I must look a right state. I groan and run my hands quickly through my hair as I go to the door.

'Hi!' Julia beams, holding up a bottle in each hand. She's certainly come prepared. She's also come dressed up. I thought I looked a state before, but now I feel even worse. She's wearing a pretty pale-yellow dress, which I'm guessing is designer, and her glossy hair is pulled up into a messy – but perfectly styled – bun. Her face is fully made up: her eyes are heavy with golden shadow and black mascara, her foundation is contoured, her high cheekbones are highlighted in a pearly satin shade, and her ruby-coloured lips are perfectly pouty, as though she's going *out* out. Not just to a friend's house. Or an acquaintance's, in this case.

I let her in, catching a waft of expensive perfume as she sweeps past me into the hallway. She turns back to face me, hesitant.

'Oh, go on in there,' I say, pointing to the lounge. Of course, she's never stepped foot inside my home; she doesn't know the layout. 'I'll grab us some glasses.'

The second I return and set the glasses on the table, Julia goes straight in for the kill. 'So, I heard there's been a development.'

'Yes, that's right. I assume all the village knows now.' My tone is curt. I'm a little put out that this is her opening line, after she invited herself to my home to offer 'support'.

'Terrible news. I'm really sorry it's come to this.' She tries for a concerned look as she glances around, but it seems a bit forced. She pops the cork from one of the bottles and pours the Prosecco to the brim of each glass. 'I hope you don't mind some bubbles. I know they're more for celebrating, which is not really fitting given the circumstances, but maybe we could drink to celebrate new friendships!' She gives a wide smile.

'Drown my sorrows, more like. God, this whole thing is devastating, Julia,' I say, honestly.

'I can only imagine,' she says, her head shaking. 'You must be so . . . *discombobulated*.'

'Good word.' I give a sharp snort. 'Although . . . angry, hurt, scared . . . *lost* – they're the current emotions fighting over themselves inside me.'

152

She smiles, sympathetically. 'Have you spoken with Tom?'

'No. I'm too wound up. Or maybe it would be more accurate to say that I'm thinking if I don't speak to him, I can pretend it isn't happening.'

'Ah, good old denial. The burying of the head. I can understand that, Beth. But you need to talk to him, surely? Find out how bad the situation is?'

'He's been charged with murder, Julia. How much worse can it get?'

'Well, without wanting to sound negative – the worst thing would be that he's found guilty. Don't you want to know what he thinks about the charge? I mean, I assume you believe he's innocent and that there won't be enough evidence to convict him, but you have to know what's going on, Beth. So you can prepare.'

Prepare. Even the word is heavy with connotation. The need to *do* something; to act. But all of a sudden I know I'm not ready for all of this. I don't want to sit here, opening myself up like this. I need to change the subject; I've been far too candid with someone I barely know.

'Yes, well – tomorrow is soon enough for reality. Now, Julia, I want to know how you manage it?'

'Oh? What?' She frowns – although you wouldn't really know it; her forehead barely crinkles.

'You've got triplets, you've got your own business, you always look spectacular. I just don't get it. How on God's earth can you juggle everything? I've only got one child and I look like . . . well . . . *this*.' I run my hand up and down myself to back up my statement. Julia throws her head back and laughs, displaying a full set of perfectly white teeth and zero fillings.

153

'Oh, sweetie – most of what you see is pure projection.' She takes a large gulp of fizz.

'Projection?'

'Yes, you know – the image I wish to project onto the world. You think I'm managing?' Her laugh is brittle now. 'You're very lovely to say so. And I'm glad I've succeeded in giving that impression – that *that's* the way you see me. You and everyone in Lower Tew.' She gives a dramatic sigh.

'Ah,' I say. 'So, not everything is how it seems?' I'm glad I've managed to make the conversation take this turn. The heat is off me for the moment.

'Is it ever?' She swallows back more Prosecco. 'We all hide behind closed doors for the majority of the time, don't we? No one knows what happens; what a person's life is really like once the door is locked. Unless we tell someone.' Tears bulge, but they don't escape her eyes. She's clearly used to being in control of her emotions. I wasn't expecting this. Maybe it's the wine talking; I think she's probably had a few glasses before coming here. Or is it her way of getting *me* to open up about what *my* life is like behind closed doors?

Clever.

'You do keep all the balls in the air, though, don't you? I mean, look at you – always perfectly dressed and made up, a successful beauty business, three mostly well-behaved children – that can't be easy – a doting husband, *and* you have a whole host of friends.' I wonder if I've overdone it; simplified everything and made her sound a bit shallow.

She gives a sad smile. 'Externally, yes – I agree my life looks pretty darn amazing. And don't get me wrong, I work hard, and on the whole I'm happy with what I've

154

achieved – what I accomplish on a daily basis. But *internally*,' she places a hand over her heart, 'so much is missing, Beth. I need to be able to share the successes and the stresses, have moments of candour and peel back my exterior to reveal the flaws beneath, too. It's quite lonely being perfect all the time.'

I'm a bit lost, and unsure how to react. Julia Bennington isn't playing me. She's just caught up in a hell of her own making. By burying her real feelings and covering her flaws, she has created an image of a completely together, successful wife, mother and businesswoman. And now she feels unable to come clean; to let others in.

'And the nursery mums? The other villagers? You haven't confided in any of those people?'

'Nope. The façade is well and truly constructed and I can't, *won't*, bring that crashing down now. I lost the one person who knew the real Julia.'

My mouth drops open. 'Oh, Julia. Not Matt . . .?' Did he leave her and no one even knows? She really has gone to great lengths to keep up the pretence of perfection.

'No. Not him. He's still the same – ignores me for the best part and uses me as the trophy wife when it suits. I don't tell him anything these days.'

'Oh, sorry – I assumed that's who you meant.'

'I meant Camilla. You know, Camilla Knight, Adam's late wife?'

'Ah, yes, sorry.' I'm taken aback. I remember they were in the same group of friends, but I didn't realise they were particularly close.

'When she died, she left a gaping hole in my life.' Julia swallows back the rest of her Prosecco and refills. I don't speak: clearly Julia is gearing herself up to share more.

It's a relief that Julia is doing all the talking, but the sadness oozing from her is making me uncomfortable. It's weird she's chosen me to unburden herself to; to share her innermost feelings, show her true self. I don't even know her. But then, maybe that's precisely why it's me she's pouring her heart out to. Is she priming me to become her next best friend all of a sudden?

'The best friend position is still vacant,' she says, as though reading my mind. She gives a wavering smile. 'No one knew me like Camilla did. None of the others, the ones I hang around with, *see* me. Do you understand? They don't look beyond the Julia with the triplets; the Julia with the business; the Julia with the designer handbags and clothes. Because they aren't bothered about anything else. They don't *want* to see anything different. Camilla did. She was actually interested in me: she asked questions, she didn't just rely on what I told her. I thought she was nosy to begin with, and I closed up even further. Then, when she asked me to go to hers after book club one evening, she told me she was worried about me. That's when I realised she was a true friend. She cared about the things I kept hidden. She was invested enough in our friendship to delve deeper and I appreciated that.'

'I can imagine. It's hard to find a true friend, isn't it? I haven't had one since uni. My mates went separate ways and we lost contact. I haven't lost anyone, not like you have, but I understand that need to have someone close you can turn to and confide in – someone who you know will always have your back.'

'Exactly. That's what I sorely miss. I assumed Lucy was your go-to friend here, though?'

'Ah, well, Lucy's lovely – but she's young. We don't

have an awful lot in common. She's brilliant at Poppy's Place – she's trustworthy, dependable. Been really good during this latest upheaval. But she's not someone I'd call a best friend, if you know what I mean.'

I'm annoyed at myself for bringing the topic back to me. I lean forward, take the bottle and top up our glasses. 'And she's loved up! She's just starting out on her journey. I would hate to disillusion her,' I laugh.

'You're right, she needs to find that out for herself. Poor girl.' Julia necks back the glass.

'She might be lucky!' I say. '*Someone* has to make it through life truly happy, don't they?'

'I'll drink to that,' Julia says, raising her empty glass. 'Oh, bugger.' She tilts the bottle towards her glass and a few droplets of wine dribble out.

'I'll get the other one,' I say, getting up and heading in the direction of the kitchen. I'm wobbling slightly; my head feels light. 'I can't believe we polished that one off so quickly.' I should slow down. I don't want to get drunk and be incapable of looking after Poppy. Adam's face pops into my mind and I feel a tug of guilt. What would he think of my parenting?

'Have you met Lucy's boyfriend?' Julia's voice makes me jump – I hadn't realised she'd followed me into the kitchen.

'Oscar? Yeah, once or twice. He's been to the café on occasion to see her.' I take the Prosecco from the fridge and pass it to Julia. Hopefully, she'll drink most of this bottle. Judging by this evening's standard, she makes light work of it. She doesn't seem too tipsy, either, which brings me to the conclusion that she drinks regularly. I shouldn't judge, but I've seen where alcohol dependency can lead.

157

'Do you think he's a bit . . . odd?' Julia says, her eyes narrowing.

'Not really. He's quiet, doesn't seem particularly confident around other people, but he comes across as pretty normal to me.'

'Hmm. Probably just me, then. He doesn't seem to have any male friends that I've noticed. Strikes me as a loner, aside from the fact he's seeing Lucy, that is.'

'Maybe he isn't keen on fair-weather friends either?' I raise my eyebrows.

'Touché,' she says.

'Tom's taken his car to his garage a few times to get a service. And he's fitted new tyres and fixed an issue with the battery apparently. He's never vocalised any concerns about him to me. I think it's just that he keeps himself to himself outside of his work, that's all. Lucy seems happy enough with him.'

'I'm projecting again, aren't I? Assuming anyone whose life looks perfect on the outside must have problems they're not sharing. I've become quite the cynic!' Julia walks back into the lounge and pours wine into both our glasses before I can stop her. I'll take mine slowly. She plonks herself on the two-seater sofa and puts her feet up.

'Cheers,' she says. 'Here's to living with secrets.'

I half-heartedly raise my glass, but I don't repeat her toast.

Chapter 40

BETH

Now

It's my first hangover for quite some time and I'm not relishing having to face the day with this lurching stomach and muzzy head. And a three-year-old. Poppy has already jumped up and down on my bed to wake me; for a horrible moment I thought I was on a ship, rolling on the waves. I'm never drinking on a weekday again. I wonder how Julia is faring this morning – I guess I'll see soon enough. Will she act weirdly with me given how much she disclosed to me last night? Will she even *remember* what she said? I'll have to play it by ear – see how she responds to me first and take the lead from her. The last thing I want is for her to feel awkward because she spilled her guts and now regrets it.

I've another missed call from Maxwell – I put my phone on silent last night. I've not been able to face a conversation with him. I know I can't put it off forever, but for now I would like to avoid it; deny the situation. *If I refuse to talk about it, it's not happening.* Such a juvenile reaction, I'm actually ashamed.

And what about Tom? He must be beside himself. Am I expected to go and *see* him? I wouldn't have thought that was possible given the circumstances. I imagine we can speak on the phone though. No doubt these are all things Maxwell is waiting to inform me of. If I were to pick up his calls, I'd know the answers.

As we're up super early, and I don't have to make breakfast for Tom, I think I'll cook up a batch of cookies. It'll take my mind off this hangover, and a spoonful of the batter will give my sugar levels a boost. Sugar always used to help my hangovers. That and a can of Coke, which, thankfully, I have in the fridge. It's one of the few things I learnt from my mother.

Poppy stands on a chair beside me as I spread the ingredients out on the worktop, and she helps by lining them up in the order I need them in. I sing along to Michael Bublé as I measure, and Poppy hums out of tune, smiling as she scoops some extra ingredients that I've given her in her own special bowl. The smells associated with baking always take me back to when I lived with my nanna. It was her who taught me the basics of cooking and baking, not my mother, who had no desire to do either. She mainly only had time for drinking, vomiting, and sleeping.

We're making my speciality – butterscotch oatmeal cookies. Poppy loves butterscotch and it's my go-to feel-good recipe for when I'm anxious or worried. As I blend the ingredients together in my Cath Kidston mixing bowl, I recall how Julia spoke about Camilla last night. I had no idea how she really felt – she certainly masks her

160

emotions well on a day-to-day basis. I can't believe I missed that they were best friends; I'd only seen them hanging around in larger groups, never just the two of them. Poor woman. I'd been a little surprised to hear about how Camilla had been so kind. If I'm honest, I'd struggled to get to know her initially – she'd seemed somewhat aloof. I was always trying to slip into her and her group's conversations, but I never really connected with her. In the end, it was over recipes that we finally bonded – if you can call it bonding. Camilla was quite an experienced baker herself and had some great ideas. In the weeks before she died, we'd started to discuss new flavour combinations and swap recipes. I remember that she even made some suggestions to help me perfect these butterscotch ones.

Of course, our friendship had never progressed much beyond that, as she died not long afterwards. Such a shame. Typically, she had been one of the only new women I talked to that Tom found bearable. He has little time for the others; he says they're shallow and false. I've tried to tell him if he gives people a chance he'd be surprised.

I was due to invite a small group of people around for a meal before all this kicked off. That won't be happening now, I realise with a sinking feeling. Will my life be anything like normal from here on in?

'Can I lick the spoon please?' Poppy says, grabbing the bowl after I dollop the mixture in even splodges on the baking tray. I know she shouldn't, not with the possibility of salmonella from the raw eggs, but it's one of the best memories I have with my nanna. She always let me take the wooden spoon and lick off the gloopy, sweet mixture. It was part of my childhood. I can't let Poppy miss out on this tradition. You have to take some risks in life, I rationalise, as I pass her the spoon.

'Ooh, thank you, Mummy,' she says, her eyes wide.

I wipe my hands on my apron and pop the tray of cookie dough into the oven. 'Right, come on, little one. Time to get ready for nursery.' I set the timer and we go upstairs. The gorgeous smell of baking fills the cottage. It's incongruous against the horror-backdrop of the situation I'm in.

We still have a bit of time before we need to head out, and Poppy is engrossed in a cartoon on telly – she sulked for a full five minutes when I told her she couldn't have Daddy's iPad – so I finally take this opportunity and pluck up the courage to return Maxwell's call.

'I was beginning to think you'd dropped off the grid,' he says. 'You know I've been trying to get hold of you, don't you?' His strained voice sounds exhausted. I remind him, wearily, how I've had a lot to deal with these past few days. He somewhat huffily informs me that Tom is in a worse position, and maybe the support of his wife would go some way to helping him cope with it. I want to hang up. How dare he take the moral high ground. Poppy and I are the innocent ones in this situation. Whether Tom is innocent or guilty, this whole situation is Tom's problem – not ours. I never even *met* Katie. He could be as pure as the driven snow and it wouldn't make any difference – it's still me and Poppy at home having to deal with his problems. I think I have every right to be angry; hurt; confused. Scared.

'Look, I understand how hard this must be,' he says more softly, obviously taking my silence as a sign he's been too harsh. 'It's not like you saw it coming, is it?

You're well within your rights to feel a whole host of emotions right now. I want to try and help navigate both Tom *and* you through this.'

'Yeah, I know. I'm sorry. You're right – I'm all over the place. But my main priority is Poppy. Tom would want that too. He's capable of looking after himself; Poppy isn't.'

'He is very worried about how this is all affecting her – and you, of course. I want to be able to reassure him, Beth. He's got zero control over what's happening outside the custody suite: I'm his only link to the outside world; to his family. I have to try and keep his hope alive, however grim it's looking.'

'Oh? It's looking grim?' It's a pointless question, I know, but I had assumed Tom's own solicitor would at least attempt to make it sound a little positive.

'The police have found other incriminating evidence, Beth. Still, nothing they have so far is irrefutable proof he had a hand in her disappearance, or murder, or anything else, but with all these separate things mounting up, it certainly helps keep the finger of blame firmly pointed at him.'

I let out a juddering sigh. 'I understand. A body would be that irrefutable evidence, wouldn't it?'

'Depends.' I imagine Maxwell shrugging.

'On?'

'Where the body has been all these years; the cause of death; whether there's any DNA linking Tom to the body, or the scene. That sort of thing.'

'But still – if there was a body, and they found evidence of someone else's DNA on it, that would rule Tom out as a suspect, surely? Every other bit of evidence is purely circumstantial, and a jury couldn't convict him on that basis. Are the police even *looking* for her body?'

'One would assume so. They'll be trying to find possible locations, but they can't search everywhere. They'd need a strong lead to begin digging in a particular area. If, indeed, the body was buried, and not disposed of in another manner.'

'Yes, I suppose.' My mind wanders and I think of the places Tom and I used to visit when we lived in London. It was only a year after Katie that we got together and I moved into his flat. The flat that Katie had no doubt spent time in. I shiver at the possibilities that I can't help imagining.

'Anyway, another reason for my call was to let you know that Tom's initial hearing is tomorrow. The magistrate will refer the case to the Crown Court because it's an indictable offence he's been charged with. There'll be something called a plea and trial preparation hearing at the Crown Court first, hopefully within about twenty-eight days of tomorrow. Tom is entering a not guilty plea, obviously, and the way it'll likely go is they'll refuse bail on the same grounds as before, and he'll be placed on remand until his trial. Any questions?'

My mind goes blank. This information dump has overloaded my tired brain; I can't take it all in. So I just say no, I don't have questions, and that I understand everything. Even though I *do* have questions, and I understand very little.

'Okay, great. Well, call me anytime if there's something you want me to clarify.' The line goes quiet, and I think this means he's hung up without saying goodbye. But then he adds, 'Tom would really like to see you.' And my limbs go weak.

Do I want to see *him*?

Chapter 41

BETH

Now

Julia isn't at nursery; it's her husband Matt I see instead. Maybe she is nursing a hangover after all. If I'd had someone else to bring Poppy, I'd have gladly allowed them to. Matt doesn't stop to converse with anyone; he just drops the triplets and rushes off. Not without first casting me a withering look, though. I lower my eyes – he must know Julia spent the evening with me. Perhaps he blames me for her state this morning. Hopefully, Julia will be collecting, and I'll be able to speak to her to get the lay of the land.

A few of the Mumsgate mums say hello, but they don't approach me or involve me in their conversations. That's fine by me. I need to get to work anyway to get the fresh goods on display early. I want to try and keep to my routine despite not feeling much like working. It would be far easier to go home; to bury myself beneath my duvet and allow the world to continue revolving without me.

But 'easier' is the coward's way. I refuse to go down that road.

Lucy is back to her usual self; I hear her singing before I even open the door to the café. It's a good sound: normal. Comforting. And I think that's what I need – even if my life has been turned upside down, if my surroundings stay the same, at least when I'm out of the house I can pretend things are fine. Be in another, safer, kinder world for a while. However brief. News that Tom has been charged with murder will circulate throughout the village quickly; 'safer, kinder' might not last.

The singing stops as Lucy sees me.

'Beth, hi. I wasn't sure if you'd be in after you left early yesterday. I texted you last night, but when you didn't respond . . .'

I pull my phone out of my bag and scroll through my messages. 'Oh, sorry,' I say as I find her text. 'I was kind of ignoring my phone. Thanks for opening up as usual. I need to try and keep things going.' I continue into the back room and hang my bag on the hook behind the door. Lucy has followed me in. I can sense she wants to ask me something.

'Are you okay? I mean, like *really* okay?'

'I'm trying my best to be, Lucy. It all feels so hopeless though. Tom wants to see me.'

Her eyes widen. 'I expect he does. I guess he must be feeling very alone. Not knowing what's going on, worrying about being sent to prison for life.' Lucy gives a little gasp. 'Sorry, that was insensitive of me.'

'No, you're right. God, it's all such a mess. How has

this even happened to us? Everything was going so well.'

'Are you going to see him, then?'

'I really don't know. That's awful of me, I know. But I can't bear to see him like that. It would destroy me.'

'But won't he want to know you support him? Believe he's innocent? You do believe that, don't you?'

And that's the million-dollar question, I realise.

Do I believe my husband is innocent? Is that what everyone wants to know?

She must've known.

'Of course,' I say. 'Right. Best get out on the floor – shouldn't leave the shop unattended.' I walk back and go behind the counter, busying myself with restacking the glasses and wiping down the coffee machine.

'A latte to go, please.'

I turn to see Adam. 'Well, hello. Don't usually see you around here during the day,' I say.

'No, I've popped out for a coffee break.' He leans forwards conspiratorially and grimaces slightly. 'I'm on a bit of a begging mission.'

'Oh, *are* you?' I raise one eyebrow and smirk.

'Yes. And I wouldn't usually ask favours from people – I *hate* being indebted – but I think you sort of offered, so I'm hoping it's not too much to ask . . .'

'Go on,' I say, guessing what's coming.

'Would you possibly be able to collect Jess from nursery when you get Poppy and have her at yours until around six?' He scrunches his eyes and puts his hands together in prayer form.

'Is that meant to melt my heart, like a puppy-dog looking at me with its big 'ole brown eyes?'

'Yeah, that's the hope,' he laughs.

I suck in a breath, giving a dramatic pause before releasing it and answering him. 'Sure. Of course I'll do it. And you're right – I *did* offer to have Jess over for tea this week. So you don't need to think of it as a favour and I won't hold you to repaying the debt or anything.'

'Thanks so much, Beth. You're a life saver. I could've asked Constance, but I feel I've called on her a little too much lately. And I think spending time with Poppy would really help Jess.'

'Sorted then. Just remember to inform Zoey I have permission to take her.' I turn my back to make his latte, and when I've finished, I hand it over, popping a freshly made cookie into a paper bag too. 'You must try these,' I say, handing it to him. 'On the house.'

'Freebies too! I'll come again.'

'Well, not too often. You'll start tongues wagging.'

'Oh, God, do you think? Maybe I shouldn't . . .' He trails off, his face aghast.

'No, Adam – I only meant that giving out free cookies too often will, not you being here,' I say, surprised at his reaction. But then I remember how he was when I dropped by his place to see him. He really seems concerned about gossip.

Is it that he's just a bit sensitive? That *is* a good quality, I guess, but surely he can't be that worried about what Camilla's friends think? I wonder if there's more to it; that maybe his intentions towards me aren't as innocent as he makes out and he feels a bit guilty.

'Ah, right.' His cheeks burn with embarrassment. 'I'm so good at reading situations,' he says with an awkward chuckle. 'You should see how I interpret emails and texts.'

We both laugh.

168

'You're better than you think,' I say. 'Now, you'd best get back to work before they think you've gone AWOL.'

'Yep, I had. I'll see you at six. And thanks again, Beth. I really appreciate this, especially given . . . you know.'

'No, what?' I say, trying to keep my expression serious.

Adam's eyes widen, his mouth dropping open. He's about to say something, then I can't prevent my smile any longer and the penny drops.

'Oh, for God's sake, Beth! I almost fell for that. *Ha ha*.'

I watch as he leaves, and a strange sensation stirs inside me.

I must be careful there.

Chapter 42

BETH

Now

The wind whips up as I head down the lane. I pull up my hood to shield from it – and anyone that I might see along the way. Some fallen leaves ahead of me lift and swirl, creating a vortex. I stand still watching the mini tornado, fascinated, thinking how this is a good representation of my life right now.

The hum of an approaching car pulls me out of my trance and I quickly back up to the wall to let a Land Rover go by. The passenger cranes his neck as it passes, staring at me. I don't recognise him or the vehicle. Does he know who I am? Whose wife I am? I suppose I should get used to this kind of paranoia. I'm tempted to take my phone out of my pocket and snap a photo of the number plate, but the Land Rover disappears before I can process the thought and put it into action. It was probably nothing anyway.

It's the usual scene when I reach nursery, bar one

exception. Still no Julia. Disappointment merges with concern. She might simply be ill, or avoiding me; but what if there's more to it? An argument with Matt? She'd had a fair bit to drink when she opened up about him and about their relationship last night. It's possible she picked a drunken fight with him when she got home. Could be why he gave me such a glare this morning.

My concern is thankfully short-lived as I see her walk out of the classroom. She obviously went straight inside – must have been talking to Zoey, rather than standing outside waiting with her usual group. Her face is practically hidden with oversized sunglasses, and, given the overcast weather, I hazard a guess she's using them as a means of disguising her hangover – dark circles; bags; no make-up, perhaps.

'Hiya, my little one,' I say, as Poppy exits the building, Zoey directly behind her. *Oh, God, something must've happened*. 'What's the matter?' My voice catches. I swallow hard.

'You're taking Jess Knight too today?' Zoey says. Of course. She's just checking before she allows Jess home with me. Nothing bad has happened.

'Yes, Adam asked me earlier. He's going to be delayed at work.'

'I just need you to sign a form,' she says. I follow her into the covered entrance, out of the wind, and scribble my signature to say I've had permission to pick Jess up. Then I take Poppy's and Jess's hands, one in each of mine, and walk to the gate. Both of them are excitable, which is lovely to see.

Luckily, I catch Julia before she crosses over. I only want a brief chat to check she's okay.

'Well, that was quite the distraction you offered me last night,' I say lightly, grinning.

'Gosh, wasn't it?' Julia leans forward and whispers, 'Maybe one bottle would've sufficed.' She flicks her hair behind one shoulder and turns away from me. 'Catch you another time, Beth. Must run.'

I watch her hasty retreat, an uncomfortable feeling in the pit of my stomach. I'm relieved she's not *off* with me, but she was quick to get away, so not exactly friendly either considering our heart-to-heart last night. I think I'll text her later; let her know I'm not going to say anything to anyone else. Put her mind at ease. She must be feeling embarrassed at having shared so much with me.

Back at the cottage, I set the girls up on the kitchen table with Play-Doh and a load of different cutters, ask Alexa to play my uplifting playlist, and begin to prepare their tea. For this moment in time, everything appears normal, carefree, and happy. I find myself loudly singing along to 'Nothing's Gonna Stop Us Now', and like any good illusion, I *feel* the emotion, despite everything.

At spot on six, there's a knock on the door.

'Daddy!' Jess shouts.

Adam hands me a bottle of wine as soon as I open the door. I let him in and take it from him, my eyes narrowing.

'A little thank you,' he says, in response to my questioning glance. 'And I didn't want you to feel guilty about drinking it, so I walked here so I could share a glass with you.'

'Oh, really?' I say. 'I'm not sure about *sharing*.'

He gives a gentle shake of his head. 'Well, obviously

I'm only going to have one. I *am* the responsible adult after all.'

'That's what I thought.'

After Jess and Poppy have run around him for a few minutes, they go into the lounge to watch some telly.

'I hope I've worn her out for you,' I say. 'Shall I pop the cork now?' I don't mention it'll be my second evening in a row to drink.

'Yes, do.' He glances around, his eyes not settling on anything.

'Everything all right?' I ask.

'Yes, sorry. I was just thinking how strange . . . *disquieting* . . . all this must be for you.'

I pour two small glasses and hand him one. 'Disquieting.' I nod. 'Good word. Yep – it really is.'

'You're doing so well, keeping it all together, Beth.' He tilts the glass to his lips and takes a sip.

'Well, looks can be deceiving.'

Adam nods. 'Very true. I'm sorry, I should've known better than to say something so stupid. Although I'm very good at stupid.'

'It's not a stupid thing to say – you're right. To the outside world I'm coping. But we both know the exterior has to remain tough, intact, for our children's sakes.'

'How long have you been building that exterior?'

I frown. His expression leads me to think he's not just referring to my current situation. 'What do you mean?'

'Tell me to get lost if you want to – but I get the impression it's not a completely *new* construction.'

Heat rises into my cheeks. I scratch the back of my neck and take a gulp of wine. Adam's eyes remain firmly on mine. What has he seen in me that no one else has?

'All my life, probably,' I say, shrugging.

'A lifetime building barriers around yourself, and now the one man who you allowed to break through has let you down. That sucks. I'm sorry.'

I feel strangely protective of Tom suddenly. It's okay for *me* to say he's let me and Poppy down, but Adam saying it makes my skin prickle.

But I'm unable to find the words to defend him.

Adam keeps his gaze on me, his eyebrows knitted together. He's leaning back against the worktop: the one Tom had me up against the last morning our lives were normal. Adam is waiting for me to say something.

I think my silence speaks volumes.

174

Chapter 43

The sex is hard, frantic. Perfunctory. No intimacy.

He's in control. She's not the focus of his fantasy, but she's the vessel for it. She'd said no to the handcuffs; no to the ties. And the stockings. He doesn't like being told no, but he quickly became aroused by it. Made her say it more.

'No, No, NO!'

He's quick to finish, which means her moment on top won't last long.

He gets off her, but she senses his dissatisfaction. He picks up his jacket and straddles her again; places it over her face. Holds it firmly. Within seconds it becomes hot, claustrophobic. Denying him the usual ways has only made him more creative – he's thinking outside the box.

She struggles against him as her air runs out. This is the part he really enjoys. The power of life or death in his hands.

He doesn't take her to the brink this time, though.

He yells as he comes again. But it's not her name that leaves his lips.

'Sorry. Sorry. Sorry,' he shouts, over and over.

He lies in her arms for ages after. Crying.

If only people realised what went on behind closed doors.

Chapter 44

TOM

Now

Maxwell seems to think Beth won't come here to visit me. He's finally spoken with her after trying to get hold of her for over a day. Why did she avoid him? Why is she avoiding *me*? I can't believe she'd abandon me here alone. Without hope. She's not like that. Not my Beth. She loves me. She needs me.

I cannot go to prison.

I need to be at home; I need to be a father and husband. Providing for my family – that's my job. They are what keep me sane. Without them, I have no purpose; no reason to live this life.

It's cold in this room tonight. Maybe it's the fear of what's ahead. Maybe it's because of the ghost here with me.

They say I killed Katie Williams.

In that case, you'd think *she* would be the one haunting

me, to ensure I get what's coming to me; that she gets justice.

But the ghost is not her.

I pull the thin blanket up over my head, like a child afraid of monsters.

Only it's me who's the monster now.

Chapter 45

BETH

Now

'I'd best be getting Jess off home. Thanks for having her,' Adam says.

'Thanks for the wine.' I hold up my empty glass. How many have I had?

'You're welcome. Glad I could share one with you.'

'It was good to have a chat; pass a bit of time at least.' I refill my glass. 'Shame to let it go to waste,' I smile.

'Will you be all right?' A concerned look flits across Adam's face. 'I feel bad now, leaving you like this.'

'Like what?' I have a terrible feeling my words are slurring. I need to get a grip.

'I've plied you with wine, talked about the most stressful thing in your life, and now I'm going. I'm so sorry.'

'I'll be fine. Don't worry. I've been left in worse states, believe me.' I'm trying to make light of it, to make Adam feel better about leaving me, but I think I've made it worse by saying that. 'Really. I'll get Poppy to bed and follow suit. I could do with an early night.'

He hesitates at the kitchen door, one foot in the hallway. 'I know it's different circumstances but, you know, I actually felt pretty let down by Camilla too.' He turns to look at me. 'Don't feel guilty about thinking Tom's let you down.'

'But Camilla didn't . . .' I'm about to say that it wasn't Camilla's fault she left them, it was a terrible accident. But I realise he's right to be annoyed, in a way. She chose not to be strict with her allergy; she chose to take a risk here and there if a packet mentioned 'may contain traces of nuts'; she got careless. She made decisions that ultimately affected Adam and Jess, and now, it's becoming clear to everyone that Tom must have made bad decisions in his past. And that's affecting me and Poppy. You don't get charged with a crime unless you've done *something*.

'Even those we love can hurt us, eh?' I say instead.

'Did Tom ever hurt you, Beth?' He's the most serious he's been. I wonder why he's asking this just as he's about to leave.

'Of course not,' I say in a whisper. 'Well, if you exclude the . . . *you know*.' I give a jokey nudge and a wink.

'No. I don't know. What do you mean?'

Do I really need to spell it out to him? I assumed he'd get what I'm referring to. I'm suddenly too embarrassed to come out and say, the *sex*, Adam – so I carry on, in the hopes he'll get my gist. 'He likes to be . . . *in control*, and stuff. You know, normal married role play games, I guess.' I wave a hand dismissively. Adam's brows rise.

'Yeah. I see,' he says, turning away again to walk into the lounge to find Jess.

His tone tells me he doesn't see at all. Maybe his marriage wasn't *all that*. Maybe I shouldn't have said anything. The wine has already made my head light, my lips loose.

The girls are sleepy, cuddled up together on the sofa. 'Ahh, that's so sweet,' I say, as I watch Adam bundle Jess into his arms.

'You've definitely done a good job wearing her out. Thanks again, Beth.' He starts carrying her out to the door, and I go ahead to open it, almost tripping over the hall table. 'Oops! Steady on!' he says.

'Clumsy me,' I say. 'Hope to see you soon,' I add, blushing.

'Yes, look – I've got the afternoon off on Friday. Maybe I could return the favour? Give you chance to have a bit of time to yourself.' His smile is affectionate, kind. I say yes without having to think.

'You're a good friend. Thank you,' I say, giving him a peck on his cheek.

Chapter 46

KATIE

Eight years ago

She had managed to get some peace – some time alone – in the toilet. That was about her lot. Tom had been acting oddly – even more clingy than usual. He wouldn't leave her side for longer than a few minutes at her flat. He wanted her to move into his, but the thought made her panic. She'd have no independence. No space at all.

The past two days had been claustrophobic. And he hadn't been the same with her, either. He wasn't as gentle or as loving. When they had sex, he glared at her, making her feel uncomfortable. It was almost as though he hated her. He'd been rough, punishing.

What had she done wrong?

***

TOM

How can she look at me? Doesn't she know what she's done wrong? It's like she's *pretending* she loves me and wants to be with me. Wants to marry me. But all the while she's stringing me along. I don't get it. Maybe she wants the both of us – me and Isaac. Or is she biding her time – waiting for the perfect moment to tell me she doesn't want to be with me?

Well. One thing's definite. If I can't have her, I'll make damn sure Isaac can't either.

Chapter 47

BETH

Now

For a moment I can't make it out over the sound of the Nespresso. Then the buzzing intensifies. It seems like it's coming closer. I look around trying to locate its source and as I'm about to pull the kitchen window blind up, the coffee machine switches off and I realise what the noise is.

'Poppy,' I call, rushing out of the kitchen into the hallway.

She's crouching down in front of the door, picking something up from the mat.

'Poppy, no!' I yell. She jumps and her hand releases its grip. Small cards flitter to the ground and she looks at me, her bottom lip wobbling. 'Sorry, sweetheart – I didn't mean to scare you. I wasn't sure what it was you had there,' I say, more calmly. The buzzing I heard is clearer here by the door. People. A cacophony of voices. And the source is outside my cottage.

I pick up the cards Poppy dropped. Every one of them is a journalist's calling card. Bloody journos. It's happening. They know about Tom. They've found out where we live, and they want their pound of flesh. *Bastards*. How dare they? I throw the cards onto the hall table, take Poppy's hand and lead her upstairs. Her bedroom is at the back of the cottage, so at least it's quiet there for the moment. What do I do?

I'm dreading going to the café now – they're bound to know it belongs to me. And what about taking Poppy to nursery? I've seen this kind of thing on telly – they'll block our path; shout questions; snap cameras. There'll be flashes going off in our faces; they'll chase us up the lane. It's awful – they shouldn't be allowed to behave in this way.

I'm shaking as I make a call to Adam. It's not as though he'll be able to do anything about this, but it'll make me feel a bit better to share my horror. It goes to voicemail. *Shit*. It's almost nine – he'll have dropped Jess and be on his way to work already. It's too late for his help. I take Poppy into the lounge and turn on the telly. Guilt sweeps through me, as I know I've stuck her in front of it way too much recently.

The commotion outside the front window intensifies. I've kept the curtains drawn and I daren't peek now in case they see me. The voices get louder; more urgent.

There's a hard bang on the door.

I ignore it.

It comes again. And again. I want to cover my ears like I used to when my parents argued. Shut it out. Shut everyone out.

'*Leave us alone.*' The words come out of my mouth in a hiss of anger.

185

'Who is it, Mummy?' Poppy's eyes are wide. This is scaring her.

'Silly people who are trying to get my attention, my little Poppy poppet. There's nothing to be afraid of – they'll leave in a minute.' I sound quite convincing, despite my pessimism.

There's a drumming at my front door again – someone's repeatedly thumping it. Then, through the noise, I hear a voice I recognise.

I unhook the chain, open the door a crack and Julia squeezes through.

'Jeees . . .' She looks at Poppy. 'Good morning, sweetie,' she says, quickly recovering.

Julia looks amazing. Like a movie star – I suspect she's in her element. She pats down her hair, straightens her cream jacket and clasps her hands together.

'Right!' she says, brightly. 'We're playing a game this morning, Poppy – are you up for it? Me and the boys have already played it and I'd love it if you'd join in.'

'If the game isn't stone the journos, she's not interested,' I mutter.

'What is it?' Poppy says.

'It's a bit like hide and seek. Do you know that game?'

'Daddy plays that with me,' she says.

'Great! Then you're already ahead. In a minute, I'm going to take you out the back door and Mummy is going to help you over the garden wall,' Julia says, giving me a sideways glance. I realise what she's doing and I'm hugely grateful, so I let her carry on. Her being here has also set my mind at ease – my worry has abated that she'd felt too awkward after the drunken night to speak to me again.

With Poppy all set, and after I've checked the coast is clear out the back, Julia takes her hand and walks her calmly to the far wall. I'm thinking it's a bit high for Julia to get up in what she's wearing, but before I can even suggest getting a stepladder, she's hitched up her skirt almost to her waist and is heaving herself up the stone wall.

'Oh, wow,' I say. 'You're more nimble than you look.'

'Cheeky!'

When Julia gets down the other side, I lift Poppy up and she scrambles to her feet, balancing carefully on top of the wall. My heart is racing – I'm frightened she'll fall, even though I'm gripping her legs. Julia replaces my hands with hers and lowers her down the other side.

Julia's head is visible above the wall. 'What a nightmare,' I say.

'It most certainly is. I saw them when I dropped the boys and assumed they'd be at your door. I hope you don't mind me coming and taking over.'

'Not at all. Thank you, Julia. I owe you one.'

'Well, if it involves wine, I think we should skip it,' she laughs. 'Okay, I'll get going before they cotton on. Are you planning on heading to the café?'

'I'll see if it dies down. Surely they won't stay there all day?'

I can't see Julia's expression clearly, but her lack of affirmation tells me she thinks they might.

'If it's not looking great, text me after lunch and I'll bring her back for you too.'

'Thanks so much, Julia.' I blink rapidly. 'I can't believe this is happening.' I force myself to smile. 'Have a good game, Poppy! Mummy will see you in a little while.'

'Shhh, Mummy. I'm hiding,' I hear her little voice say. I'm glad she really does think this is a game, because I'm not finding it fun at all.

'Speak later,' Julia says. 'And take care. Maybe ring that solicitor and see what he can do.'

I tell her I will. I hear rustling leaves on the other side, footsteps growing fainter. I wait until I can't hear them at all, then fall back against the wall, tilting my head up to the sun. It's quiet out here. Perhaps I should stay here all day and avoid reality.

It's a nice thought, but I know I can't. I've things to organise.

I go inside, ask Alexa to play my uplifting playlist, and cry along to the songs.

Chapter 48

BETH

Now

My own car's blocked by the mob of journalists, but Tom's is still sitting outside the gateway. The detectives searched it at the same time as the cottage, but they mustn't have found anything of interest because it wasn't impounded. I'm free to drive it. If I want to leave the house without being hounded, I think it's wise to take it. They can still follow, of course, but at least I'll be cocooned inside a metal shell. Windows up, doors locked. Safer than walking.

I peer out through the slit in my bedroom curtains. The crowd has thinned out; some of them have clearly got bored and have better stories to chase. Good. The remaining reporters and journalists are relaxed, off-guard, lolling around, their cameras inactive. If I go out the back door and creep around the front, I should be able to get into the car before they notice me. I can avoid the worst of their 'investigative' tactics. For today, anyway.

But what about tomorrow? The next day? The next week; month? How long will this go on for? I dig my nails into my palms, hard. Tears sting my eyes. Maxwell seems to think I should be worried about Tom, alone in a cell, anxious about what his future holds. And I *am* worried about him. The uncertainty of what the police have against Tom is a huge weight on both our shoulders. He must be feeling so isolated and afraid; it's not unheard of for an innocent person to be found guilty and imprisoned. But I'm afraid too. Right now, I'm the centre of attention – the focus is on me. Tom is safe, at least. *He's* not the one dealing with the locals. He doesn't have to keep showing his face knowing people are talking behind his back. And he's not the one the journalists are scrambling to get a glimpse of; take photos of. He's not being followed.

He's left me to deal with this alone with a three-year-old.

He's left me.

The thought hits home; it's a smack in the face. It doesn't matter how, or why – what matters is he's abandoned me, just like my father did.

He's abandoned Poppy.

I run downstairs, snatch Tom's keys from the pot, sneak out of the back door and dart around the front to the car. I don't stop to think – I just act. If I hesitate, then they'll spot me and I'll have to scurry back inside like a mouse into its hole. I open the passenger side, as that's closest, and scramble across the seat. I'm on the driver's side, central locking activated, by the time one of the journos clocks what's going on. I accelerate hard and

190

speed away, my tyres screeching like a scene from *Starsky and Hutch*. The journos scatter, probably afraid I'll mow them down. Let them be afraid. They shouldn't be in the road in the first place. Idiots.

My entire body shakes as I continue to drive, slowly now, through the village. I don't want to go to Poppy's Place – they'll assume that's where I'm heading and be there within minutes, and I can't have Lucy getting stressed out about the attention. I carry on driving, out of the village, taking a right onto the main road. I've no idea where I'm going, but I am compelled to keep going. Anywhere out of Lower Tew will do.

It's times like this I wish I had family I could drop in on. A safe haven to crash at, even if only for a few hours. Having no one wasn't an issue when I first met Tom – he took the place of my family. He was my everything. I didn't need anyone else. Tom would tell me that all the time. He said I was all he needed, too.

But I don't think that was entirely true.

I'm in Banbury before I know it, parking up at the train station.

This is part of Tom's daily commute. Perhaps I'll follow his steps – the ones I thought he took on Tuesday morning. Why was Tuesday different? It can't have been a coincidence that he chose the day after he'd been questioned about Katie to take the day off. Perhaps he just couldn't face work after a long, emotional night. I've no reason to think he hadn't planned to go to work as usual when he left me and Poppy at six fifteen that morning. Perhaps he got here and decided in that moment to go off and spend time alone.

Did he drive, leave his car at Banbury, in this car park,

then take a different train somewhere for the day? DC Cooper said they'd checked CCTV and they hadn't seen him getting a train into London. And surely, if he'd driven somewhere, they'd have picked him up on a camera – they have those ones that automatically recognise number plates, so they would've checked, wouldn't they?

After sitting contemplating, watching people head to and from the station, I make my mind up. I'm going into London. I'll drop into Moore & Wells myself; see if anyone there will tell me why Tom didn't show for work on Tuesday. Someone must know. I'm not entirely sure why I'm doing this – I think I just need to find out what Tom's been hiding from me. If I know, I can protect myself. Protect Poppy. Because in my gut I know he wasn't just taking a bit of time out. He was up to something. And he didn't want me to find out what.

Chapter 49

TOM

Now

The initial hearing, a formality, is over. Maxwell had already explained my case would be referred to the Crown Court and that I wouldn't be bailed because their enquiries regarding my whereabouts on Tuesday are ongoing, so there were no surprises. I'm being taken to Belmarsh prison to await my trial. A remand prisoner. My stomach rolls and twists. I don't want to spend a single night in a prison cell, let alone years. Maxwell has reassured me I won't be treated as a convicted prisoner. Yeah, right. I might not have to follow the usual regime or wear prison issue clothing, but I'm going to be incarcerated. With convicted criminals.

I can have a one-hour visit three times a week.

Please, Beth. You must see me. I need you.

Chapter 50

BETH

Now

The train rattles into Marylebone station and I rush to exit before I get caught up in the crowd, weaving my way towards the Bakerloo line. It's been a long time since I've used the underground: I'd almost forgotten how busy and congested it could be.

I don't have a lot of time to spare. I called Julia while I was travelling, explaining the situation. She kindly agreed to collect Poppy for me and look after her until I get home. It seemed a big ask, but she didn't hesitate – she said she was expecting to pick her up anyway after this morning's escapade.

Nerves take root as I think about what I'm doing. Why do I think I'll find out what Tom was doing on Tuesday from one visit into London? If the police haven't uncovered his whereabouts, I doubt I'll have better luck. But I have to try. I have to feel like I'm doing something. If I do discover where he was, though – what he was up to – what am I going to do with the new information?

It depends what you find out.

I'm carried off the tube with a dozen other passengers. We all surge to the door at once, then along the platform and up the escalators. My body goes with the flow. It feels I have little choice in the matter. When I finally break away from the river of people, I stand on the pavement outside the station, taking a moment to gather my thoughts and to figure out exactly where I am. My starting point has to be the bank. I can't remember the last time I set foot in there. I can barely recall any specific names or conjure any faces in my mind's eye, but hopefully there'll be a name that rings a bell. Someone willing to talk to me about Tom.

As soon as I'm through the main door of Moore & Wells, I begin scanning the lobby floor for an employee I recognise. For an uncomfortable moment I think I might have wasted my time, but relief washes over me as I'm approached by a familiar-looking man dressed in a charcoal-grey suit. A flash of recognition passes across his face, too.

'Good morning,' the man says. His eyes are wide-set, the bridge of his nose spread – a boxer's nose. It's that which has sparked a memory. 'Do you have an appointment here today?'

I gaze at the silver name badge on his lapel. *Andrew Norton.* Andy. New to the banking business when I was last invited to one of the firm's dinners. I got stuck chatting to him about investment banking – an exhilarating conversation it was not. I won't forget having it, but I would never be able to recall a single thing he'd actually said if questioned. Several hours of my life I'll never get back.

I'm reminded now of how Tom always talks about his day in relation to how he felt about it, rather than specific details, precisely because he's aware of how dreadfully boring banking talk is to anyone other than a banker.

'Hi, Andy,' I say, raising my eyes to his. 'Beth. Tom's wife?' I wait for a beat. 'I don't have an appointment – I was only dropping in as I was close by.'

'Ah of course,' he says, enthusiastically. 'I *thought* I knew your face.'

'Are any of Tom's usual colleagues about?' By usual colleagues I'm meaning those he considers his mates, but I don't say this explicitly as, for some strange reason, I don't want to hurt Andy's feelings by assuming he's not one of them.

'They very rarely come down to this level,' Andy says with one brow arched. He's clearly fully aware he's not 'one of them'. 'I'll take you through security and get you a visitor pass, then if you go up to level three you'll be able to find someone who can help.' His face darkens suddenly, his eyes flitting around. 'I'm . . . er, sorry. You know, to have heard about his—'

'Yes, thank you.' I interrupt quickly, not wishing to hear him say the words. 'As you might expect, it's come as rather a shock.'

'Yes, yes. I can imagine.' His eyes widen. He looks as though he's about to add something, then thinks better of it and closes his mouth again. He remains silent as he escorts me through the barrier and sees me into the lift. 'I'll let them know you're on your way up,' he says, giving me a lop-sided smile. 'Nice to see you again.'

'You too, Andy. And thanks.'

The lift doors close. I look out the corner of my eye at the mirrors – they're on every side of the lift, so it's difficult to avoid my reflection entirely. I pinch the material of my blouse at the shoulders, lifting it and straightening it, then run my fingers through my hair and pat to neaten it. I don't have time to reapply my lipstick before the door swishes open.

'Beth! This is a surprise.' I'm greeted before I've fully stepped out of the lift by a thick Scottish accent. Tom's boss.

Thankfully his name comes to me as soon as I see him. 'Hello, Alexander,' I say. 'It's been a while.'

'Look, I've got several appointments, but I can fit you in quickly – as it's you,' he says, laying a large, purplish hand on my shoulder and guiding me across the floor to his office. I can feel the heat of his palm through my blouse and I twist slightly to escape it. Why must he touch? I remember *that* from the last dinner, too.

'Do take a seat. Drink?'

I'm about to decline, but then I decide it might be a good idea as it will buy me some extra time to grill him about Tom. 'Yes – white coffee, no sugar, thanks.' I sit with my back to the door at his heavy wooden desk. I smile to myself as I note he has his name engraved on a mahogany and brass desk sign: *Alexander Robertson, Director of Portfolio Management* – with a bunch of letters after it. So old-fashioned and conceited. From what Tom has told me, he's quite the chauvinist, too.

Alexander strides to the machine in the corner of his office and sets about making two drinks. I'm almost surprised he hasn't called for a female colleague to come in and do it for him.

197

'I wondered if you'd pop in,' he says. His back is to me while he stirs a wooden stick in the cardboard cups. 'After the detectives showed up and began asking questions, I imagined you'd be close behind.'

'Oh, really? Why?'

'I know you, Beth. Or, rather, I know what Tom tells me. I had a feeling a determined woman like yourself wouldn't take any of this lying down.'

I find it odd that this man, who – bar a few social gatherings – is a stranger, is talking about me in this way. I suppose Tom has probably talked about me – maybe about my determination in setting up the pottery café – but I'm doubtful it would equate to enough for Alexander to think he knows me, or what I'd do in this situation.

I don't know how to act in this situation. How could he?

'If I'm honest, Alexander, I have literally no idea *how* to take it. Lying down or otherwise. It's why I'm here, really. To try and fill a few . . . well, *gaps*.'

'What kind of gaps?' He places a cup in front of me and then sits in his chair, shuffling it forwards. 'You know the police have already been here, and we weren't able to help them past the basics – the hours he worked, who he was pally with – that sort of thing.' He steeples his fingers together, elbows on his desk.

'That's fine. Basics are a good place to start.' I lean towards him. 'Starting with Monday. He was here then I believe – what hours did he work that day?'

'The usual – he gets in for half eight, leaves at half four, so he can get back to see Poppy before she goes to bed. He arranged those hours when she was born and always makes up any shortfall by working from home,

198

as you know. He's very much a creature of habit, Beth. I told the detective woman that.'

'Yes, which is why it's odd that he was late home that evening. But even more odd that he didn't show up to work at all on Tuesday.'

'As far as we knew, Beth, he was taking the day off sick. He called in at eight thirty to say he'd been taken ill on the journey and was going back home.'

'The police didn't tell me,' I say, more to myself than to him. He *wasn't* at home that day – I know because I stopped by at the cottage to pick up more cakes before collecting Poppy. 'He didn't go home again, Alexander. Did he speak with anyone else here that day?'

'He didn't actually speak with me at all. It was Celia who took his call and passed the message on to the team.'

'Is she here today?' I turn in my seat, craning my head to see through the glass partitions of his office to the wider floor.

'Hang on, I'll grab her.' Alexander gets up and beckons to a smartly dressed woman in her forties standing on the far side. She immediately stops her conversation and heads over.

'Yes, Alex?' she says, popping her head and shoulders around the doorway. Her eyes narrow when she sees me.

'Come in, Celia; close the door,' Alexander says. 'Beth is Tom's wife. She's wondering what Tom said to you, exactly, when he called in sick last Tuesday.'

'Oh. Well, not a lot really. He was very abrupt. I had to tell that to the police, too, I'm afraid.'

'Why are you afraid?' I ask, unable to stop myself.

She blushes. 'Well, I mean, I had to say how he came

199

across. Like there was something bothering him. And I realise it might've added to their . . . concern, I suppose.'

'Why did you think he sounded as though something was bothering him? If he told you he'd come over ill, didn't you think it was just that?'

'I've worked with Tom for a number of years now, and I picked up that something was a little off in his tone. It didn't seem like it was because he felt unwell. He sounded panicked.'

'Did you happen to pick up anything useful? Like where the hell he was?' I squeeze my hands together, focus on gripping them to try and distract myself from my rising frustration. Celia looks taken aback at my abruptness. She licks her lips and swallows. Pushes her shoulders back.

'I could only hear what sounded like a radio in the background. So nothing helpful. He could've been anywhere.'

'A car radio?'

'Well I assumed at the time he was driving back home, so yeah. Must've been.'

Celia shrugs then ducks back out again, and I watch her through the glass as she returns to her desk.

I know Tom didn't return home – the police seemed certain of that. Was he driving somewhere else?

Was my husband having an affair? The thought makes me sick. No. He wouldn't do that.

'How has he seemed to you, lately?' I turn back to Alexander who I catch in a yawn. 'Sorry, am I keeping you up?' I smile.

'Had a long, sleepless night.' He sips from his cardboard cup. 'He's always kept pretty much to himself, Beth. You know how he is. Rarely shares anything too personal with us lot – he tends to just talk about you and Poppy. Jimmy might know more; he chats with Tom more than anyone else.'

I recall Tom talking about Jimmy on several occasions, sharing funny anecdotes and office banter. It would be fair to assume that if Tom confided in anyone here, it would be him. 'Great, can I have a quick word with him?'

'Not in. He's on annual leave until Friday – in Cornwall with his wife and kids. Sorry.'

'No worries.' I sigh. I can't say I was expecting much really, but I'm disappointed I will leave here without a single lead as to what Tom was up to on Tuesday.

'Maybe you're looking for something that's not there, Beth.'

'Maybe,' I agree. 'But I don't think it's a coincidence that the day after he's questioned about the disappearance of an ex-girlfriend, he goes AWOL. Do you?'

'It happened – what – eight years ago?' He leans back in his chair, fingers drumming on the armrests. 'I don't see how the two things *can* be linked. Other than maybe he was upset and wanted time out on his own. To process it.'

'Perhaps,' I say.

But I know that's not it. I know there's another reason he lied to me. And I won't rest until I find out what it is.

Chapter 51

BETH

Now

I wander aimlessly for about half an hour after leaving Alexander, my hopes of finding some nugget of information dashed. Without knowing how, I find myself outside our old flat. I stand on the pavement, head tilted, looking up at the third-floor balcony. It looks just the same from the exterior. Moving in with Tom had been the obvious choice back then because the rent on my flat was extortionate given its size. 'Dingy', Tom had said. I guess he was right, although I loved my little flat. Probably because it was the first place I could afford to live in alone, without uni housemates or a flatmate. Full independence. It was brilliant. It took a while to adjust to living with someone again.

We had happy times here, though. My memories are good ones, on the whole. I was thrilled about being able to upsize when we moved to the Cotswolds, but it didn't stop me feeling apprehensive about packing up and leaving here. I remember that Tom was stressed in the weeks prior to us moving out, so I suppose he also felt some reluctance to make the huge move. We had Poppy, though, and we knew we were doing the right thing for her future. I do question now, as I stand here, whether there was more to Tom's stress than I thought. This was the flat he and Katie had also spent a lot of time in. She practically lived here, from what he told me when we first met. It wasn't just his memories of *us* he was leaving – it was his memories of her, too. We even found a few things of hers when we were packing.

I shiver.

Don't think about it.

I pull my thoughts away from the past and cross the road. I should think about making my way back to the station so I'm not too late picking up Poppy from Julia's. I'm frustrated that I'll be going home without any new inkling as to what Tom was doing and why he felt the need to lie. I should've thought this trip through and made a plan. Maybe I'll visit again. If I leave it until next week, Jimmy will be back from his holiday. Perhaps he'll be more helpful than Alexander.

As I weave through people on the walk back to the station, I feel my mobile vibrating in my pocket.

'Hey, Lucy. Everything okay?' I duck down a quieter road, leaning against the wall to take her call. 'Sorry, I'm in London – just . . .' *Just what?* What should I tell her?

Her voice cuts in anyway, so I don't need to think up a reason.

'Beth. The police have been asking questions.'

'Oh,' I say. 'At the café?' My mind goes blank for a moment, unable to imagine a reason why they'd be there.

'No, not here. Not me.'

I pull at the neckline of my blouse, suddenly feeling hot. 'Who, then?'

'They were wanting information from Oscar.'

'What?' A flurry of anxiety sweeps through me. 'What's Oscar got to do with all of this?'

'I've no idea, Beth. But they were particularly keen to hear about the borrowed car.'

My mind is a whirl of confusion as it attempts to make sense of this statement. 'We haven't borrowed any car from Oscar.'

'It appears Tom did.' Lucy pauses. I hear her draw breath. 'On Tuesday morning.'

Chapter 52

BETH

Now

Julia's expression is both tense and relieved when I get there to pick up Poppy.

'Oh, thank God!' she says as she flings the door open. 'Who knew one extra child would make such a difference? People assume because I "cope" with triplets that I'll find another a breeze.' She turns and heads to a room off the hallway. I follow, feeling terrible. I've clearly caused her harried state by asking her to have Poppy.

'I'm so sorry, Julia. I've over-stepped the mark—'

'No no, sweetie, not at all. I really was – *am* – happy to help any way I can. I just need a stiff drink and a lie down after it, that's all. Four little ones running riot isn't exactly calming.'

I laugh. 'I'll be sure to drop around a few bottles of fizz as a thank you.'

'A secret getaway, alone, to a spa would be better.' Julia

sweeps her hair up and secures it with a scrunchie into a ponytail. Even stressed out she looks as though she belongs in a beauty advert or something. She shouts for Poppy, then brings her attention fully back to me. 'Did you find what you were looking for?' She smiles sympathetically.

'Er . . . no. Not really.' I sigh. I don't tell her about Lucy's call. I'm still too wound up and I haven't been able to get it straight in my head despite my long journey home. I need to digest it; try and figure out its relevance. Why would Tom borrow a car when he had one in perfect working order?

The reason can only possibly be a bad one.

'That's a shame. Maybe it's a good thing, Beth,' she says, her face serious. 'No telling what you might unearth. Sometimes, ignorance is bliss.'

A cold sensation claws up my spine. 'So, you think he did do the terrible thing he's accused of,' I say. I don't pose it as a question, as it's clear she thinks Tom's guilty. She wouldn't have said that otherwise. Her face pales.

'I'm sorry. Look, I have no idea if he is or isn't capable of . . . hurting someone. All I'm saying is, do we ever really know a person? I mean, *everything* about them? What goes on in the darkest recess of their minds? There has to be a question in your head that it's a possibility, or I assume you wouldn't have jetted off to London today. I'm not judging, Beth. I'm in no position to do that. All I'm saying is, leave it to the police. Let them do their job. The villagers of Lower Tew have got your back regardless.'

Tears prick my eyes. I'm grateful for the support Julia is giving me – and it's reassuring to hear her say she'll be on my side whatever the outcome. But it does worry me that she thinks Tom is guilty. And it worries me that although she is saying the right things to me – to my face – she could very well be saying entirely different things to people behind my back. The fact the nursery mums were saying I must know, that I must be aware of what Tom's done, sits heavily within me, like a malevolent spirit crouching, waiting.

'Thanks, Julia. I really can't thank you enough for what you've done today.' I decide not to embellish further.

'What are friends for?'

Poppy rushes up to me and flings her arms around my legs. 'I thought you were gone,' she says, burying her face in my jeans.

'Of course not, Poppy. I had to work longer today, that's all. I'm sorry.' I lift her up, squeezing her tightly and nuzzling my nose into her neck.

'Are we climbing the wall again?' Her face lights up. I'm glad she saw that as a bit of an adventure earlier, but I'm hoping it's not something we'll have to repeat daily.

'I'm a little tired for climbing. Maybe we can just go in the front door now,' I say, looking to Julia with my eyebrows raised, mouthing '*Can we?*' She nods. Thank goodness. I assume the journalists will be back, though. I'm certain they won't give up that easily.

Reaching the road to home, we walk slowly towards our cottage. Cautiously, in my case. I relax when I note there are no extra cars parked, or people outside. The place is in darkness. I immediately take Poppy upstairs to bed. It's been a long day for her. It's been long for me, too.

I think about my next move while listening to the gentle hum of the microwave – yet another meal for one.

Tom borrowed a car from Oscar's garage. Why? As

much as I'm loath to admit it, I think Julia is right. Do we ever really know everything about a person? I know the answer: of course we don't. I know a lot about Tom; he knows a lot about me. But he certainly doesn't know every little thing about me, so therefore it's safe to assume I don't know every little thing about him.

I'll call Maxwell after I've eaten.

Tomorrow I want to go and visit Tom.

Chapter 53

BETH

Now

The hall somehow manages to smell clean and dirty at the same time. I've got here as quickly as I could – I set off as soon as I'd dropped Poppy at nursery. But apparently, I was lucky to be given admittance seeing as I was late and in future I have to ensure I'm here to check in between 8.30 and 9.15 a.m.

I sit gingerly on the bolted-down chair I've been directed to, to await Tom. I give a furtive glance around the visiting hall, filled with convicted criminals and those, like Tom, who are awaiting their fate. I can't even do this for the next few weeks, let alone years. There are children here, but I won't be dragging Poppy along. She's not mingling in that play area with kids of killers and the like.

The pulses in my wrists bang against the tabletop as I lean on it to try to regulate my breathing. I've never been so nervous to see my own husband. How will he look?

Maxwell told me he's not sleeping and he's unable to eat – worry must be gnawing away at his stomach. It's been nine days since I last set eyes on him or spoke to him. What must he think of me that I've been unable to even accept a call from him? I wring my hands together, keep my eyes forward: I don't want to make accidental eye contact with anyone. I could buy a drink from the tea bar, so I at least have something to keep my hands busy, but anxiety prevents me leaving this seat.

Movement at the far side catches my attention. I swallow hard. I almost don't recognise him as he walks towards the table with slow, hunched movements. When he sits opposite me, I see his complexion is grey and his face is drawn. His eyes appear hollow. Ghostly. I look away.

'Thank you,' he says. Even his voice seems strange; alien to me. 'God, Beth, you've no idea how desperate I've been to see you.'

The words I want to say – *should* say – are frozen inside my voice box. I force myself to look up and focus on his face, but my lips remain stubbornly tight. He frowns and I see tears gather at the corner of his eyes. Rather than their usual clear, beautiful peacock-blue, they now seem hazy and dull; staring and soulless.

Tom is allowed three visits a week and I'm here on his first day in Belmarsh. Although that makes me seem like I'm the dutiful wife – loyal and supportive – I can't even speak. I don't tell him I love him, or offer words of encouragement, and I know this will upset him.

'I'm so sorry, Beth. This is the worst situation – I can't imagine what you and Poppy are going through.' His hands edge closer to mine, his fingertips brushing against my skin; it sends tiny electric shocks up my arms. I with-draw quickly, positioning my hands on my lap beneath the table. I was told you could have minimal contact at the beginning and end of the visit – not during. But I know that's not the real reason I'm pulling away.

My stomach ties in knots as I see the hurt on his face. *Speak. Say something.*

Tom shifts awkwardly in the chair, his eyes darting around him. Then he hunkers down, leans forward a bit more and, with his voice lowered to almost a whisper, says, 'I should've spoken to you about all of this on Tuesday morning. Like you wanted. I really regret not listening to you.' He pauses, takes a breath. 'You've always known best,' he says with a small laugh.

'Why did you lie to me?' I say, my eyes narrowed, the words coming out in a hiss. That flippant comment of his has sparked my anger and caused me to finally find my voice.

Confusion spreads across his face. 'I haven't lied.' His cheeks flush red: he knows I'm not stupid.

'Where did you go on Tuesday? Why did you let me think you'd gone to work?'

'Seriously? That's what you're worried about? Why are you getting hung up on that? It's not important, Beth.'

'It's important to me!' I sense curious stares turning towards my raised voice, but the diversion is fleeting; heads quickly turn back as their focus returns to their own tables.

'What have you told the detectives?' Tom's being defen-sive now; he's scared about what I've let slip, no doubt. I shake my head.

'Nothing, Tom. Because I can't tell them what I don't know, can I?'

Silence stretches between us, the chatter from other prisoners and visitors filling the void.

'There's more pressing things to be concerned with,' Tom says eventually. He indicates around the visiting room. 'Look where I am, Beth. I can't be here.'

His vulnerability in this moment tugs at my heart. If the detectives hadn't shown up on Monday evening, we wouldn't be in this situation now. We'd be carrying on our lives as normal: a happily married couple with a daughter. Wouldn't we?

'Maxwell is doing everything he can,' I say, softly. I move my hands towards his now, guilt replacing my anger, but I stop myself before they make contact. I don't want to inadvertently break any rules and draw the attention of the prison officers. 'He doesn't think the prosecution will have enough evidence for a jury to convict you. He reckons he can at least show there's reasonable doubt. You could be home within months.'

'It feels like everything is down to chance. I don't like that. I've no control over anything.'

'I don't know what you want me to do.'

'You have to help me.' His eyes plead with mine. And then he whispers: 'We've been through this. You're the only one who understands.'

I clench my hands together, preparing for what's coming. The truth I've been trying so hard to hide, even from myself.

'You know I didn't mean for her to die, Beth.'

Chapter 54

TOM

Now

Nine days desperately needing to see my wife and that's all I get.

The door clanks shut behind me, keys rattle as it locks, and I'm left in my cell. Alone again. It was good to have a change of scenery; the visiting hall is the least prison-like area here, if you don't look too closely.

Once I spotted Beth, though, she was all I could see. The urge to pull her to me, smell her, feel her warm body against mine, was incredible. Overwhelming. So much so, it took me a while to settle, to stop the images penetrating my mind. I wasn't expecting her to be ecstatic to see me, but I admit, I thought she'd be a little pleased. Not a single thing about her body language – the way she looked at me, spoke to me – showed any hint of that, though.

Why is she withdrawing from me? I don't understand – it's like she doesn't *want* to help me. I know I let her down – God knows, I should've talked to her after the police interview – and I've been sweating buckets since my arrest wondering if she'll accidentally say something to incriminate me. Had I spoken to her when she asked, we could've worked out a story between us to tell the detectives. I fucked up, big time.

Of course, some would say that it wasn't my first fuckup. That killing Katie Williams was.

But those people would be wrong.

Chapter 55

BETH

Now

I've come away no closer to knowing why Tom lied to me. He was far more intent on making sure I wouldn't divulge what I knew to the police than on telling me what he'd been doing on that Tuesday instead of working. Funny how he considered it important I should know about an event that occurred eight years ago, but not what happened just over a week ago.

What is he hiding from me?

I wrap my arms around myself, gently rocking in the driver's seat, radio on, waiting to feel calm enough to drive home. I wish I hadn't gone to see him now. It's strange, but I'd convinced myself I was as shocked as anyone else when he was arrested – and without seeing him, I was able to keep up the illusion, to others *and* myself. Apart from a few times when the whispers from the nursery mums got to me, I'd mostly been able to hide

215

my knowledge away in the depths of my mind. Self-preservation.

Julia, of course, came worryingly close last night.

I must keep up the charade now, though. I can't afford to let it slip. Because in everyone else's eyes, that'll make me as much of a monster as Tom. I felt awful saying I can't help him. How can I, if it means telling the police I knew? I can't risk being implicated in this in any way; I have Poppy to think about. I tried to explain that it doesn't help his case in the slightest. I think he is hoping, if it comes to it, that me telling the jury how it was all an accident will in some way clear his name; stop him being convicted. He's not thinking straight. All that will do is categorically confirm that he did kill Katie, accident or not, and that he kept it hidden all these years. Kept *her* hidden. Never allowed her family and friends to mourn her or bury her. There's no closure for them. No body to lay to rest.

Tom's only hope of coming home is to continue to proclaim his innocence and pray for lack of evidence.

And I can't help with that, either.

My mind drifts back to the day last year. The day that changed everything.

It'd been breakfast time and I'd let Poppy use Tom's iPad to watch an episode of *Moon and Me* while I tidied away the dishes. I'd promised him I wouldn't use it after he caught me the last time but I really needed the extra help today. 'Come on my little Poppy poppet,' I'd said, sliding the iPad out of reach of her sticky little fingers. Her face had screwed up in an angry pout and she'd stamped her feet. *Terrible twos are real*, I remember thinking. It was six thirty and Tom had left only moments before. I'd needed to get a move on as I was laying on a special coffee morning at the pottery café that day to help entice new customers.

I'd been about to close down the iPad, but I'd realised Poppy had managed to access Tom's emails. I'd hoped she hadn't accidentally sent some random letters to one of his clients or anything. I scrolled down his inbox, squinting, hoping nothing had been altered, or worse, deleted – cursing under my breath for causing myself undue stress. But it had got worse.

Something on the screen hadn't looked right.

I'd slowed down the scrolling, confused at the email subject headings.

Then it had hit me. What I was looking at *wasn't* Tom's email account.

I'd stared at it, bewildered. The email account was definitely someone else's.

My breath had caught, and my heart rate increased two-fold. The name on the account was familiar.

'Katie Williams.' Speaking it had felt strange on my tongue.

I didn't understand. Why had Tom got his ex-girlfriend's email account on *his* iPad?

My mobile vibrates in the glove compartment and catapults me back to the present. I'd stuck it in there when I went inside the visiting hall. I open the compartment and reach for it now, and stare at the name displayed on the screen for a moment.

Adam.

I accept the call.

Chapter 56

KATIE

Eight years ago

'Am I not good enough for you?' Tom said. His eyes were wide – manic – as he held the mobile inches from Katie's face. She turned to the side, backing up until she was pinned against the wall. 'Eh? Well, am I?'

His spit felt damp on her cheek. She closed her eyes tight; she didn't dare speak.

'Fucking hell! Don't you have anything to say for yourself? Aren't you going to even *try* and explain? Say sorry? Beg for forgiveness?'

Still, Katie remained silent. Her refusal to engage when Tom was shouting at her made his anger spike. He pushed away from her, flinging her mobile across the floor. Katie let out a shuddering sob.

'What are you crying for? I'm the one who should be upset. I'm the one you've lied to. Cheated on. After everything I've given you. All I've done for you. You

218

ungrateful *bitch*!' Tom launched towards her again, his right hand raised. The blow caught Katie on her left cheek. Pain exploded from it, causing white sparks to flitter in front of her eyes.

'Please . . .' she whimpered. She slid down the wall into a crouching position, cradling her already swelling face.

'I don't want to hurt you, Katie. I love you. You know full well I love the bones of you. But how could you betray me like this? With *him*?' Tom moved away and reached for the discarded phone. 'What is this?' He shoved the mobile up to her face again. 'Read it,' he demanded. 'Go on! Read that bit of the fucking message out loud. Let me hear you say it.' Tom jabbed his finger at the screen – at the last part of the text.

'I don't . . . want . . . to,' Katie said. Her voice was thick with tears. Fear.

'Read. It.' His voice was low, menacing.

Katie did as she was told.

'You . . . mean the world to me—' Katie gave a hiccupping sob, then sucked in her breath, trying to continue, '—you know that . . . And after the other night, I thought things might have changed.'

Tears streamed down her red, bloated face.

'I don't need to ask what he means, do I? It's obvious. Am I not man enough for you, or something? You *look* like you enjoy sex with me. Surely it can't be that?'

Katie shook her head, her eyes lowered. She didn't want to see his anger. She dared not say that sex with Tom sometimes scared her; that it could be too intense. Too rough.

Tom lunged for her, grabbed her under the arms and

hauled her into a standing position. Then he dragged her, like a ragdoll, into the bedroom. He threw her onto the mattress.

'You're going to have to be punished for this. You do realise that? I can't just forgive and forget this betrayal, Katie.'

Katie lay on her back, her eyes screwed up. She should fight. Run. Scream. Anything.

But she couldn't move. If she just let him hurt her – get it out of his system – maybe it would be quick. Then she could make her escape afterwards.

***

TOM

I'd held it all in for as long as I was able. But it's always been the case that when the red mist descends, there is little I can do to stop it; something deep inside of me takes over. It doesn't happen very often. Probably just as well.

I scrolled through Katie's messages again, finding the ones from him. For a split second I wondered if I'd over-reacted; read too much into them. Then, like a nagging eye twitch, the voice inside my head told me I'd been right. They'd been planning on going behind my back.

Chapter 57

BETH

Now

I drove home in a daze, not thinking about Tom, the visit or his trial. Those thoughts flood my brain now, though, as I sit on my bed. I don't feel capable of anything – all my energy has been zapped. Lying down and pulling the duvet over my clothed body, I shut my eyes against the brightness of the sunshine blazing through the window. Tom's face hovers behind my closed lids, his features distorted with worry. Desperation radiates from his eyes as they plead with mine – just as they had the day I confronted him.

'Tom, why have you got Katie's email account on your iPad?' I'd asked him when Poppy was in bed that evening. My heart hammered as I waited for an answer. I saw the tell-tale flicker of panic cross his face; caught the distinct bob of his Adam's apple as he swallowed hard. I waited for him to give me an elaborate explanation – something benign; a simple reason. But it didn't come. Instead, Tom's face crumpled he dropped down on the sofa as though he could no longer hold his body weight up. And he cried.

After a while, he calmed down enough to begin explaining. He didn't even try to lie. He told me everything and I listened in complete silence, too stunned to interrupt. It'd been an accident, he said, the repercussions of which had spiralled out of control – first one lie to cover up what he'd done, followed by another to cover the first, then another and another. I wanted to scream at him to stop talking – whatever he was going to tell me couldn't be unsaid. His mistakes couldn't be undone. I didn't say a word, though. I let him continue his story. It was as though I was listening to a radio play; fiction. Or someone else's life.

Tom spoke of how he'd momentarily lost control – he was jealous when he found out Katie had cheated on him. He'd only been trying to stop her from leaving the flat – he'd wanted to discuss it, to try and make things right. He'd thrown the paperweight at her from a distance – he hadn't even meant for it to hit her, only to act as a warning. It was supposed to be a shock, to give her pause and to give him enough time to put up a good argument as to why they should stay together, work things out. He'd told her he'd forgive her for her error of judgement – but she'd ignored him and carried on. When it had made contact with her head and she'd collapsed, he'd frozen. Hadn't thought straight.

It had been an accident. A terrible, catastrophic accident he'd immediately wished he could reverse. In his panic, he'd left her there, in her flat, bleeding on the ground.

Wandered the streets around Bethnal Green for an hour freaking out. He knew he should've called an ambulance, despite it being obvious she was dead. He should've called the police, but he'd been scared, as anyone would've been in that situation, he'd said – he was afraid no one would believe he didn't purposely hurt her, especially as she'd just told him she was leaving.

Tom had convinced me it was a terrible accident. He'd been beside himself, crying as I held him; his shame, grief and regret seeping from him. When I pushed him away, the gravity of what he'd told me had sunk in, and a sense of horror had replaced the initial shock. Tom had begged me to forgive him. Not to think badly of him.

'I need you,' he'd said. 'Like you need me, Beth. And you wouldn't want Poppy growing up without a father like you did. She'd be devastated – her life would be altered forever, affected by my one poor decision.' He had known how to get to me; how to bring me around.

'I'm the same person you've always known, Beth,' he'd pleaded. 'You *know* me. You know I wouldn't ever purposely hurt anyone. Have I ever laid a finger on you? Poppy? Have you ever had cause to think I was capable of anything bad?'

And no – *of course* the answer had to be no. He hadn't hurt me – not in the way he was referring to. Just as I'd told the detectives, Tom is the perfect husband and father.

Something that happened eight years ago, an event I'd had no clue about up until that point, wouldn't change our relationship. It'd been an accident. And for Poppy's sake, it was one I knew I'd have to learn to live with as well.

Wouldn't I?

223

Chapter 58

KATIE

Eight years ago

Katie was vaguely aware of Tom close by. Every inch of her hurt. He'd said he was going to punish her, and he had certainly lived up to his promise. But what would come next? His breathing was still rapid. Very slowly, Katie turned her head towards the sound. He was sitting on the floor, his back to her. There'd be no way she could edge off the bed and leave the room, the flat, without him stopping her. She'd have to try and talk her way out of this situation. She'd got Tom all wrong. Isaac had been right – she should've trusted him.

Her movement caused the mattress to creak, and Tom snapped his head around to face her.

'I'm sorry,' he said, standing up.

It was too late for apologies. And she wasn't going to say sorry back. She'd done nothing wrong.

'Whatever,' she said. Her face was stiff; no doubt it was bruised. Maybe a broken cheek bone if the pain was anything to go by. She pulled herself into a sitting position, crying out as she did so.

'It only happened because you went behind my back, Katie. I can't be blamed for that. You brought this on yourself.'

Katie didn't respond. Sliding her legs off the bed, she cast her eyes around for her mobile.

'Looking for this?' Tom held it up. 'Going to go running to *Isaac*?' He smirked, and in that moment, Katie hated him. With what little strength she had left, she lunged at him, grasping for her phone.

Tom ducked out of her reach and laughed. 'Don't worry. I've already sent a heartfelt message from you to that pathetic loser.'

Katie's brow creased. Her stomach contracted painfully. What did he mean?

'Cat got your tongue?' he smiled.

'Give it to me,' she said.

Tom held her mobile up above his head, his hand stretching to the ceiling. 'Come and get it.' He danced around the bedroom, the bizarre scene making her sick. Every one of her muscles tensed.

'Fuck off, Tom.' She couldn't care less that he had her phone; she just wanted to get out of her flat. Let the police deal with him. She waited until he was on the far side of the room, then she ran, as best she could, towards her front door. For a brief moment, she thought she'd make it. But time slowed, and a sharp pain in her skull stopped her in her tracks. She put her hand to her head. Slowly, she brought it back down in front of her. Blood. Covering her hand. Dripping down her face. She watched, stunned, as blobs of deep red splashed onto the floor.

'Oh, no you don't. You don't get to leave me,' Tom said, dragging her backwards. 'Come on. Let's have a little fun.'

'My head,' Katie said. 'It's bleeding.' Her voice sounded strangely disconnected.

'Yes, babe. I know. Don't worry, I'll look after you.' Tom placed Katie on the bed and left. She was too dizzy to move. She winced as he pressed a towel against the back of her head. 'It's just a cut. Might need some stitches. But, first, I think we need to make up, don't you?' He lowered himself onto the bed.

Confusion clouded her mind. Was he going to try and have sex with her in this state? She wriggled beneath the weight of his body, a searing headache causing her vision to blur.

'No . . . Tom . . . not . . . now . . .' She felt weak. Helpless.

'It'll be okay, my darling. Just let yourself go. Give yourself to me.'

His hands, hot, soft, grasped her throat. His grip tightened.

Katie's lungs burned. She found a final spurt of energy from deep within her and bucked, clawing at his hands. He didn't release her.

'I love you, Katie. Never forget that,' were the last words she heard before darkness descended.

* * *

TOM

A satisfying sense of relief – a calmness – came over me as her life ebbed away in my hands. A calmness I hadn't felt in a long time. Seven years, in fact. I sat for a long time afterwards just staring at her lifeless body. It was beautiful. If you looked past the bruises, that is.

I knew I had to shake myself free of the trance and figure out my next move. I let myself take one last look into her eyes, then sent another message from her phone.

Hey guys, sorry for radio silence lately! Hope you're all doing OK. *Long message alert* (You might want to make a coffee . . .) I've been having a rethink about my career, and as you know, I'm keen to become a yoga teacher . . . so . . . I'm going to go to India to do it! I realised I've been procrastinating enough, and I really want to put everything into doing this – for me! You know, while I'm young and supple 😂 I know you'll all be super happy for me. It does mean a fairly long time without contact though, as I want to fully immerse myself in the experience – no distractions or bloody social media – that sucks the soul right outta you! I'll keep you updated as and when. Sorry there's no time for a farewell party – some things need to be done with minimum fuss (and before I chicken out).

Love and miss you all! Take care my wonderful friends. K xxx

PS. Be kind to Tom for me. I put the engagement on hold and although he understands and supports my need to do this, he is pretty gutted.

I really hadn't meant for it to happen. Of course I didn't want her dead. But I had wanted her for myself – *to* myself – with no interference from Isaac or anyone else. I think she'd had fair warning – enough chances to make it right. To put us first. She chose to go against us. She was going to choose him.

It was a shame. I'd had high hopes she was the one.

Although, that said, I'd thought the same about Phoebe too.

Chapter 59

BETH

Now

God, what time is it?

I must've drifted off, forgotten to set an alarm. Sleeping during the day isn't a good idea at the best of times, although I have no idea how I even managed to drop off. Thank God it's only two thirty. Still time to get my shit together and make myself presentable enough to collect Poppy.

I have several text messages – two from Lucy, wondering if I'm going to bother to turn in today; one from Julia asking if I need her to pick up Poppy again; and one from Adam, confirming the play date he arranged with me when he called earlier.

I'd been shocked to hear from Adam so soon after our last meeting, when he'd suggested he would have Poppy on Friday. He asked for me to have Jess again this afternoon, which means he must trust me. It's reassuring to know he's still willing to be friends with me. At this stage, anyway. I imagine he'd change his mind if he knew the truth. Now I've faced Tom, I'm hoping I can keep up the façade for everyone else. I might not have known about it until relatively recently, but that doesn't excuse my decision to keep it to myself. I'm well aware I could help end the pain of Katie's family and friends, but to do that I'd have to create pain and suffering elsewhere. I can't in all good conscience swap one for the other. Poppy is my priority. I refuse to hurt her.

And besides, I must play the dutiful wife.

There's a low, droning noise outside. I concentrate, listening intently. Voices. Lots of voices.

Shit. They're back.

I peep outside my bedroom window and see them, grouped together like a pack of hyenas. There must be about twenty reporters, or journalists, whatever they call themselves, all itching to get a photo of the killer's wife. Anxiety shoots through my body. I'm going to have to face them; they might be hanging around until Tom's trial. God, I hope not, though. Please let a bigger news story break.

I choose my plain blue chiffon top and smart black trousers to go out in. Conservative. I may well be judged for my husband's crime, but I won't be judged on my clothes. With a light coverage of foundation, minimal make-up – I need to appear as though I'm distraught yet classy – I edge towards the front door. I can't even hear their chatter above my pulse whooshing in my ears. Nerves rise inside me; their tingling is more than the usual butterflies. More intense; more painful. Enough to create doubt.

I can't do this.

They're going to see through me. I'll be vilified. Crucified. And they don't even know the half of it.

Chapter 60

BETH

Now

It's now or never, I guess. I'm taking a leaf out of Julia's book and donning a pair of sunnies – at least they won't be able to read what's behind my eyes.

Stand tall. Don't let them know you're scared of them.

I burst from the door like a cannonball, shooting up the path to the lane outside the cottage before they even know what's hit them. But then I hear the clamour of mass movement and clicking camera shutters. As much as I intended to hold my head high, reality and the onslaught of attention hit me and I lower it instead, tucking my chin onto my chest. I keep walking, concentrating on putting one foot in front of the other as I attempt to drown out their shouts with the voice in my mind – the one repeating *everything's okay, you'll be all right, this will be over soon*. I don't believe it, but it gets me to the nursery gate.

It also gets *them* here too. I can't believe they've followed me to my daughter's nursery. How fucking dare they. I turn sharply to face them. I know as soon as I open my mouth a torrent of foul language will gush out of it, which won't help the situation at all and certainly won't keep me in a good light – there'll be no sympathy from anyone witnessing my outburst; it'll likely confirm their suspicions of me. But some things can't be held in – their behaviour is abhorrent, and they must be called out on it.

'Hey!' I shout. Blood rushes to my face. 'What the—'

Before I can say anything further, I feel hands on either side of me, roughly turning me away from the flashing cameras.

'Don't,' Adam says. 'Let me.' And he leaves my side and struts forward, approaching the journalists, seemingly unfazed by the long lenses being thrust near his face. Isn't he worried he'll be somehow linked to this shitstorm? To me? He's been so reluctant to be seen with me in public before – afraid of the repercussions. Scared people would get the wrong impression. Surely he's directly inserting himself into this now by confronting the press?

I don't hear what he says; he's speaking very quietly. Calm and assured, unlike me. I take a shaky breath in.

Within moments Adam is back by my side, the group dispersing.

'What on earth did you say to convince them to leave?' I remove my sunglasses so I can see Adam clearly.

'Oh, I just reasoned with them. And said the nursery would sue each of them, individually, for taking pictures of their premises where any of their pupils might be snapped without permission.'

'Good one,' I say, managing a smile.

'You're shaking,' Adam says.

I look at my trembling hands. 'Adrenaline.'

'I'm glad I turned up when I did. You looked like you were about to explode – and as much as it would've pleased me to watch those lowlifes get what was coming to them, I don't think they'd have come off well, which means you wouldn't have either.'

'I was pretty angry.'

'And rightly so. Bloody vultures.'

'I was going to pop into the café on the way back because I promised Poppy some banana bread. Do you and Jess fancy joining me?' I ask, then I remember. 'Oh, God – sorry. They were meant to be having a play date – you'll want to be making the most of the time on your own.'

'No, actually. Why do you think I'm here?'

'Oh, yes.' I shake my head, confused. 'I was supposed to be picking Jess up, not you.'

'That was before I heard about the mob outside yours.' Adam raises a brow. 'I figured you might need backup.'

'Thanks, Adam. I'm seriously grateful you stepped in when you did. That could've been a very ugly scene otherwise.' I look around at Julia and the other yummy mummies. All of them are casting wary glances my way. 'I need to do the rounds before the girls come out. Do you mind?' I indicate towards Julia.

'Absolutely – you go ahead. I'll just be here, waiting. I don't want to be a part of *that*. I'd rather face a pack of journalists,' he says, giving a mock shudder.

'Hah! You do make me laugh,' I say, as I leave him sitting on the low wall away from everyone else. I do wonder why he doesn't try and chat with the other parents.

I know he says people treat him with kid gloves, that they avoid him because they still don't know how to *be* around him following Camilla's death, but I get the feeling it's not them: it's him. He doesn't want to converse with the parents. It's him hiding away avoiding them, not the other way around.

The nursery door opens within a moment or two of me approaching Julia and her posse. None of them have time to mention the scene moments ago, or to ask questions about Tom and how things are going. A quick 'hello' is as far as it gets, which works in my favour.

The walk to Poppy's Place is laboured. Both the girls dawdle, stopping every few steps to gabble on about something they've seen, but it's fine. It's great to see Poppy being this friendly with another child; it's reassuring. And anyway, Adam and I are happy to amble. The leisurely pace is restful in comparison to my earlier journey to nursery. I'll take slow and uneventful any day.

'How are you doing?' Adam is walking in the road, and I'm on the pavement. Our heads are almost at the same level. I look into his eyes and see the same warmth and kindness which enabled me to open up to him before. I purse my lips together, contemplating. I turn to check where the girls are, and, happy they're close but not likely to hear me, I take a breath and tell Adam about my visit with Tom.

Well, I tell him the basics, anyway. I daren't share the entire truth.

'Oh, Beth. I'm so sorry, that must've been really stressful. If that's even the right word.'

'It's one word,' I say. 'Although stress wasn't the over-riding emotion. Honestly, Adam, the way he looked at

234

me. Pleading eyes.' I drag my hands over my face. 'I don't want to think about him.'

'Change of subject then?'

'Yes. Please.'

'I can offer up the following topics for conversation,' Adam says, turning and side-stepping alongside me. 'Ready?'

I laugh. 'Possibly not, but go on. I'm intrigued at least.'

'Cheeky. I have in my arsenal: bedwetting trauma; dead pet trauma; work trauma,' he puts his finger to his lips, 'and . . . my pièce de résistance . . . getting stuck in a lift for three hours trauma.' He stops to take a bow.

'Oh, no! Really?' I can't help but laugh. 'All of those ordeals – are you receiving therapy?'

'You're it.'

'Oh, the pressure! In that case, I feel we should cover each topic in the order of severity. Which would you consider to be your most traumatic?'

'Hard to say. The worst for Jess is the dead pet.' His face takes on a serious expression.

'Which pet? And does she know yet?'

'Moby the goldfish. And no. I've managed to lie, like every good parent, and say I took him to have his water changed.'

I cover my hand with my mouth to prevent the giggle, but it's too late.

'Oh, thank you very much. Laughing at my misfortune.'

'Adam – that's the worst lie ever!'

'I know, I know. I hang my head in shame.' He does just that and I start laughing again.

'Most parents would lie by replacing the deceased gold-fish with a brand new one?'

'I'm not good at lying. I couldn't think anything up on the spot. Rubbish, aren't I?'

It's a simple statement, but it holds so much significance. I put my hand on his arm. 'It's a good thing, you know.'

'What? A dead fish?'

'No, Adam. That you find lying hard.'

'Doesn't everyone?'

I shake my head. Is he that naïve? 'I'm afraid not.'

'Oh? You sound as though you're speaking from experience.'

It's my turn to hang my head in shame now. Real shame. For some unfathomable reason, I find myself wanting to tell him. Suddenly, I'm eager to unburden my guilt to *someone*. It's a huge risk, though. I'll be opening myself up for judgement. Putting a new friendship under enormous strain. But in this moment, it's something I feel needs to be done.

I stop walking and Adam does the same, his eyes narrowing, searching mine for a clue as to what I'm about to say.

'I don't really know where to start, or how to say this.'

'Maybe you shouldn't, then,' Adam says, concern flickering over his face, pinching his features. I can hear an uneasy edge to his tone. I hesitate. I should backtrack. Maybe I've got Adam wrong after all.

Then he looks to the girls and back to me. 'Sorry,' he says. 'Go on. It's okay – you can trust me.'

I hope he's right.

'I've got a confession to make,' I say.

Chapter 61

TOM

Now

If I close my eyes, I can still see her face the moment the life drained from it. The memory isn't one hundred per cent accurate now – years of thinking about that night, turning it over in my mind, recalling the sensations I experienced when I realised what I'd done – they've altered the original slightly. It's like re-watching an old favourite movie that's been digitally remastered in high definition: the images are sharper, the colours are brighter, but over the years I'm likely to have embellished the incident – edited it. It had been dark – I couldn't *really* have seen her face clearly enough to watch the life slip away from it. And the fact she ended up in the water, drowning, means I didn't actually witness her dying breath as I imagine it in my head. All my fantasies must've mixed in with the real events and become part of my memory.

Phoebe was my first.

You never forget your first, do you? It's said you never truly get over them either. Phoebe assumed our meeting had taken place by chance, but I'd seen her around campus. I'd watched her during our first year at uni with her fresher mates: confident, loud, excitable; her long honey-coloured hair hanging loosely around her shoulders; her impish face alight with curiosity; full of life. She fascinated me right from the off. But I kept my distance and our paths didn't cross that year.

It wasn't until the second year – freshers' week – in a club in town that fate gave a helping nudge. She'd lost her friends. Lord knows how; I'd been watching and they had stuck together like glue for most of the night. We were both drunk when she came back to mine, and we shagged like our lives depended on it. As dawn broke, I made love to her again, this time sober: slowly; sensually.

At first, anyway – then it became clear she enjoyed the wilder side. Rough sex was her thing too. I couldn't have been more satisfied that night: she blew my mind. She'd left before the sun rose fully; before I was even awake. No 'it's been great'; no goodbye. No promises we'd meet up later. But I knew she would want me again. I bet no one had screwed her like I had.

'Hey, Phoebe,' I'd said casually when I saw her out at a club later that week. I'd told her it was the one my mates and I went to regularly, so I knew she'd turned up there hoping to bump into me. But her face hadn't shown her usual enthusiasm. She'd given me a look of disdain, which I hadn't expected or appreciated.

'Oh hey, you good?' she'd said, before walking off without waiting for my response. I'd lingered at the end of the bar until I saw her heading to the toilets on her own, then I'd chased after her.

'Thought we could hook up again after?' I'd said to her. She'd frowned, and her pretty features had puckered into an ugly expression.

'Um, *no*,' she'd said, in a tone that smacked of repulsion. Like it was the most ridiculous suggestion of all time. 'Oh, come on. You and I both know it was a drunken one-night-stand . . . er . . .' she'd hesitated, opened her mouth to say my name, but then didn't bother – clearly she'd forgotten it. Perhaps I hadn't told her, I'd tried to convince myself. She'd walked off, leaving me standing there like a twat. My face burns now as I remember.

The slag.

Phoebe had spent the rest of the night hanging off some bloke – snogging him openly, just to belittle me. I hadn't wanted her to know she was getting to me, so I found my own bit of fun. Got drunker and drunker to cover up my humiliation.

I'd left the club before her, but I didn't go far. I waited for her along the path by the river that I guessed she'd take back to her accommodation. Luckily, she hadn't left with the guy she'd been with, and her friends had done another disappearing act – what kind of friends were they anyway? I'd jumped out in front of her as she walked along the riverbank. The shock, then fear, that crossed her face was satisfying. I let her know what a slut she was, leading me on that way, then discarding me.

'You're fucking insane, mate,' she'd said, pushing past me. I ran to catch her up; darted in front of her again.

'Oh, for Christ's sake,' she'd slurred. 'It was one night – get over yourself. You do know about uni life, don't you? You're bloody deluded if you think I'm seeing you again. You're a weirdo.'

It was a hard fall.

I'd watched it happen in slow motion, adrenaline pumping fiercely through my veins as she bumped and bounced like a ragdoll, tumbling down the embankment. The end of her journey was marked with a sickening thud. I'd only shoved her once. I swear she was just trying to make it more dramatic than it was – she must have wanted to make it look like I'd been violent. Backfired on her, though. She must've broken her ankle on the way if the *snap*, followed by the scream, was anything to go by.

It hadn't taken a lot to finish her off; she barely put up a fight in the end as I gently held her face under the water. Her alcohol level must've been off the scale, let alone whatever drugs were undoubtedly in her system.

I'd realised it would look like a drunken fall. No foul play. There were no CCTV cameras along that path back then. I'd wondered about fibres from my clothes, but from the way she'd behaved in the club, I knew mine wouldn't be the only ones they found. The water would probably make it difficult to collect samples, too. Or that had been my hope when I rolled her in bodily, anyway. Mainly I was confident because there was no reason for the police – or anyone – to suspect me. As far as I was aware, no one even knew we'd met. No one had seen me with her – she hadn't even remembered my name, so it was doubtful she'd told her friends about me.

The only thing that could link us was her uni sweatshirt. She'd left it in my room after she snuck out. I'd intended to burn that, but when it came to it, I was unable to. I kept it as a reminder. Some might say it was a trophy.

Her scent remained on that sweatshirt for years: I could get off on smelling it; reliving the night she fell, over and over. Beth had found it once, but I'd said it was mine – that it'd shrunk in the wash. She always used to believe everything I told her.

I really hadn't intended to kill Phoebe – not before the opportunity came up. But once it happened, something inside me, which must previously have been dormant, reared up and fought to be released. I pushed the urges away; struggled with my desire to replicate the feeling that had surged through me that night; tried to carry on a 'normal' life. I kept it all under control.

Until Katie.

Then, the night it came out she'd cheated, the demon inside me came out again too.

Chapter 62

BETH

Now

I can't say the words out loud.

'You all right, Beth? You've lost all your colour,' Adam says.

It's the fear – of opening a box I can't close again. 'Yes, sort of. I . . . well.' I sigh deeply, my eyes averted. A car drives slowly past us, and any other words I had are stolen from my mouth by a shout from the window.

'You're her, aren't you?' the man in his mid-twenties yells through the half-open driver's-side window. He doesn't wait for an answer, though; he just spits at me as the car screeches off. I wipe the back of my hand over my cheek, mopping away the stringy blob of saliva. I gag.

'Jesus!' Adam runs into the road and after the car. It's a waste of time, I think – he'll be long gone. But I realise Adam's got his mobile in his hand. As he comes back to me and the girls, breathing heavily, he says he got the registration number. 'Sorry, girls.' He crouches down beside Jess and Poppy and smiles. 'That was a very rude man and he shouldn't have done what he did.'

'He is a bad boy,' Poppy says, her eyes wide. She comes to me and wraps her arms around my thighs. 'Don't worry, Mummy. *His* mummy will tell *him* off.'

After some smoothing over and encouraging words from Adam, my shaking subsides. I don't want them to know how angry I am; how hurt. That has got to be the most gross thing that's happened to me.

'I think he'll be on the naughty step for quite a while,' I say, giving Poppy a squeeze. 'Right, let's get that banana bread. Put a step on it, girls – or the café will be closed before we get there!' I try to sound unaffected; light-hearted. Looking at Adam's face, I know I'm not fooling him.

Lucy seems stressed when we walk into the café. Without her usual bandana, her hair is wild; strands of loose hair are falling around her face. Her red face. She's flustered – rushing from table to counter, her movements jagged. Oh, God. I've caused this.

'You guys take a seat. I'll get some drinks and treats,' I say, smiling at Adam and the girls, then hurrying over to Lucy.

'I'm so sorry for leaving you to cope with all this, Lucy.' She doesn't even look at me; her head is bowed as she makes a latte. 'Yeah, well – it's not been easy.' I can hear the threat of tears in her voice.

'I should shut up shop for a week, give you some recovery time. I know you've had an awful lot of stress thrust on you – I really am sorry.' I put my hand on her shoulder, but she shrugs it off.

'Whatever you think,' she says. Then she turns to face

243

me, her expression softening. 'Or perhaps reduced hours instead? I don't want your hard work building this place up to go to waste.'

'Oh, Lucy. You're such a star. I couldn't have done any of this without you.'

'I'm sorry for being a grump. What with the Tom thing, then the police asking Oscar all sorts, it's set me on edge. I know any other time I'd be fine with working here on my own, it's just—'

'No, Lucy. You shouldn't have to.' Her mentioning Oscar reminds me about the car Tom apparently borrowed – I need to try and contact Jimmy, his mate from the bank. He should be back tomorrow. 'I'm wrong to put that on you – increasing your responsibilities at such a challenging time. It's not like I've just left you to it while I go on holiday, is it?'

'Nope. It really isn't,' Lucy says, her blue eyes watery. 'I know it's not easy for you. I can't imagine what you're going through. I heard someone saying just now that there were journalists hanging around the nursery. Poor Poppy – she must wonder what's going on.'

'Yes, it's awful. I'm managing to keep her fairly sheltered from it all, I think, at the moment. Although I have literally just been spat on by someone in a passing car.'

'No! Oh, Beth – I hope you're going to report that to the police?'

'I don't think I can face seeing them,' I say. 'Plus, I have a bad feeling there'll be more where that came from. I'm going to be a target, aren't I? For people's hate.'

Lucy looks away. She doesn't need to respond.

After the silence has stretched for too long, she asks me a question. 'When will this all die down?'

I desperately want to tell her soon. I want to say 'it'll get better'. But I don't want to lie any more than I have already. All I can do is shrug.

Back at the table, I dish out the drinks and some banana bread, which the girls immediately begin devouring.

'Wow! Jess – it's as though I've never fed you,' Adam says. Then he looks me in the eye and my insides shake. 'So? You want to come clean?'

I gulp down a mouthful of hot chocolate, then look around me at the customers sitting at three other tables. One is a table of two women; both are engrossed in painting plates. The others are also couples, sitting and chatting over a coffee. They could easily overhear me talking.

'I will. But not here. Somewhere more private,' I say in hushed tones. Adam looks disappointed. He must think I'm chickening out.

Maybe I am.

'After we've had these, why don't you come back to mine?' he says. 'The girls can play and we can chat.'

I draw in a long, slow breath, then release it just as slowly. I sound like I'm breathing through labour pains. The comparison comes close in this scenario.

'If you're sure,' I say. My initial bravado, and my desire to confess, is diminishing with each passing moment. By the time I get to Adam's I will probably have bottled it altogether.

Chapter 63

BETH

Now

Back at Adam's, the girls rush up to Jess's bedroom and I hear the thuds, thumps and clatter of toys being strewn all over the floor. Adam follows them up to check on them while I stand and wait, nervously, in the kitchen. It's neat and minimalist; Camilla's touches are evident in some of the accessories. I eye the expensive, top-of-the-range food mixer and remember the conversations about baking we'd had, and how Camilla had enjoyed coming up with new nut-free recipes. One of the last times I'd seen her we were talking about cookies. What a shame that's all we'd ever really spoken about.

On the upright fridge-freezer, I note the photos of the three of them – happy family snaps. Moments captured for eternity. I hadn't had the chance to absorb the smaller things last time I was here. Being on my own for a few minutes enables me to really take everything in.

'Right, they're happy,' Adam says as he bounds back into the kitchen like an excitable dog. 'Lounge would be more comfortable to chat in.' He leads me out of the kitchen and into the room opposite. I sit hesitantly on the beige upholstered three-seater sofa, its large cushions enveloping me. Now I'm here, I've lost my gumption. I wish the damn cushions would consume me, so I could disappear and forget everything.

'I know we've just had a drink, but can I get you another?' He tries to catch my eye. 'Or do you need something stronger for this conversation?'

I give an awkward laugh. 'No, I'm fine. Thanks.'

'I'm all ears, then,' he coaxes.

I wring my hands together; try to swallow. My throat is dry, the texture of sandpaper. 'Actually, I will have a water, please.'

Adam smiles sympathetically and leaves the lounge, returning with a tumbler of iced water.

'Thanks. This isn't as easy as I thought it would be.'

'Difficult subjects rarely are when it comes down to it, Beth.'

I sip the water. The only sound is the ice cubes clinking against my teeth as I tilt the glass. The room has a stillness that reminds me of horror films – the creepy atmosphere prior to a shock reveal. Apt.

I've gone over this moment a lot. The pros and cons of what I'm about to disclose, listed and edited, added to or deleted, depending on what I think the effects will be. The desired outcomes. I need to be careful, or the only outcome I'll get is to be ostracised. By Adam; by the community.

Think of Poppy's future.

She's what matters.

Of course, her future *is* dependent on safeguarding my own, though.

'I haven't been entirely honest with you – with anyone. Not even Julia. Probably not even myself,' I say, my words rushing over themselves like water babbling over rocks in a river.

Slow down.

Adam doesn't say anything, so I carry on. 'About Tom.' I leave a gap here. I'm still not convinced I should be doing this. I need to tell someone. I can't keep this inside any longer.

'It's fine, Beth. This is obviously a big deal, and you telling me means a lot.' He slides off the chair opposite and kneels in front of me, taking my clenched hands in his. I relax them, comforted by Adam's expression of support.

'Please, don't think badly of me. It's not straightforward.'

'I understand. Go on,' he says.

'I know more than I've let on to the police.' The words hang between us for a moment before I add the bombshell. 'About Tom. About Katie. About her death.'

I can tell he wants to retreat. Withdraw his hands from mine. I feel a slight tug, but he doesn't let go. Instead, he releases a long shaky breath.

'Okay. That's a big shock, I give you that.' He presses his lips together into a tight line, and I'm biting my own – hoping, praying he doesn't throw me and Poppy out. 'When you say you know more . . . I mean . . . like, as in you know *now*, because of something the police have said . . . or you've *always* known?'

Here it is. The make or break. I could say I've only just found out, and maybe I'll salvage our friendship, and my reputation. But it matters to me what he thinks. I need him on my side – so I should be truthful. Do my best to explain.

'I found out last year,' I say. Tears have begun dripping down my face and now land on the front of my top. Tiny, dark circles appear in the pale blue material. I watch as they blot, grow larger. 'I didn't believe it at first; then shock gave way to devastation. It felt like our life was one big lie. He'd literally lied to me from day one.'

'Have you told the police now?'

I look up sharply. 'No! How can I? I'm the only one who knows, so he'll immediately realise it's his own wife who's gone against him. And if I tell them everything, Tom will definitely spend his life in prison. It'll ruin Poppy's life. And I'm scared if I tell them, I'll go to prison too!'

'What did he *expect* you to do?'

'It was a terrible accident, Adam. He was broken. And if I didn't go along with keeping it quiet, there's no telling what he'd have done.'

'What do you mean?'

'He'd have been so angry, taken it out on me . . .'

'As in . . . hurt you?' His eyes are wide, his expression filled with shock.

'Yes, and I couldn't take that chance. The thought of what he might be capable of terrified me.'

'Beth, I'm so sorry. I had no idea.'

'No one did,' I say, my eyes lowered. 'It's surprising what you can hide behind the image of a perfect life. I guess I learned how to be happy despite his behaviour.

Tom has always been pretty controlling, but at the beginning it was more subtle.'

'It sounds as though you've been manipulated by Tom for your entire marriage then. You're the innocent party in all of this. The police will understand why you didn't come forward sooner.'

I let my emotions flow; I'm sobbing now. It's the first real release I've experienced for the past year. Holding onto secrets, whatever your intentions, is damaging – slowly but surely they flow through the blood in your veins, spreading their poison until they take over. If I don't let this out, I'll be consumed by guilt forever.

Adam stands, leans forward and pulls me to my feet, his arms wrapping around me in a tight, comforting embrace – the heat from his body radiating through mine. My body sinks into his. This feels the most natural thing in the world, but I know it's not right. I should pull away. Adam is being friendly and supportive – that's all.

Without speaking, he places his fingertips under my chin and gently lifts it so my face is upturned towards his. He wipes the tears from my cheeks. It is such an intimate gesture, my heart's in my throat; for a moment I think he's going to kiss me. I search his eyes, looking for a clue as to what he's thinking. Then, just as his lips lower, the spell we're under breaks. He hastily backs away, leaving me breathless. Breathless and, if I'm being honest, disappointed.

Chapter 64

BETH

Now

When I got home from Adam's yesterday, I realised I'd had a voicemail from Maxwell saying he needed to speak with me. By the time I'd got Poppy some tea and settled her in bed, it was too late to call back. This morning, I know I can't put it off.

'Tom mentioned you'd visited,' he opens. From his tone, I infer I'm being told off.

'Yes, it wasn't easy, but I went. For his sake.'

'I thought that would've given him a boost, but it appears to have had the opposite effect. He was very quiet when I spoke to him. Dejected. Didn't it go well?'

'It went okay, considering,' I say. 'But I'm at a loss as to what he expected if I'm honest. Hard to be cheerful and chatty as usual when your husband is facing a life sentence, wouldn't you say?'

'Of course, of course. Challenging times for sure. But

251

please try and be positive around Tom. It isn't good for him to go back to his cell from a visit – especially as you've been his only visitor bar me – in such a negative place. Mentally, I mean.'

'Funnily enough it's not great for me, either, Maxwell.' My heart rate increases and blood rushes to my face. I shouldn't lose my temper – not now – it would look very selfish. But in reality, I'm pissed off that *I've* been put in this situation by something *Tom* has done, and with all the sympathy going to him, it's becoming increasingly hard to hold it in. It's enough to make anyone angry. 'I know Tom is suffering at the moment,' I say, as calmly as I can, 'but he must accept I am too. What am I going to tell Poppy when her daddy doesn't come home?'

'I'm still banking on the evidence for conviction being too weak. Although we can't be certain how the jury will go, of course, if they're swayed by the prosecution. They have numerous pieces of circumstantial evidence, including incriminating emails from Tom's iPad. Though that in itself doesn't prove murder outright, it doesn't look great either. With a good solid account from you, Beth, and no criminal record, there's a strong possibility it could swing his way. That's the positive spin.'

'Right,' I say, my mind drifting.

'Have DI Manning and DC Cooper spoken to you again yet?'

'No, why? Will they? I gave them a statement already.' Even though I'd wondered about it early on, I'd not given it further thought. The suggestion now that this might happen makes my throat constrict, and I can't quell the rising panic. I've said all I want to say to them.

You haven't, though, a nagging voice in my head reminds me.

Adam was determined I should go to the police and be honest about what I know. I left him just before five yesterday with a promise I'd contact DC Cooper – I thought she'd be the most sympathetic, despite her icy exterior. Not because she's a woman – although I suppose I'm hoping that'll make her more likely to relate to what I say – but because the way she's questioned me so far has instilled a certain amount of trust. I have more faith in her than I have in Manning, at any rate. There's something behind his eyes that unnerves me; like he can see right through me. Imogen Cooper would be the one I'd confess to if I had to. And as far as Adam is concerned, I have to.

I feel despondent this morning. The spitting incident was probably a drop in the ocean compared to what I can expect from here on in. It'll be worse once the trial starts. Will I have any friends left by then? Will Adam still be supportive? Deep down I know he's right about going to the police – it's just scary. They'll be suspicious about why I didn't relay this information to them sooner. From what I've told them so far, my marriage with Tom is a good one, and he is the model husband and father.

Will they believe my reasons for telling them a different story now?

Journalists are outside again when I step through the front door with Poppy. There are several yelling for my attention and others that get in my face, bombarding me with questions. I grip Poppy's hand and drag her through them, saying nothing. I've given Poppy the best explanation I could think of about why these people are camping outside our house, asking us lots of questions and following us, taking photos. I told her it's about her daddy, that something has happened in his job in London and people are very interested about it. She asked if it was a good thing he'd done, and I came very close to breaking down there and then.

I pulled myself together and I lied to her. I said he'd done something very important. It's not such a big lie really – I suppose murdering someone is an important thing, in a way.

We don't get followed to nursery – that boundary appears to have been upheld, thanks to Adam's intervention yesterday.

I think about the almost-kiss and my heart flutters wildly. Afterwards, there'd been several minutes of awkwardness; neither of us had known what to do or say. We had both probably realised how close we'd been to taking a huge step into the unknown; crossing the boundary of friendship. Adam had reacted by muttering an apology; saying he felt bad, that he was taking advantage of my vulnerability. Of course, I firmly denied he'd done that, and explained how mine and Tom's relationship had been crumbling long before the current events had come to light. He seemed to relax a little once I told him I'd been waiting a long time for the truth to come out – for Tom to be arrested. I wanted Adam to know he was in no way taking advantage.

I wonder how we'll interact from now on. Will something happen between us? Where it goes from here is anyone's guess, but Adam is free to do what he pleases, and I am not.

I'm married. I might need to do something about that. I sneak back to the cottage via the back lane, climbing over the wall to avoid detection. Safely inside, I make a call to Moore & Wells and ask to speak with Jimmy. I know he's not likely to be there as Alexander said he was on leave until today, so he probably won't be at work until Monday. But I'm hoping I can wangle his mobile number from one of his colleagues.

It takes all my powers of persuasion, but finally I'm given his number and I'm speaking with him.

'Jimmy – sorry to bother you. I know you've only just come back from holiday. It's Beth Hardcastle, Tom's wife—'

'I'm not back, actually. I've still got the weekend.'

'Oh, er . . . I'm sorry. I can call another time?' I hesitate – I don't want to wait any longer really, but I don't want to annoy the man.

'Alex said you'd been into the office asking questions.' His attitude is off; he's immediately on the defensive. I wonder why Alexander told him. But anyway, he hasn't ended the call yet, so that's a good sign. I need to ease into this conversation if I want to gain anything from him.

'Yes, I did pop by on the off chance I'd catch one of Tom's mates. It's been such a traumatic couple of weeks I couldn't think where else to turn.' I lay it on thick, ensuring my voice sounds weak and teary. 'Tom only ever really talked about you, Jimmy. I guess you were the only friend he'd made a connection with at the bank.' I know this isn't quite true, but maybe if I massage this bloke's ego, he might be happier about opening up to me.

'Look, I'm really sorry about what's happened. I can't believe they've dragged Tom in about this missing woman.

How can they even be certain she was murdered? It's madness. But I don't think there's anything I can do to help his case, Beth. I'm sorry.'

He sounds as though he's wrapping up the conversation. I have to keep him chatting. 'I understand, Jimmy. I think I was just hoping to fill in the gaps and find out what was troubling him before this all kicked off. He hasn't been himself for a while and I'm worried something happened . . .'

'What do you mean?'

'Well, what if they're right, Jimmy? What if he murdered her? You never really know a person, do you? I have to accept there's a possibility the police are right. As far as I knew, he went to work on the Tuesday – but he never showed. Apparently he phoned Celia to say he had been ill on the commute and he was on his way home. But he *didn't* come home as far as I know – not until later. He could've been trying to cover something up in that time. Maybe he was concealing evidence of him murdering Katie before the police came down hard on him. It's the only thing that makes sense, isn't it?'

'God, Beth,' Jimmy lets out a long sigh. He stays silent for a while.

I prompt him. 'What's wrong? Did you know he was trying to get rid of evidence?'

'No, no. Nothing like that. None of this is what you think, Beth. Tom's a good man.' He pauses. 'Or, he's not a killer, anyway.'

He clearly doesn't know Tom well, then. 'Then what?' I say.

'He wasn't destroying evidence that day. Or concealing it, or whatever. He was . . .'

256

I hear Jimmy scratching his beard. He's clearly torn between his loyalty to Tom and telling me what he knows.

'He was what?' I ask, impatiently.

'I'm sorry, Beth. I can't believe I'm going to tell you this, but it's the lesser of two evils . . .' He lets out a puff of air. 'I can't have you thinking he's a murderer. Please don't shoot the messenger.'

I'm suddenly worried. What could be worse than destroying evidence of a murder?

'I won't. I promise. Please, Jimmy, I need to know.'

'He wasn't at work, because he was visiting someone.'

'Who?' My pulse bangs in my throat.

'He's been . . . seeing someone. He made me swear to keep it to myself.'

'A fucking *affair*?' I momentarily lose all grip on my emotions. That can't be right. 'He wouldn't . . .'

'Beth, it's been going on for a while. Like, years, I reckon.' Jimmy's tone has altered dramatically, going from defensive to sympathetic. I don't want his sympathy. The room spins; my head is getting lighter and lighter. Jimmy must be lying. Tom loves me; only me. He's always been faithful. He's the jealous type – he wouldn't cheat, because he loathes people who do.

Like Katie Williams.

'Do you know who with? Where?'

'Only that he'd sneak off at lunchtimes to see her, so it had to be close. And occasionally he'd leave work early and I know he didn't head home to you.'

The words sting. An affair was the last thing I'd been expecting to find out.

Do I know my husband *at all*?

* * *

257

I sit in the darkened room in silence, absolutely still. Only my mind is active. It's working overtime as I consider how, why, Tom cheated on *me*.

I wish he were here now so I could yell at him; tell him what a bastard he is. A lying, cheating, murdering bastard of a husband. He doesn't deserve a loving wife and daughter. Why would he ever put the life he supposedly loves in jeopardy by having an affair? It doesn't make sense.

Jimmy must be wrong. He didn't say Tom had categorically disclosed this affair to him. In fact, Jimmy seemed to be guessing based merely on Tom disappearing at lunchtimes. Although he did say that he'd promised Tom he wouldn't say anything. No. It's more likely that Tom didn't want to socialise with his work colleagues and made an excuse, so he didn't have to suffer them for the entire day. I know he often ordered gifts from the London Zoo click and collect service and then walked across to pick them up to bring back for Poppy.

That was his cover. His alibi.

I can't prevent the thought, and now I've had it, it grows. It casts a different light on everything. Have I been made a fool of?

Shaking myself from my trance, I make another call.

It goes to voicemail.

'Hi, DC Cooper, it's Beth Hardcastle. I need to see you.' Rage gives my voice an edge. I pause, knowing that once I say this, there's no return. Anger, hurt and humiliation all take over and I carry on. 'I need to tell you something,' I say. 'It's urgent.' I don't embellish; I hang up.

Now I wait.

Chapter 65

He cried for twenty minutes; she didn't think he'd ever stop. It was as if a plug had been pulled on all of his pent-up emotions, all of his long-held pain, and now he was releasing them. She wonders: why now? What made this moment any different from the others? It can't have been anything she said or did. Something has happened. She wants to ask him about his wife, but she daren't – she doesn't want to anger him, or upset him any more than he is already. So she silently strokes his hair as he recovers from his outburst. He's like a child, she thinks, being comforted by his mother. She gets the feeling his relationship with her wasn't a good one either; nor with his father. In her experience, damaged people like him tend to be born from broken families.

'Sorry,' he says, finally moving away from her. He leaves a damp patch on her belly which she wipes with the corner of the duvet. 'Thanks for listening.'

'You didn't really say anything.'

259

'I don't have to with you,' he says. He begins pulling his trousers back on, then tugs his shirt from beneath her clothes on the chair in front of the bedroom window. She watches him intently as he dresses, wondering if he'll come back. A strange feeling in her gut makes her doubt it. She thinks perhaps they've run their course; her usefulness has come to an end today.

'That's why you keep coming back for more?' she asks, softly.

He turns to her, his face solemn. 'It helps,' he says. 'But mostly I keep coming back because you let me do what I want.'

His bluntness – his honesty – hurts her a bit. And he's wrong, she thinks, because she doesn't let him do all that he wants, sexually. But she nods, guessing he gets more from her than his wife, at any rate. She can't blame her – it's not everyone's cup of tea to be strangled during sex.

'When will you be back?' she calls as he heads towards the door.

'Very soon,' he says, without looking back.

Maybe her gut was wrong then; although that's seldom the case. He does still want to see her. She knows she shouldn't let this happen any more. Each time, she swears it's the last. But she can't help but find him intriguing. It's like being addicted to drugs – one high needs to be followed up with another – and despite the downsides; the fear he can provoke; she needs him as much as he needs her.

Chapter 66

BETH

Now

'Adam, could you possibly pick Poppy up from nursery today?'

'Yeah, sure – I offered to anyway, remember? Are you okay?'

I take a deep breath. 'I've agreed to meet Imogen Cooper in London. I'm going to tell her.'

'The detective? Oh, good. I'm glad. You're doing the right thing, Beth. Really. You have to think of yourself and Poppy.'

That's what I have been doing. All I've been doing since the day Tom told me.

'Thanks for the push. I wouldn't be able to do this if it weren't for your support, Adam. I mean that. You've been amazing.'

'Ah, it's nothing,' he says. I can imagine his face flushing red. 'I've enjoyed spending time with you and Poppy – it's been good for me and Jess. So, thank you!'

'Strange how it's two awful events that have brought us together.' I immediately regret my wording, and stutter and stumble over my attempts at rephrasing. I didn't mean to imply we were in any way 'together'.

'No, you're right,' he says, interrupting my rambling, saving me from further embarrassment. 'It feels wrong that it's other people's misfortune now that's finally enabled me to open up to someone again, though.'

'Yeah, I know. Anyway, thank you again. I'll pick her up from yours when I'm done.'

As soon as the call ends, I grab my bag and jacket, and with my head down to avoid catching the eye of any of the press hanging around outside, make my way to the car. I release my breath when I'm safely locked inside, then drive at a snail's pace through them all to get out of Lower Tew. This trip to London means I've now officially been to the city more this past week than in the previous two years.

I park outside the city centre and get the tube in, reaching the coffee shop we'd agreed on a few minutes early. After a sweeping glance around to check if Imogen Cooper is already here, I find a table near the back, away from the attention of passers-by and seemingly quieter than the front. For now, anyway. We should be able to talk here with relative confidence of not being overheard.

I spot a head of strawberry-blonde hair bobbing through the customers to get to me. My stomach drops. How stupid to have this reaction when I know she's coming to meet me. Maybe a part of me had hoped she wouldn't show up.

'Beth,' she says, giving a curt nod and sitting down opposite me. She looks around, then lifts her hand to gain the attention of a waitress. She orders an espresso, I ask for a latte. Cooper asks if I want anything to eat, and I decline – I feel sick enough without adding solids into the mix. 'Right. Let's get down to business, shall we?'

'Sure,' I say, trying to force my lips into a smile. My palms are sweating, and my t-shirt clings uncomfortably to my back. The leather seat is increasing the temperature, and a layer of heat has trapped itself between it and me. I shift position.

'No need to be nervous, Beth. You're not in any trouble, you know.'

Not yet, I think.

An awkward silence settles. It's Cooper who starts the ball rolling by asking me what I wanted to talk about.

'I . . .' *I can't do this.* 'It's difficult.' I place my elbows on the table and drop my head into my hands, fingers splaying across my forehead. I study the grain of the wooden table, debating how I should phrase what I want – need – to say.

'I understand, Beth. It's been a hell of a few weeks for you, I'm sure. But you obviously have something on your mind you'd rather be rid of. I can help with that. A problem shared, and all that.'

'It's really not like that, though, is it. You're the police – you've got a job to do. You want to secure a conviction for my husband. Anything I share with you is not a problem halved – it's another nail in his coffin.'

Cooper raises her eyebrows sharply and leans forward. 'A nail in his coffin?' Her interest is piqued; her pupils have dilated to twice their size. 'How do you mean?'

I exhale loudly. 'Hypothetically, if I were to tell you something that I already knew but didn't feel *able* to tell

263

you when first questioned – something I failed to say in my statement – would that make me some kind of accessory? Or mean I was guilty of withholding evidence and obstructing justice? Would I be charged too?' I've clasped my hands together now and interlaced my fingers. I'm squeezing them so hard they're turning a deep red.

'*Hypothetically*, yes,' Cooper says. 'But if there were mitigating factors, of course they would be taken into consideration.'

It's not enough. There's no security in having 'mitigating factors' taken into account. I need something solid before I spill. I've made a mistake asking to meet.

'How about we talk unofficially,' Cooper says, eyeing me cautiously.

'What does that mean?'

'Off the record.'

'I thought that only happened in journalism. Or in dodgy crime dramas.'

This makes Cooper smile. 'You'd be surprised. And anyway, I think what you have to say is important. Pertinent to the case. So obviously I'm interested. Having something more concrete to work with would be helpful.'

'You're making it sound as though I'm going to go against Tom; help you convict him.'

'Well, aren't you?'

I'm stumped for a moment. Is that what I'm doing here? Is it what I want?

'I'm trying to tell you the truth about what I know. I was afraid before, but I know if anything ever happened to Poppy . . .' The waitress comes over with a tray and puts our drinks down. I wait for her to leave again. 'If someone hurt her, I'd want to know everything. And I'd want justice to be handed out to the monster who did it. I was torn between protecting her, protecting me, and helping you get justice for Katie.'

'You were scared of Tom?' Cooper asks. 'As in, if you had said anything, he'd have hurt you?'

'Yes, that's what I was afraid of. I'd have been risking a lot if I'd opened up straight away. I had to play it cautiously. I'm sorry.'

'Okay. Well I understand your reluctance to come forward. Now is better than never, so . . .'

We both take sips of our drinks, but our eyes don't leave each other's.

'Where do you want to start?' Cooper asks, after a minute or so passes.

'I think I have some evidence that might help. Evidence you can use against Tom.' My mouth is dry; my heart is hammering. I've gone too far to turn back now. Cooper's eyes are wide.

'You know we already have the emails, right? And we suspected you knew about those, given you admitted using Tom's iPad and you had his passwords.'

So I *am* under suspicion. I'm the wife – I guess it was inevitable. Now seems like the perfect time to come clean.

'Yes, I know that. I mean other stuff.'

'What type of evidence do you think you have, Beth?'

'A sweatshirt,' I say. 'Maxwell said all you have, or all you're letting on to him that you have, are the emails sent from Katie's account on Tom's iPad. Nothing physical. Nothing conclusive that links him to a murder.'

Cooper doesn't respond to that, so that makes me think they do have other evidence. But I'm guessing it's not

265

substantial enough. She does now ask the obvious question, though.

'Why would Katie's sweatshirt be relevant, unless it has blood on it?'

'No. No blood.'

'Then I don't think—'

'It's not Katie's sweatshirt.'

Cooper's brow creases and she sits back in the seat. 'So, why are you telling me this?'

'It's not Katie's. It's Phoebe Drake's – her university sweatshirt.'

Cooper's upper body lurches forwards. I have her full attention now. 'Who is Phoebe Drake?'

'She was a victim of a drowning incident fifteen years ago. Only it wasn't an accidental drowning. Phoebe was Tom's first victim.'

Chapter 67

BETH

Now

Cooper sighs, drains her espresso and leans on the table, staring straight into my eyes. She's silent. I know what she's thinking – how does a sweatshirt help with anything and how do I know any of this. I fill her in on what Tom told me – or most of it. I hold back certain information – I'm too afraid of the repercussions. I have to make sure I'm not going to receive any backlash for having withheld this information first.

'Shit,' Cooper says. 'So, at the time, no one even suspected foul play, because she'd sustained a broken ankle and had alcohol in her system?'

'That's what I've gathered. Tom said it *was* an accident, though. He hadn't meant to kill her.'

'And you believe that?'

I purse my lips. I wanted to believe it when he told me. When I found out about the emails he'd been sending pretending to be Katie, it hadn't taken long for the rest to come out too. Had Tom's confession about Phoebe come first, believing her death was accidental would've been easier. After all, Tom gave a feasible account of the incident. But it was how he'd kept it from me, lying for so long, that had tipped the balance. If I hadn't come across those emails, would he ever have told me? It made me reassess and dissect everything. How could I believe he'd accidentally killed *two* women?

Seeing him in the prison yesterday had unlocked something – the memories I'd buried *and* the realisation that I was married to a killer. Of course I'd known. But I'd loved him. He was my Tom.

I didn't want him to leave me and Poppy.

But I also know I have to secure a future free from fear. Free from being let down.

If what he did ever came out, I knew we would be destroyed; our family unit would be broken. Things always come out in the end and I'd rather it be now, while Poppy is too young to understand – while I'm young enough to build another, brighter life for us – than to live a life worrying about the truth surfacing. It has to be done.

I must make sure they have enough evidence to send Tom down.

'I want to believe him, DC Cooper. But I know even if they were accidents, the end product is the same. Two dead women; two families unaware of the truth. I should've reported what I'd found out immediately, but Tom is so good at twisting things, manipulating me, making me feel it would be my fault if our lives fell apart. My fault if Poppy ended up being without a father. And . . . well, he can be . . . aggressive sometimes. I was too afraid I'd become his third victim. I couldn't risk it for Poppy's sake.'

Imogen frowns and I wonder if she's trying to reconcile this information with the picture I previously painted of my perfect marriage. I'd worried this might be the case. But then her face softens. I think she accepts that this happens with people in abusive relationships; she's bound to have seen it many times before.

'Where is this sweatshirt? We didn't find anything like that in the search of your property.'

'I told Tom I was taking it to burn. I have it in the storage space in the loft of Poppy's Place. I can get it for you.'

'Good, yes. And with this new information and evidence linking Tom to Phoebe, we'll reopen the case and charge him with her murder too. It'll definitely help when it comes to the trial.' Cooper's cheeks fill with air and she blows it out in a slow hiss. And, almost under her breath she says, 'Of course, Katie's body would be even better.'

Chapter 68

TOM

Now

Maxwell tells me new evidence has come to light.

He says it's come from Beth.

I shake my head violently from side to side – my brain feels as though it's crashing against my skull. If I do this for long enough, maybe I'll faint, or give myself a brain haemorrhage. It's the only way I'll get out of here now.

'Tom, no! Stop!' Maxwell's words sound strangely distorted in my head.

Hands are on my shoulders. 'Come on, fella – relax.' The prison officer's voice is calm. I recognise it; he's from my wing. Another officer strides across from the hall – backup in case I get out of hand. I haven't the energy to put up any kind of fight.

'Maybe this legal visit should continue another day?' the second officer says. I'm vaguely aware of Maxwell rising from his seat and speaking in a low voice. He's likely telling them I've had bad news, to keep an eye on me.

Put me on suicide watch.

Yes, I want to shout – put me on suicide watch because my fucking wife has just betrayed me. Has she found out? Is that why she's decided to go against me now? I trusted her. She said she'd stand by me; she knew it was only an accident. Knew I hadn't meant to harm them.

But I did. I did mean to hurt them. And although Beth believed me when I said otherwise, there's a possibility that something she's found out has changed her mind. About the supposed accidents. About me.

I slam my fists against my temples. Again and again.

I don't believe she'd give the fucking police evidence that would help convict me. She needs me. Poppy needs me.

They have no one else.

It's a game, isn't it? Manning and Cooper are doing this to see how I react. It's lies.

They've got nothing.

I let my arms hang loosely at my side.

'Sorry,' I say to the two officers either side of me, who have started manhandling me out of the hall, back to the wing. 'I'm okay. Really. It was nothing. I'm over it now.'

'Do you want to see a listener? Or the chaplain? I think it would be a good idea, Tom.'

The words wash over me.

Beth hasn't sold me out; she'd never do that.

Those lying fuckers. I'm not falling for their games.

Chapter 69

BETH

Now

My knees scrape against the rough wooden slats as I crawl through the roof space to reach the box. DC Cooper was keen for me to hand it over, but she allowed me to wait until this morning – she refrained from seeking a warrant to search the premises herself, which I'm grateful for.

Cooper shines her torchlight through the loft hatch, but I don't need it. I know exactly where it is – there are only a few cardboard boxes stored here. I hesitate once I find it, my fingers feeling around the outer edges and picking at the brown parcel tape I used to secure the flaps. Inside it is the link to Phoebe Drake – a second-year university student Tom met at Leeds. The girl he 'accidentally' pushed to her death.

I'd looked up everything there was to know about her after Tom told me. There wasn't a lot. Cut and dried – death by misadventure. No one knew Tom had anything to do with it. No one knew they'd been together, albeit very briefly. No witnesses came forward to say they'd seen him with her that night, or the one evening previously when he'd taken her back to his accommodation. He said he hadn't even been questioned – he'd only 'heard' of her death on the uni grapevine. A tragic accident, people said. A warning to students not to become so intoxicated that they were no longer aware of their surroundings; of the danger of being on their own.

Tom got away with it. He'd been lucky.

But that luck has just run out.

'Here you go.' I lower the box through the hatch and climb back down the ladder.

'Thank you,' Cooper says. Her eyes are alight, her pupils dilated. Excitement evident.

'I'm sorry I didn't give it to you earlier. Tom told me it was his when I first found it. Shrunk in the wash, he said.' I let out a short, sharp laugh. 'I kept it even though I'd promised to burn it.'

'What made you hold onto it, then?' Cooper's eyes narrow.

'A small part of me didn't believe Tom's account – a big enough part to prevent me destroying it. I thought it would be wise to hold onto it, for a little while at least. Then I forgot about it.'

'Really?' Cooper eyes me suspiciously. 'You forgot about your husband telling you he'd killed two women?' The scepticism drips from her tone.

'No, I didn't forget that. I mean the sweatshirt – I put it to the back of my mind. I've had to get good at burying things.' I curse myself for my choice of words, expecting more reprisal from Cooper, but she remains pensive, cradling the box in her arms as though it were a baby.

'All done?' Adam pops his head around the corner. He's kindly keeping an eye on Poppy – I set the girls up with some plates to paint while they wait. Being early on a Saturday, it's only them – Lucy doesn't open until nine, so there's no one to witness Imogen Cooper walking out with further evidence.

'Yes, I'll be back with you in a moment,' I say. He nods and leaves. His interruption has broken whatever trance Cooper was in.

'He's been supportive, then?' she says, jerking her head towards where Adam had been. I don't answer immediately, and my hesitation probably goes against me.

'His daughter and Poppy are in nursery together,' I say by way of explanation. 'I've had to call on him to pick her up a few times while I've been at the station or visiting Tom.'

'Yes, of course. Good that you have someone to lean on. Does he know?'

I'm wary of the question – what she's implying. 'I mentioned to him that I knew something I hadn't yet informed the police of, yes, and I confided in him about how frightened I was of the repercussions. He was the one who encouraged me to talk to you. He said it was perfectly understandable that I'd held back given I was living with a manipulating, controlling man, but now was the time to break free.'

'Good. That's good,' she says, moving towards the door. She seems perplexed, but she doesn't say anything else.

Back in the café, I slide into the seat next to Poppy and start to talk to her about the plate she's painting. There's

274

a large splodge of yellow in the middle, which she informs me is a sunflower. I give a sideways glance as Cooper walks past us to head out.

'Thank you for this, Beth. We'll be in touch,' she says as she turns and closes the door.

'Well done. That can't have been easy. You've done the right thing, you know, Beth. I'm proud of you.' Adam reaches his hand across the table, laying it on mine. Poppy pouts and glares at me. I pull my hand away, smiling at her.

It's as if she knows I've just betrayed her daddy.

We've betrayed each other now – so I guess that makes us equal.

Chapter 70

BETH

Now

It's hard not to let the images flood my mind. All those things I've imagined, ever since Tom confessed to ending two women's lives. After I found Katie's email account and he broke down and told me about her, things began to unwind. *He* unwound. The subsequent confession about Phoebe, although it came as a shock, felt almost inevitable. I think I'd been expecting it.

'Are there more, Tom?' I'd asked, hoping against hope he would say no. I was so relieved when he said he'd told me everything. That there were no more secrets.

I'd been stupid enough to believe him.

The sound of breaking glass and muted thuds on the carpet releases some of my pain: a silver-framed photo of me and Tom lands face down, and a glass jewellery box lies in bits at my feet where I've swept them off the dressing table with my arm. A book and a ceramic lamp crash on top. The damaged pile lies there, silently accusing me.

Our first year in Lower Tew set me up for what I imagined was going to be the happiest life. Even when he tried to ruin it with his bloody confessions, I continued to hold us together, to keep the dream alive. I wanted to succeed here; I wanted the happy, village lifestyle I'd craved since being a child.

Tom has destroyed my dream. Destroyed my dreams for Poppy.

I have to make up for his failures.

And I will. I'm determined to make sure she and I have the life I'd envisaged for us; that I've worked every hour for.

Even if it means being without Tom.

My husband.

Poppy's daddy.

A murderer.

Adam is a good man. A good choice. Loving, stable, secure.

Not a murderer.

I flop down on the bed, listening intently, wondering if the noise from my outburst has stirred Poppy. It doesn't seem to have. I slide my phone off the bedside table and check my messages.

How are you doing? If you need me, call. A xx

My pulse skips as I dial.

'Thanks for your message,' I say. 'I'm taking you up on your offer.'

'Good, I'm glad.' Then, unexpectedly, and quietly, he adds, 'I've been missing you.'

'Really?' I sit up, my mood lifting immediately. 'You

only saw me yesterday.' I almost say that I thought that would be enough, given the circumstances, but I don't want to put that idea into his mind. He was so supportive yesterday at the café, when I gave Imogen Cooper what I hope is hard evidence, so I'm assuming that means he doesn't hold my failure to act on my knowledge sooner against me.

'Yeah, I know. Look, I know things aren't exactly . . . usual – for want of a better word – but I want to be here for you. I'd actually quite like to see more of you . . .'

I inhale sharply.

'Beth? I'm sorry, if this is too soon – if you think I'm being inappropriate—'

'It's not,' I say, tears stinging my eyes. 'Inappropriate, I mean.'

'That's a relief. Spending the last two weeks with you has been the best I've felt for a really long time.'

'Since Camilla, you mean?' Of course that's what he means, but for some reason I ask the question.

'Yes. Since Camilla. A dark cloud has hung over me every day since she died. I've allowed unanswered questions to eat away at me. It was like a cancer, slowly killing me. You've changed that.'

'By replacing your darkest thoughts with my own?'

He laughs. 'No. By giving me a reason to smile again. I let you in, and at first it frightened me; your intensity, my feelings for you . . .'

I hear him swallow. He's letting his words sink in now, before he continues. He wants me to confirm I feel the same way. That won't be hard.

'It can be scary letting another person in, can't it?' I say.

'Yes, and the timing is particularly challenging. What do you think will happen now?'

'To Tom, you mean?'

'Yeah – will what you've given them be enough, do you think?'

'I really don't know. I suppose it'll depend what they can gain forensically from the sweatshirt, but ultimately, they'll need more. This helps them collect the bigger picture – but really, he could say he found the sweatshirt. It doesn't exactly prove anything, does it?'

'But the detective seemed so pleased to have some more evidence.'

'As I say, it's building the case, but what she really needs is a body. And maybe DNA evidence that irrefutably links Tom to the killing of one or both women. Then there's no doubt they'll get a conviction.'

'You sound as though you've thought this through.'

'I've had lots of lonely nights to think about it.'

'Ditto,' Adam says. 'My mind has actually been in overdrive.'

'Oh, why?'

'It's daft,' he says. I hear a heavy sigh.

'No, go on. I've shared so much with you – do feel free to share your madness with me.'

Adam gives a nervous titter. 'Well, it's just – it struck me, when it first came to light that Tom had been charged with a woman's murder, that he may have had a hand in—'

'Oh, God! You're not about to say you think he had something to do with Camilla's death, are you?' I can't keep the shock from my voice. He said it was daft, but really – why would he make that leap? 'Tom barely knew her, Adam. And her death was different – an accid—' I stop speaking, recalling how Tom had called Katie and Phoebe's deaths accidents too.

'It was a stupid thought, I know. It was only because I didn't find her EpiPen near her and she usually carried it everywhere. The spare was still in the bedside cabinet . . . I guess she couldn't reach that in time.'

'I'm not saying it's stupid,' I say, bringing the softness back to my tone. 'But highly doubtful.'

'Yes, probably. I guess in some way, believing that Tom had killed her would almost be better than knowing she *chose* not to take her allergy seriously enough. She'd been flippant; she kept buying stuff she wasn't one hundred per cent sure didn't contain any traces of nuts. Just because she'd got away with it once or twice, didn't mean it was no longer a risk. A trace is a trace – they put that as a warning on everything for a reason.'

'To be fair to Camilla, that might be *why* she ended up getting a bit complacent. As you say, they label practically everything with *may contain traces of nuts*. I have to put the sign up for all of my food at the café, too.'

'Yes, true. But still. She didn't only have herself to look after. She should've been more careful, for Jess's sake. It was pretty selfish of her.'

I can hear his bitterness – an emotion I've not noticed before. I know it's the grief talking. He doesn't really think Camilla was selfish – he loved everything about her; that was obvious even to an outsider. I get what he means, though – if she'd been taken from him by someone else, he wouldn't be able to blame her. Unfortunately, the way it had happened, he couldn't avoid thinking that Camilla

280

simply hadn't taken enough responsibility. Her death was avoidable.

'We're all guilty of being selfish sometimes, Adam. It makes her human.'

'Made,' he says simply, correcting my tense. We both fall silent. I'm worried I've upset him by not giving any credence to his thoughts.

'Anyway,' I say to break the awkwardness. 'You have any plans for tomorrow evening?'

'We usually have a film night – well, late afternoon – every Monday. And we have a picnic in the lounge. Not exactly enthralling, I know, but Jess loves it.'

'Sounds lovely. Can we join you?' I ask, hopefully.

'If you promise me one thing.'

I tut. 'Oh, I see. Well – I'm not sure about that. If it comes with conditions attached, then one might have to decline,' I say, in a mock posh voice.

'Get you, turning down an invitation to be with the youngest widower in Lower Tew! You won't get a better offer you know.'

'I think one might be getting ideas above his station.'

'Ahh, it's so good to partake in some light-hearted humour, Beth. You've no idea. Anyway, the condition is only that you have to bring the snacks – nothing earth-shattering!' he laughs. Finally, he sounds at ease. Clearly, talking about Camilla puts him on edge. I must steer the conversation away from her in future.

'I think I can manage that,' I say. 'I need to cook up a batch of muffins for the café tomorrow anyway, so I'll do a few extra.'

'A few? I was hoping for a dozen at least.'

'You drive a hard bargain,' I say.

'You'd best get used to it – you know, if we're going to be seeing a bit more of each other.'

The instant warmth his words cause makes me happy and sad at the same time. Life seems to be like that at the moment – filled with contradictions. And I feel as though I'm the biggest contradiction of all.

As I'm drifting into sleep, Adam's words float back into my consciousness. The fact he'd considered, however briefly, that Tom might have had a hand in Camilla's death blindsided me. But her death wasn't like the others, so why did Adam even contemplate it? Visions whir, blurring, mixing as they shoot through my mind. They mix with Jimmy's words, too: *Tom was having an affair*. They all combine, and I dream vividly. Tom, Camilla, lying in each other's arms. Blood-soaked sheets, blue-tinged lips, deep red gouges around a pale neck. Arms and legs bound to bed posts, Tom thrusting himself into her, shouting out her name as he climaxes, his hands around her throat. Camilla struggling to get air into her lungs, thrashing her body, grasping at her throat as she takes her final breath.

I awake, drenched in sweat, to a scream piercing through the stillness of the night.

Chapter 71

She's barely had time to shower before he comes back. Seeing him at her door again so soon confuses her.

'Did you forget something?' she asks, letting him in.

She notices he's carrying a briefcase; he hadn't had that just now.

He sets it on the floor and closes the door, locking it. Her insides quiver. What's happening? He never visits her more than once in one day, and never after four.

'I think the seven-year itch might well be a thing, you know,' he tells her as he bends down and snaps open the metal clasps on the case. There's something about the loud clack as each one springs open, like a bullet being fired from a gun, that steals the saliva from her mouth.

She swallows hard. 'Is that how long you've been with Beth?' she says, instinctively backing away as she speaks, unsure of his intentions. Her gut tells her this situation isn't one she'll have control over.

He lets out a prolonged sigh. She catches its almost

283

*sarcastic tone, and realises too late what's in store. He's
pulling out a piece of rope – slowly, deliberately twisting it
in his hands. He stands up, smiling. 'You know too much.'*

*'No. No . . . I don't . . . I don't know what you mean.'
Panic grips to her words.*

*'You know my wife's name. You know why I come here.
And I've shared too much.' He moves swiftly towards her
now, and as she turns to run, she screams. His hands are
over her mouth in a split second – so fast she swears he
must be superhuman. As he stands jutted up against her
back, he whispers, 'Shh, don't,' into her hair, then inhales
deeply. The rope loops around her neck. 'You know I can't
do this with Beth. You're the only one I can be myself with.'*

*The rope isn't tight yet – she can still get out of this,
if she stays calm. She's been ready for this type of situation for a while now. She must keep him talking. Make
him believe she's on his side.*

*'I've always let you do the things you can't with your
wife. Like you say, you can be yourself with me. You need
me. I need you, too, as it happens.' Her words are shaky,
but at least she has the ability to speak. For now.*

*'Yes, I can tell. I can see you. Properly, I mean. Not
what you show other people, but what's inside you. You
really did mean something to me.'*

*The past tense. She no longer means something to him?
Or is the past tense what she's to become? 'I'm thirty-four
years old and I'm saving up to get out of this place – I've
got dreams, things I want to accomplish. You and me –
we could carry on seeing each other. And not just here,
somewhere better; somewhere classy. I could give you
what you want.'*

His laugh stops her speaking.

'Don't worry. You are going to give me what I want.' He runs his tongue from her neck to her ear. 'You are giving me your life.'

Tears bubble and fall. She's not going to talk him around. If he wants to end her life right here and now, there's nothing she can say or do to stop him.

Apart from the gun in her bedside table. If only she could reach it.

'Why don't we take this into the bedroom. You can tie me to the bed?'

It's a risky move, but her only hope. He pulls her backwards roughly by the rope and her legs grapple on the floor to get traction while her hands grasp the loop, trying to keep it from strangling her.

'I've been with Beth for eight years. But it's when I hit that seven-year mark that things became more of a struggle. Keeping my desires to myself; my real self hidden; it was problematic – which is when I found you. It struck me recently – I don't know why it took so long before the thing inside me wanted more. I killed Phoebe in a fit of rage and hated myself for years. But when it happened again, when Katie cheated on me, I knew I needed to kill again. And I enjoyed giving her what she deserved.' He pulls her to the bed, yanks her up. 'It'd been seven years since Phoebe. See the pattern?'

She rolls to one side, closer to the bedside cabinet. This is her chance.

'Hey, what are you trying to do?' He wraps the rope around his forearm and jerks it hard, snapping her head backwards.

She groans, falling onto her back.

This is it, *she thinks as she stares up at the ceiling. At* the damp patch that's still there, despite asking her landlord a thousand times. It's my fault. She knew Tom was bad news from their first encounter. Her own weird, twisted thinking had brought her here. The danger was exhilarating at times; the highs had seemed worth the risk.

Not now, though.

'Thank you for helping me. For keeping me on the right path for this long. My wife and child appreciate it.'

'Your wife and child will leave you and you'll die alone.'

He puts all of his weight on her, pressing his thighs against hers, squashing her. The rope begins to tighten. She only has moments left. Her thoughts lose focus. He's left his suit jacket on. He's fully clothed. He's not going to have sex with her? The strangulation part was always a sexual thing for him. Why not now? Maybe the killing doesn't do the same thing for him. Maybe he'll have sex with her lifeless body.

'They'll never know,' he says, bending over her, smiling.

She laughs – it comes out as a constricted gurgle. 'That's what you think,' she manages to say, before swiping her hand up, digging her nails into his neck. He whacks it away, cursing, then pulls the rope again. Harder still. Her eyes bulge; they feel as though they're about to burst out of her skull. Her vision blurs and her head feels light. Perhaps in her next life she'll make something of herself. And avoid men like Tom.

She tries to gasp for breath but nothing comes: her airway is totally blocked. She doesn't want to give him the satisfaction of seeing her panic; struggle; thrash – but she can't resist the compulsion. That survival instinct you hear about – how even when death is inevitable, you fight it to the last.

She hopes he doesn't get away with this.

Chapter 72

BETH

Now

Was the scream mine? Or Poppy's? I leap from the bed and run across the landing to Poppy's room.

Her bed is empty.

'Poppy!' I fall to my hands and knees to check under it. It's not deep enough below her princess bed for her to be hiding there, but for some reason I check anyway. I call her name again, my blood whooshing in my ears so loudly I probably wouldn't hear her answer me. My feet sound like rumbling thunder on the stairs as I descend.

'Poppy, what's the matter?' I launch towards her, taking her in my arms. 'Why are you downstairs, sweetheart?' Her little body is rigid as she stares at the front door. I glance to where her eyes are focused. 'Are you having a bad dream, Poppy?' My hands are on her upper arms; I shake her gently to tear her from the trance. She's never had night terrors, but I had them as a child, so I wonder if this might be the start. It wouldn't surprise me, given the last few weeks. As much as I've tried to shield her from what's been happening, she's still witnessed the journalists; the spitting incident – she's likely internalised it. And this is how her little brain is coping.

'Why are you crying, Mummy?' she says, finally turning her head up to mine. I give her a tight hug.

'I'm not, my little Poppy poppet. My eyes are just tired.'

Another lie. I seem to be telling so many that they come easily now.

'Mine too,' she says, rubbing them. 'The bang woke me.'

'Oh, I see. Was the bang down here?'

'Think so.'

'You should've come and got me first, Poppy. Always come to Mummy first, okay?'

'Oookay!' She buries her head in my chest and I lift her up and take her back upstairs. After tucking her in and waiting with her, stroking her temple until she falls back to sleep, I go downstairs. I whack on every light and do a thorough check of each room, wondering what the noise she heard could've been. I can't see anything that may have fallen – there are no items out of place. She must have heard it in her dream.

Before heading back up the stairs I peer out of the lounge window, which overlooks the garden. The sky is inky black, the moon full. Its glittery illumination casts enough light for me to see what caused the bang. My body freezes and goose bumps spring up on my arms. An icy-cold fear clamps down on my heart.

Why the hell would someone do that?

I can't leave this until morning – this can't be ignored, or flippantly cast aside like the spitting man. I run back upstairs, taking two steps at a time, grabbing my mobile from the bedside table.

She picks up her phone on the second ring. 'DC Cooper? It's Beth Hardcastle. I need you to come to the cottage. Now.'

'Beth, what's happened?' Cooper's voice is groggy. I've obviously woken her.

'Some creep has been in my garden,' I say. Before I can explain further, Cooper says she'll get the local police to send a car over to me.

'Thanks. The cowards will already be long gone. But I need the police to do something – it's getting out of hand. I don't feel safe here.'

'Okay, Beth. Try and keep calm. Obviously I won't be able to get to Lower Tew very quickly, but let me call them now and then I'll call you right back.'

It's only a few minutes before my phone rings.

'Two PCs – one male, one female – are heading over to you now, Beth. They're called Hopkins and Mumford. Only answer the door to them – no one else.'

'Okay, thanks DC Cooper.'

'It's fine to call me Imogen, by the way. Makes a change from Cooper. Or Coops.'

She's trying to keep me chatting, to keep me calm. But nausea is squirming away in my stomach. 'Sure. How long will they be?'

'I'm guessing about twenty minutes.'

'*Twenty*! Perhaps I should've called 999.' It's a long time to wait for a response. What if an intruder had got into the cottage? So much could happen in twenty minutes.

'Sorry. It wouldn't be any quicker, though – not to get to your location. The joys of living in the sticks.'

'There's no joy at all lately.'

'I know you've been having a tough time. And this will be some idiots trying to scare you—'

'They've succeeded, DC . . . Imogen. You need to see what they've left for me.'

'You haven't been outside, though, have you? Stay indoors, Beth. Just to be on the safe side.'

'Nope. I can see it plainly enough from my window thanks. I just want it gone before Poppy gets up again. She heard it, you know. She was screaming because the noise frightened her. She was right by the front door when I found her!' My voice is clipped, and my words speed up as I feel hysteria begin to take hold.

'What is it? What's in your garden?'

'Someone has erected a *gallows*, Imogen. Complete with hanging body.'

'Jesus,' she whispers. 'How awful.'

'Not a real one, thank God.' As I say those words, I'm suddenly not so sure I'm right. An icy-cold sensation skitters down my spine. I hadn't even considered that possibility. 'I assume it's a dummy, anyway. Surely to God no one would go as far as to hang a *real* person to make some macabre point?'

Imogen doesn't respond. She doesn't want to say it's plausible. That she's seen worse. The fact it's even crossed my mind sets it racing. If this is what some people will do *now*, what the hell will they stretch to if they find out I did know about Tom's past – that I knew he was a murderer?

Is the gallows a warning to me? Are they saying I'll be the next one hanging?

No. It must be Tom they are aiming this at. They can't

get to him, so they're targeting me. It's a scare tactic, not a threat.

Either way, I can't stay here alone with Poppy any more. I won't be a sitting duck.

My next call is to Adam.

Chapter 73

BETH

Now

'Someone went to a lot of trouble with this.' PC Mumford walks around the gallows, his torchlight illuminating the morbid structure. He tilts the torch upwards, the beam shining on the hanging dummy. It casts an eerie, yellow light on its head. He continues to step carefully around it, and despite the darkness, I can see him frowning. I wonder if this is the most exciting incident he's dealt with for a while. He looks sluggish around the middle, like he hasn't had to pursue a suspect for a number of years. He was calm and effective when he turned up, though – keen to put my mind at ease. His smile was confident and warm, the opposite of his colleague PC Hopkins. She gave me the impression I was wasting police time with her slow, uninterested manner. 'I'll do a perimeter check,' she had said as soon as they arrived. Didn't even introduce herself.

'Looks to me like potato sacks,' PC Mumford says, poking the middle section with a gloved hand. 'Filled with sand,' he suggests. The relief is short-lived for me, though. Tied to the head is a laminated picture. A blown-up photo of a face.

My face.

This is about me, not Tom.

'Why would someone be doing this to me?' I ask the question, but I'm afraid I already know. PC Hopkins answers. She's been looking around the outside of my cottage for the past ten minutes or so, but now she's back standing beside me. 'Some people get hooked on cases like this. Invested. I suspect they think you're getting away with something.'

I turn sharply. 'What! Me? What the hell do you mean?'

She's not perturbed by my abruptness; her face remains stony and she merely shrugs as she begins to usher me back inside. 'Have you got somewhere you can stay for a bit? Until this dies down.'

I almost laugh at her choice of words. 'Yes, I'm going to be staying with a friend.'

'We'll take the address, if you don't mind.' She takes a notebook and while she leans on the hallway table, I rattle off Adam's details. As I'd already planned to go over to his for film night, I'd asked if we could stay the night. I hadn't needed to suggest it might be best if we stayed more than one – he extended the invitation himself.

Her gaze lifts and she eyes me questioningly over the notebook. 'Oh, really? Just around the corner. Is that wise?'

'I don't know! I assume you think not.' My stomach knots. They're worried that the freak who's doing this is serious. That this is a threat, not some silly prank, and that there could be more to come. This could be just the start, and from here on, the threats might become actions.

'It's fine. But don't you have family elsewhere?'

'No. No family.' I don't elaborate. 'What are you going to do about that . . . that *thing* in my garden?'

'DC Cooper has requested it be dusted for prints. It'll be photographed in situ, then removed and retained as evidence in case it's required at a later date.'

'If this escalates, you mean.'

'Yes.' PC Hopkins is not one to sugar-coat anything, I realise. Usually, I like straight-talking people, but in the dead of night, feeling alone and scared, I really would appreciate a lighter touch, a hint of empathy. Mumford is the sensitive one in this duo. He's older, probably has a family, whereas Hopkins is barely out of her teens by the look of her. She's likely new to this and has less life experience – and even less police experience.

'How long will it take? I can't have Poppy seeing it when she wakes up.'

'We'll be as quick as we can, Mrs Hardcastle,' PC Mumford says, his voice making me jump as he sneaks into the hall behind me. The name makes me feel suddenly uneasy. It's the first time I've experienced repulsion from hearing the surname I've had for the past seven years. Right here, right now, I decide I will be changing mine and Poppy's names by deed poll – I don't want us to be forever associated with a killer.

'Thank you. Can I leave you to it, then?' I'm exhausted. I know I won't sleep, but I need to lie down.

'Just a few questions first, please,' Hopkins says. I nod, rolling my neck to release the stiffness. 'DC Cooper mentioned there'd been a few other incidents recently.

Could be linked – do you know the perpetrators of those?'

'No. There was only really the one – some guy in a white estate car wound down his window as he drove by and spat on me. He shouted something about me being "*her*". My friend got a photo of the car. I could get him to send it to you.'

'That would be helpful. Anything else you can think of? Other people flinging abuse at you? Anyone from the village being particularly off with you?'

'Not at this moment, no. Most people have been very supportive. I don't think this would be anyone I know. Not anyone local. Poppy's Place had a fair few new faces at the beginning of all this. Like you said, some people get invested in these stories. Like to see where the people involved live. It's weird, but I suppose it's like those rubber-neckers who slow down to gawp at accidents.'

'Okay, well if you think of anything, give us a call.' She tears off a piece of paper with a telephone number and a crime report reference.

'Thank you, I will.'

She and PC Mumford both turn to walk back outside, but Hopkins pulls up short. She watches Mumford walk up the path, then says, 'Oh, by the way. DC Cooper said she'll be here in the morning. You need to stay in until she's seen you. Then you can move in with the widower.'

I'm taken aback by her tone, but too tired to counter it. I close the door, lock it and go back upstairs. I check on Poppy again before climbing into bed. In the daylight, everything will seem better. Plus, tomorrow night I'll be with Adam.

With Adam, I'll feel safer.

Chapter 74

BETH

Now

I peep out of my bedroom window at five a.m. The sun hasn't risen yet, but I can tell that the hideous structure has gone. I breathe a sigh of relief that PC Mumford kept his word. Poppy hasn't stirred yet – her disturbed night's sleep has clearly had an effect. I pull on my silk dressing gown and pad down the stairs to switch on the Nespresso machine.

There's a tremor in my hand as I take the cup. It's Monday morning; I really should go to the café. Leaving everything to Lucy is unfair, and if I don't think I can manage, then maybe I should hire someone else to take up the slack. I'll sound her out about it once Imogen Cooper has been over.

Adam said last night he'd come over after work and help me collect enough belongings to cover me and Poppy for a few nights. This development fills me with nerves, and I know he will be battling with conflicting emotions too. It's not as if we're moving in together – he's only offering a short-term solution – but I doubt others will see it that way. The village gossips will be tripping over themselves.

I notice the unread message on my mobile as I sit down to eat breakfast with Poppy. She's as bright and alert as she usually is, so the slightly later start to her morning hasn't affected her. I eat a croissant with one hand and open the message from Julia with the other. My heart sinks.

> God, Beth, I'm so sorry. Just heard a nutter left a gallows in your garden last night. Wow – who'd even think of something so gruesome? Let alone putting your face on it! 😱 Makes me shudder – can't imagine how you're feeling. Give me a call if you need to chat. J xx

I reread it several times, my face muscles tense. How had she heard so quickly? The neighbours didn't make a peep last night when the police were here. No doubt there was some curtain-twitching going on, but only one of the neighbours can see into my garden from their window, and that's Gretchen Collins and she rarely leaves. She wouldn't have been calling the residents of Lower Tew to share the gossip – she's not the type.

But, then, who am I to judge?

Maybe Julia was aware of it so quickly because she knows who did it.

The thought clouds my mind while I get Poppy ready for nursery. I don't want to get into any conversations about it when I drop her off. A weight feels as though it's pushing down on my shoulders. If Julia knows, the others will too – and that means the press will.

I hate being right. Of course they're here, waiting for me to give them some juicy titbit, like dogs waiting outside the butcher's. I've never liked the sensationalist spin that news journalists put on their stories, but now I have a newfound hatred. Maybe today would've been a good day to sneak out the back way with Poppy, but it's too dangerous without someone helping her over the wall. Besides, my anger has reached a new peak and I find myself wanting to face the baying crowd.

As soon as we open the front door, the onslaught begins. I pick Poppy up and with her on one hip, her head buried in my chest, I begin to push through them. I get a few feet from the cottage before my temper soars. Furious they have been the ones to allow some lunatic to get a photo of me, to get to me here at my home, I have the overwhelming need to yell at them.

'It's thanks to you lot they were able to find me! Can't you see what you're doing?' My voice is high-pitched; adrenaline is pumping through my veins. Flashes blind me, a cacophony of voices and camera clicks fills my ears, and I can't block out the loud buzzing in my head. I close my eyes, surging on through the crowd. They don't care. They have zero respect for my privacy and my security. Perhaps they want something bad to happen to me to give them more to report – a breaking story.

'You are animals!' I stop walking and turn to face the ones behind me. There are some alarmed faces – they weren't expecting me to react so strongly after my relative silence over the past week. 'How can you sleep at night knowing you're ruining our lives?'

'How do *you* sleep at night knowing your husband murdered an innocent woman and you did nothing about it? Or don't you care? Is it because you helped him?' The accusation rides above the heads of every other reporter and journalist, quick and bold. I'm caught out – a rabbit in the headlights. I can only gawp; my lips move wordlessly as I try to formulate a comeback. And now one person has asked, more accusations rain down on me. I grip Poppy more tightly in my arms and march away from them. Their voices follow me.

A woman shouts, 'Did she get in your way, Bethany?'

'You helped to dispose of Katie Williams, didn't you, Beth?' says another.

I begin to run, but I'm afraid Poppy will hear the awful things being said, so I lower her down and thrust both hands over her ears. Together, somewhat awkwardly, we carry on walking.

'Why are you protecting a killer?'

'Does your daughter know her daddy is in prison?'

I'm horrified at this last question. I'm glad I've covered Poppy's ears.

The awful realisation hits me: this won't stop by moving to Adam's. They'll find me and follow me there, as will whoever it is who's intent on frightening me. PC Hopkins was right.

But I don't have a better option.

If they see I'm helping the investigating officers, will they stop hounding me?

Maybe Imogen Cooper will be able to help me. She might be the only one who can.

Chapter 75

TOM

Now

The TV in my cell is small, but it's a luxury in here and at first, I was grateful for it. It didn't take long, though, before a feeling of loathing took over – watching the outside world, knowing I wasn't going to be a part of it again, irked me. As much as Maxwell tries to be optimistic and spouts ridiculous positive phrases like those ones on mugs that basic bitches have, now I know Beth has supplied some evidence against me, there's little hope of a not guilty verdict. Despite my hurt and anger, seeing her on the news earlier was frustrating because I still want to help her. But there's nothing I can do. I caused this.

But *she* will be my downfall. *She* will cause my lifelong imprisonment.

Maxwell said that a piece of evidence linking me to another historic death has been 'found'. And I don't need to guess what the evidence is, or how they came upon it.

I know it's Phoebe's university sweatshirt. I'm assuming they no longer think it was an accidental death – they'll be looking at it again in a different light now. Another murder they'll be hoping to pin on me.

Beth told me she'd burn it. The traitor.

My wife, the liar.

Chapter 76

BETH

Now

'I'm so scared, Imogen,' I say, the second I open the door to DC Cooper. The noise outside confirms that there's still a crowd of reporters gathered, despite my outburst only an hour ago. Did they shout questions at Imogen when she arrived? Did she answer any of them?

She's wearing a dark-grey linen trouser suit today with a white shirt beneath. Its over-sized collar tapers to a sharp point. She gives a fleeting smile and a nod of her head in greeting, then heads straight into the kitchen, where she shrugs off her jacket and hangs it deftly over the chair before she sits down. She's yet to utter a word.

'Coffee?' I'm on edge, wondering if she's about to inform me of something bad. Her serious expression doesn't waver. But then, it rarely alters, so maybe I shouldn't read much into that.

'Yes, thanks.'

I shift my position so I'm side on to her while I prepare the drinks, rather than having my back to her. It's not because I think it's rude to turn my back – I just need to have eyes on her. I realise I'm not as trusting of her as I'd first thought. She is merely the better of two bad options.

'I appreciate you coming here. It must be a drag travelling from London.'

'It's my job, Beth. I'm working on the murder case and you are involved, so . . .'

Shit. *Involved*. Her wording makes me shudder, as does the realisation she's not really here for my benefit.

'Has something else happened?' I venture.

'What, in addition to your midnight caller?'

'Yeah. It's just you seem . . .' I rack my brain for the right word. 'Preoccupied.' That is the wrong word – it implies I think her mind is elsewhere, that she's not up to the job or something. I can't afford to alienate her. 'Like there's something you need to tell me,' I add.

'I'd like to ask further questions, but no – I don't have anything further to tell you. You're clearly concerned there's more, though. Which means there must be more to know.'

I fell into that trap.

'There's always more, isn't there?' I say, eyes widening. 'It's like being in an ITV crime drama here these days.'

'The bad guys usually get their just deserts in those shows. That's not always the reality.' Her cool, grey eyes penetrate mine. I'm the first to look away.

'If this were a show, I'd probably be the next victim.' I say it half-jokingly, but it's met with a serious expression.

'Why do you think you weren't one of Tom's victims? Why has he spared you?'

303

'You make it sound like some ritualistic sacrificial killing I managed to escape from!'

'Poor wording. But if you say Phoebe was his first victim, then seven years later, Katie – why did he stop?'

'He said they were accidents – that he didn't intend to kill them. They both wronged him – belittled him – and he lost his temper. Lost control. I guess I've never caused him to behave in that way.' I shrug and put the drinks down on the table before I sit. 'Then we had Poppy. She means the world to him. He's always craved a happy family unit. I don't think he had that himself when he was growing up – although he's never told me much about his childhood. He always somehow turned it around and asked me about mine instead. He thought it was better just the two of us. He didn't invite any of his family to our wedding.'

'That seems strange,' Imogen says, her eyes narrowing. 'Why?'

'Because I didn't have any and he didn't want me to feel bad. He kept saying it was our day anyway, that we didn't need anyone else. He maintained that over the years – the fact we had each other, so outside interference was never welcomed. Tom was all I needed. I was all he needed.'

But now I know this to be a lie.

I wasn't enough. Tom had someone else.

I battle with my conscience over whether to mention this to Imogen now. For some reason, I want to keep it to myself. It's not relevant to the investigation.

Not unless he's murdered her.

My heart slams against my ribcage.

Why hasn't this crossed my mind before now?

He was late back on the first Monday, when this all began, then he disappeared for the entire day on Tuesday. He borrowed a car from Oscar's garage. To remain untraceable on CCTV and avoid his number plate being recognised? If he were merely visiting his lover, why the need to have a different vehicle? As far as I'm aware, he's never done that before.

I sense the weight of Imogen's gaze.

'What are you thinking, Beth?'

'I'm thinking there could be another reason I've been targeted.'

'Oh? What?'

'When you told me Tom didn't go to work on the Tuesday, I did a little bit of digging.'

Imogen's sculpted eyebrows raise. 'Go on,' she says, leaning forwards.

'I spoke with the bank, as you did, and his boss, Alexander, said that if he was going to confide in anyone, it would be Jimmy, his colleague. He was away the day I visited, so I spoke with him on Friday, and he was convinced that Tom was having an affair.' Telling her feels right.

'That's interesting,' Imogen says, her sharp elbows resting on the table, her chin on her clenched fists. 'If that's true, it might explain the missing day we haven't been able to account for in the timeline. We know he borrowed a car and we've been scouring hours of CCTV footage to figure out where he went after he drove it to London . . .'

My heart drops. Imogen has just confirmed Tom *did* go to London on Tuesday. It seems likely Jimmy was right, then. Suddenly, things begin to make sense.

'It might account for why I haven't been the next victim,' I say, quietly. I'm almost afraid of what reaction I'll get.

Imogen slams back in her chair, letting out a long stream of air. She stands abruptly, sending the chair sliding back on the limestone-tiled floor.

'Did Jimmy give you a name?' She's jabbing at the keys on her mobile as she speaks.

'No, he promised me he didn't know who she was, only that he reckoned he'd been seeing her for a long time. Years, he said. But I can't believe that. Tom hated cheaters; he'd never do it to me.'

'Maybe he didn't class it as cheating.'

'Having sex with someone other than his wife? I'm pretty sure that's cheating.'

'And I'm pretty sure he might see it differently if he wasn't actually in a relationship with her.'

'So, just because it's only sex, that doesn't count as infidelity?'

'It's what some men, and women, believe, yes. It helps them carry on doing it without feeling guilty. They justify it because they aren't emotionally involved.' She's walking into the hallway now.

'You're going? I thought you were meant to be talking to me about the gallows?' I'm at her heels, dangerously close to physically dragging her back into the kitchen. I don't feel at all confident anything will be done about the threat to me if she leaves.

'Sorry, Beth, something important has come up. I'll catch up with you later.'

As she rushes to the front door, I catch what she says to whoever she's just dialled.

'I think we've had a breakthrough,' she says, before

opening the door and running up the path towards her car.

What did I say to invoke this reaction from her?

All I can assume is that what I've just told her now has enabled her to make a link to another case.

Has there been a third murder?

Chapter 77

BETH

Now

The visit from Imogen Cooper was much quicker than anticipated, which means I've enough time to pop into the café. I keep my head down when I leave the house as the reporters shout their questions. Mostly they're the same questions as earlier. Apart from one.

'Who do you think has it in for you, Beth?' a male voice calls.

So they *do* know about the gallows. I cast my eyes upwards as I pass the neighbouring properties. I can't imagine any of the occupants have spoken willingly to this mob. And then a thought occurs to me.

What if it was one of *them*? One of the journalists themselves?

Some of them have practically been camping out – one of them would've seen the culprit, surely. Maybe the reason they're not coming forward is because they're covering up for one of their own.

'Didn't you see who did it?' I shout. 'Or was it one of you?'

I'm met with a stony silence, which is a surprise. Maybe my accusation has hit a nerve. None of them offer any information, so I turn on my heel and carry on. They've lost interest by the time I dive inside the café.

'Ah, Beth. How are you doing?' Shirley Irish asks. 'I haven't seen you for days.' She's got a bulging paper bag in her hands, which will be filled with her usual order of cookies.

'I've been better,' I say. No point trying to pretend otherwise at this point.

'I don't like to poke my nose in, but I was thinking,' she says. I hold my breath for what's to come. 'I don't think, given the circumstances, that it would be wise to run your book club, do you?'

This isn't what I was expecting her to say, and I'm relieved to the point I almost laugh. 'Er . . . no. You're quite right, it wouldn't. If I'm honest, I'd forgotten about it! You know, I've had such a lot on my mind. But rest assured, it's cancelled,' I say with feeling.

'Good, good,' she says. I assume she's finished now she's got this off her chest, but her face becomes even more serious. 'I keep hearing terrible updates,' she says, her eyes widening. 'Awful business with Tom . . .' She trails off, but I get the impression she wants to add, 'How could you not have known?' I'm scared, now that I've told Adam and given a fuller account to the detectives, that my knowledge of Tom's actions will become public. And what will everyone think of me then?

I may have to rethink my strategy.

'It's devastating, Shirley. I'm trying to do all I can to help the police,' I say. Tears prick the back of my eyes. I blink them away, but Shirley notices them.

'Come now, love.' She puts her free hand on my shoulder and squeezes it. 'I'm sure everyone in Lower Tew knows it's nothing to do with you. None of this is your fault. We don't always know everything about a person, do we? It's shocking what some people hide.'

I can't look her in the eye.

'Thank you – I appreciate that. Right, best get on,' I say as I move away. I don't turn back until I hear the door close. An icy-cold sensation shoots up my spine. Why did it feel as though she'd been looking right into my soul?

'Ah, Beth – it's you!' Lucy's sing-song voice brings a smile to my face.

'Hi, Lucy. I'm like one of the lost sheep, aren't I?'

'I hope you don't mind, but I drafted in some free help.' Lucy puts her arm out towards a teenage girl with a punk hairstyle and a dozen or so face piercings. 'This is Emmy. She's doing some work experience and we thought this was the perfect opportunity. She's my cousin,' she adds, by way of explanation. I'm pleased Lucy has some help – I've neglected her and Poppy's Place badly.

'Brilliant!' I reach forwards to shake Emmy's hand. 'Glad to meet you, Emmy. How are you finding it so far?'

'S'good.' She gives what I think is a smile, but it's difficult to tell due to the line of small silver balls surrounding her lips. Lucy instructs her to clear a table, and once she's ambled off, explains to me how having

310

her to tidy up is helpful, despite her not being the most enthusiastic worker.

'Honestly, whatever makes your life easier is fine by me,' I say.

'Any updates?'

'Apart from a threatening "gift" left in my front garden last night, no.'

'Christ, Beth. What was it?'

'Oh, you know – just a gallows with a fake body hanging from it.'

Lucy's face pales. 'You're joking! That's so scary.'

'Unfortunately, my sense of humour is in dramatic decline. So . . . no – I'm not joking. We're going to stay at a friend's for a few nights – or maybe a bit longer – until this blows over.' I don't feel it's wise to mention that Adam is that friend for now.

'And you think it *will*?'

Lucy's negativity crushes me. It's what I've already been thinking – that there's no end in sight for this – but hearing her question it feels like a stab to the heart.

'God, I hope so. We can't go on like this, can we? I'd have to move away.'

'Don't do that, Beth. I love this job.' She eyes me cautiously, probably wondering if she should start looking for another position, but then she adds, 'Oh, God that sounds so selfish of me. I'm sorry. Thinking about myself again.' She lowers her eyes.

'You've every right to think of yourself, Lucy. But don't worry, your job here is safe. Even if we were to leave, I'd keep Poppy's Place going. You're practically running the whole show anyway – I'm sure you could manage it for me.'

'Thanks. But don't go. Don't be run out of this place by a few haters.'

'I'm surprised you don't want me gone – especially given that Tom dragged Oscar into his . . . mess. And maybe you wouldn't feel as compassionate if he'd been accused of murdering one of your family members, would you?'

Lucy doesn't answer.

I don't blame her.

To lighten the mood, I ask if I can do anything while I'm there. Lucy suggests I check the kiln and make sure the trays are clean. It feels a bit weird to take instruction from her, but she really has been the boss lately. I'm glad to be of some assistance, and even more glad to be out at the back, away from the public glare of accusation.

I potter about, my mind wandering from one thing to another: why Imogen ran off so quickly after I mentioned Tom's affair; who the third victim, if there is one, is; how to manage the developing situation with Adam; how to keep up the façade, or whether I should come clean right away. It's been relatively easy up until now to keep the truth from spilling out. But it won't last. I can't stay quiet indefinitely.

Chapter 78

BETH

Now

Imogen Cooper's phone went straight to voicemail several times during the day, so I'm surprised to see her name pop up on my mobile now – it gives my heart a jolt. It's probably about the third victim. Am I ready to hear what she has to say? Will *she* be ready to hear what *I* have been reluctant to share?

'Hi Imogen,' I say. 'I've been trying to contact you.'

'Been tied up.'

She doesn't elaborate, and the line goes quiet. Odd – she was the one to call me. I stay silent, waiting for her to speak again. I want to know what's going on, but I'm hesitant to ask. I wait out the silence.

'Where are you right now?' Imogen asks. She sounds tired – her voice is strained.

'I'm just at home, packing a bag ready to stay at Adam's for the next few days. Why?' My mouth goes dry. I wonder if I'm still under some suspicion. Did Imogen believe me? My reasons for not telling her sooner about Tom's confession? She could be gathering evidence of *my* involvement, or getting ready to arrest me for perverting the course of justice. I only have her word that what I divulged wouldn't be used against me. If they've found a third victim, she might easily retract that. My pulse quickens. I look out of the bedroom window, half expecting to see police cars screeching to a halt outside.

'I'm on my way to you,' Imogen says, then hangs up.

Am I right? Could she be on her way to arrest me? Serial killer couples have been known before – might the detectives be thinking that Tom and I are the new Fred and Rose West?

I pace the room as my thoughts spiral.

Relax. They can't have any proof of wrongdoing by me.

Apart from the fact I knew he'd done his victims harm and I didn't tell anyone. That's clearly bad enough.

Do they think I know the most recent victim? Perhaps that's why Imogen is coming here.

With a thumping heart, I realise someone might have been killed while Tom's been in custody. In which case, will they think it's me?

No, of course they won't.

I have an alibi for the last two weeks – I've been seen every day by someone, and there's a mob of reporters documenting my every move. Well, almost every move. I must calm down. I haven't done anything.

I stuff a few more items into my holdall, then go into Poppy's room to pack her things. She's happily playing. She's so independent; I love that about her. She's content with her own company. A thought creeps into my mind.

Tom is a killer. Do these tendencies run in families? Will Poppy have inherited the genes that could make her a killer too?

No.

She hasn't experienced trauma, or abuse, or any of the factors attributed to people who kill later in life. With my help, she can get over the loss of her father. I didn't have a loving, caring mother to make up for my dad walking out and abandoning me, but she has. I will make this right – she'll have a secure, loving upbringing and she'll be a well-adjusted, emotionally stable adult. I'm determined she will.

The banging at the door makes me jump.

'Just stay there and play for a bit, Poppy. I'll be back in a minute to help you pack some toys.'

She doesn't look up from her animals, all lined up in size order, but she says brightly, 'Okay, Mummy.'

I rush down the stairs, almost forgetting to duck under the wooden beam in my haste – knocking myself out now would be bad timing. Although missing all this drama might have its advantages. I swallow hard and take some deep, steadying breaths before I greet Imogen. I catch a glimpse of flashing cameras before I close the door quickly behind her.

'What's the matter?' I ask immediately.

'Why don't we take a seat?' Imogen walks directly into the kitchen. I feel a twinge of annoyance that, yet again, she doesn't wait to be asked.

'I need to check on Poppy first.' I force myself to walk calmly back up the stairs. I know I don't really need to look in on her again, but I'm being a coward. Poppy is playing with her café set and kitchen now, making food for each of her animals. She'll be fine upstairs on her own for a little while longer.

'Right – I have some news,' Imogen says as I return.

I nod, momentarily mute. Anxious.

'When you mentioned Tom's suspected affair earlier, a few things slotted into place. Two weeks ago, on Wednesday, a body was found in a flat in central London. From the post-mortem it was concluded the victim had been killed sometime between four and ten p.m. two days previously.'

'Monday,' I whisper.

'Yes. The Monday Tom was late home.'

'H– how did she die?'

'Strangulation.' Imogen delivers this information abruptly, with no attempt to soften the blow. 'Crime scene investigators collected various samples. We'll be able to see if any DNA matches with Tom's.'

'That's good,' I manage. My whole body feels weak; tiredness is swooping in to steal what little energy I had left.

'It is, and it isn't,' she says, her brow knitting together. 'The victim was a sex worker.'

I shake my head. A sex worker? Why on earth do they think Tom killed her? I remember hearing the news about it now – and how it had made me glad to be out of London and in safety in Lower Tew. Yet here I've been all this time, living with a murderer.

'And you think Tom killed her?'

'I do, yes. The location is close to Tom's workplace, so he'd be able to visit her in lunchbreaks. Or, if he left earlier than he told you, after work too. CCTV in the surrounding area will be able to confirm. And from the bank statements, we think we can link a regular payment to the victim.'

Those missing bank statements from the kitchen drawer. I'd always assumed Tom didn't use the account, so I'd never checked them. 'So that's what you meant,' I say. 'When you said you thought Tom wouldn't see it as an affair. If it was just sex and he wasn't emotionally involved.'

'Yes. And the fact he'd been seeing a sex worker fits with the profile.'

'The profile?'

'The profile of the type of killer we think Tom is,' Imogen says. Her eyes soften. It's almost as though in this moment she feels sorry for me.

She shouldn't.

'He'll be charged with this murder, too I assume. That's definitely enough evidence to be convicted then, isn't it?'

'Well, that's where it's not as cut and dried as one might hope. As I say, the victim was a sex worker and that brings its own challenges. Not least the amount of DNA retrieved from the scene. It won't just be Tom's. And if he was careful, her body itself might not provide conclusive evidence that he was the perpetrator.'

'Oh, God. So back to square one, really, then. All this circumstantial evidence but nothing a good lawyer wouldn't be able to explain away. He's a vile, cheating husband, but not necessarily a killer.' Hearing these words as they leave my mouth shocks me – something about putting Tom's actions in a nutshell like this leaves me cold.

'I'm afraid you're right. We still have a strong case – there's a *lot* of circumstantial evidence stacking up. I'd rather have conclusive proof, though. Make it watertight. Your husband shouldn't be allowed out of prison for the rest of his life.'

317

Strangely, I still have the urge to defend Tom. 'But he was seeing someone for sex, and I imagine it was to act out the fantasies I was never keen on – so that he wouldn't hurt me. He was trying to protect me and Poppy from himself.'

'Maybe, yes. It's possibly why he went so long without committing another offence. But, ultimately, it seems his urge to kill became too great. He lost control.'

'He only ever lost control when he felt let down, though. Phoebe and Katie made him feel worthless. And Tom said their deaths were spur of the moment accidents. Strangulation doesn't strike me as accidental. Why would he kill this woman if he was only seeing her for his sexual fantasies?'

'I think he's the only one who can answer that now.'

A thought catches me. 'Could it have been a sex game gone wrong?'

'It's a possibility.' Imogen doesn't add anything. She probably knows more from the post-mortem than she's letting on.

Part of me is shocked at hearing Tom had been paying for sex, but the other part feels a pang of guilt. I don't know whether to count this as an affair. I'd believed he was cheating on me, so I acted out of anger. I've betrayed his trust and led the detectives to more incriminating evidence. And it seems he was doing it out of love for his family instead. To keep himself from hurting me.

Now, though, there's only one way to go. I've come this far – I need to give Imogen everything. I take a deep breath.

'I think I know where Katie Williams' remains might be,' I say.

Chapter 79

TOM

Now

Nerves consume me.

They've linked me to Natalia. I knew her body would be found, but was confident they wouldn't look at me for it.

I'd left her flat and gone home afterwards, assuming no one would find her before I returned the following day to properly clear up. At the time, I'd been more concerned about ensuring the arrangement she'd made with her friend to meet the following day wouldn't go ahead – I'd used her finger to access her phone and sent a message to Mandy cancelling their shopping trip. Natalia had told me about her day off before our session.

Having been questioned about Katie's presumed murder that evening, it was a huge risk to go back – but I couldn't chance leaving the scene as I had. Couldn't leave *her* as I had.

I'd planned to dispose of her body as I had Katie's. I'd gone to see Oscar at his garage – I gave him some story about my car having a flat battery and needing one ASAP to get to work. He let me borrow a car that was due to go to auction. I was going to bundle her into the boot and drive somewhere remote, but once I got to her place, I didn't fancy my chances. It was daytime in a busy London borough – there were people everywhere. So I'd bottled it. It's not as easy to get away with things in this digital world. There's CCTV everywhere, and people with mobile phones posting anything that looks remotely unusual to social media. It's not like it was back when I'd killed Phoebe, or even Katie. Life is more complicated now.

Or maybe I'm not as daring. After all, I've a family to consider.

Going through my actions for the millionth time, I conclude there should be nothing to say categorically that I'd been the one to *kill* Natalia. Any DNA evidence only confirms I've been there, at her flat – touched her, had sex with her – just like the half a dozen or so other men she'd had that day. Of course, if the police manage to track these other men down, they may well have alibis for the time of death, which would leave just me. But I'll bet they won't easily trace them – the draw of seeing Natalia was that she wasn't your standard sex worker. It was all very private – she didn't flout her wares, didn't advertise what she did – it was through word of mouth only. No details, nothing traceable. Unless she told someone, like her friend, about the men she had visit her, no one would know. She managed herself; didn't have someone looking out for her.

Her mistake.

But she did scratch my neck.

The recollection makes my pulse rise.

No. I cleaned her body, scraped her nails – I'm sure.

Breathe.

I should try and stay calm. Maxwell will be able to get me off the hook with this one easily enough. Everything is explainable.

Of course, now I think about it, I wasn't so careful with Katie. I suppose the adrenaline, the sexual gratification I experienced when killing her, took over my senses. I think I'd probably call it a crime of passion.

I hadn't been thinking as clearly when I disposed of her. I hadn't worn gloves; I hadn't bleached her body. But it would be badly decomposed by now – possibly only a skeleton – so that won't matter. What I buried with her, on the other hand? That will be crucial evidence; might tip the balance towards a guilty verdict. That was *my* mistake. Among others.

The knot in my gut suddenly intensifies.

Beth has supposedly given the detectives evidence to help their case against me. She's handed over the sweatshirt in an attempt to link me to Phoebe's death.

What if she leads them to Katie's body?

Breathing slowly, I try and keep in control of my emotions. I didn't outright tell her where I'd buried Katie, although from what I did say, it wouldn't take much to figure out. But she's never been to the location, so even if she does betray me, they might not find it. I hold onto the hope that Beth still has love for the father of her child. That she wouldn't put our family life, our future happiness – Poppy's security – in jeopardy.

321

If she does talk to them about it, and if they do find Katie – and prove I killed her – I *will* make sure Beth pays for her betrayal. I'm not letting her have a future with my daughter if I can't.

Chapter 80

BETH

Now

'I'm sorry, *what*?'

The three words cut through me – Imogen speaks them with disbelief and exasperation. Her lips purse together tightly and her eyes narrow as they lock with mine. She's not as happy about this information as I'd hoped. I thought the news of a possible location for Katie's remains would outweigh her anger towards me not having disclosed this at the same time as everything else. I'd been holding my suspicion back, partly because it was only a hunch, but partly out of fear. Imogen's expression makes me realise that was a huge mistake.

I've judged this badly.

'I was scared, before, to say anything. I'd already given you the sweatshirt – if Tom got off, he'd come back and kill me for going against him,' I say in a garbled rush.

'No, Beth. You were scared you'd be hauled in and

charged too, weren't you? And let me guess – you thought you'd keep the whereabouts of Katie Williams' body from us because you figured by holding it in reserve you could make a deal so you would get off lightly.'

Imogen's revulsion is plain to see. It's too much for me to bear: the emotions of these past weeks pour out of me. I try to stifle my sobs; I don't want Poppy to hear me and be scared. 'I – I . . . I'm sorry. I wasn't sure enough . . .' I get up and tear off a piece of kitchen roll to blow my nose, and then I pour a glass of water, taking sips to calm myself down. 'Imogen, I swear I only want to help. You're right, I did hold back – because I'm only going on something Tom told me and he wasn't specific. I didn't want to send you off on some wild goose chase.'

'But you're telling me now. The goose chase could be the same, so why bother? Guilty conscience?'

'Tom manipulated me for so long, I suppose I've become expert at keeping my mouth shut. This whole thing has been my worst nightmare, Imogen. For a while after finding out, I was afraid of what he'd do to me if I stepped out of line. Can you imagine being told by your husband – the father of your child – that he killed *two* women prior to meeting you? I was so shocked that for a while I blocked it out. And then shock gave way to fear.'

'I understand the fear, Beth – trust me on that one. But you should've disclosed everything that you knew when you told me about the sweatshirt. *That* was the time to tell me. That was your opportunity to make sure he doesn't ever come back to hurt you. Didn't you see that?' Imogen's hands slam down repeatedly on the table as she speaks. I blink at each slapping noise.

'I saw my life falling apart,' I say, my voice thick with

324

tears. 'I saw Poppy's future in ruins, with abandonment issues just like I had, if I was taken from her too. I panicked! And the thought he could still be released and come back here to make my life a living hell – or worse, kill me – well, it made me hold back. I'm so very sorry I didn't tell you everything, I really am.'

'You're going to have to come in and be questioned and give a new statement, Beth.'

'Okay,' I say. Fresh tears blur my vision. 'Will I be charged with anything?'

Poppy runs into the kitchen and flings herself at me. 'When is Daddy coming home?' Her big, round blue eyes are glistening as she looks up to me. I catch Imogen's expression out of the corner of my eye; she's watching this moment intently.

'A little while yet, Poppy.' I try and hide my tear-streaked face.

'You stay with me, Mummy, won't you? You won't go away.'

I glance at Imogen and see her stiff posture give a little.

'I'll always be here for you, my little Poppy poppet.' I give her a hug, then ask her to go and play in the lounge for a moment and that I'll join her in a minute.

Imogen waits for Poppy to toddle back off before speaking again.

'Right, Beth. You'd best tell me where you think Katie is.'

325

Chapter 81

BETH

Now

Adam knocks on the door at dead-on six.

It takes a few minutes to load his car, then half an hour to fill him in on the day's developments. We sit in the car in silence once we get to his place, Poppy and Jess jabbering away in their car seats behind us. I gather from this that he's still in shock about me knowing, or at least thinking I know, about the location of a murder victim's body. My husband's victim. His second of a suspected three.

That we know of.

Imogen had been keen to point out that if Tom is capable of three murders, there's no telling if there have been more. He chose to tell me about the two 'accidents', she had said, probably because I'd forced his hand by finding Katie's email account on his iPad. I know now that she's right. Tom wouldn't have ever confided in me if I hadn't rocked the boat. If I hadn't confronted him with what I'd found and pushed him into a corner.

To have killed people and – up until now – got away with it, shows he's good at lying. Good at covering his tracks and getting on with a normal family life. He manipulated me. Everyone. If it hadn't come to light now, when would it have done? Next year? Five years? When it was too late to start my life over? When it completely ruined Poppy's too?

I was stupid to have kept my suspicions about Katie's body from the detectives. It's a move that could cost me a lot. But I hope Imogen will keep her original promise; that the mitigating factors still stand. She strongly hinted that they'd protect me and Poppy, as long as I gave them everything to make sure Tom could be put away for life.

So, if she gets what she's looking for, then I imagine it'll go in my favour.

I am praying she does. Until I get confirmation, I won't be able to settle. If I'm wrong about where Tom took Katie's body, and if the other circumstantial evidence isn't enough to convict him for life, then all this will have been for nothing.

Adam's hand is on my thigh. Its heat is penetrating to my skin. I turn my head to look into his eyes. 'Are you sure about us staying for—'

'I'm completely sure,' he cuts in. 'I'm sorry. This is all a lot to take in, that's all. I'll be fine once we're inside.' He turns his attention to his house, and I see him look up and down the road. He's checking who's around – checking who might see me and Poppy go inside with bags.

'If you're this worried about what people will say, Adam . . .'

'I'm not. Not really. Old habits, I guess.' His face relaxes into a wide grin. 'Come on then – let's get film night on the go. I do hope you've remembered those snacks, Beth!'

It's nine thirty when I get the call.

'They've found her.'

My world tilts on its axis. I don't have the words to respond.

Will this body be the evidence that finally reveals the truth about my husband and ensures he spends the rest of his life in prison?

Chapter 82

TOM

Eight years ago

The wind cuts across the garden, biting at my face. But I don't feel the cold. Each one of my four million sweat glands is working in overdrive – every inch of my skin is slick with salty liquid. I can taste it as it drips onto my lips, and I unconsciously lick it away as I bump the suitcase over the uneven ground.

Before reaching this final destination – the location that is to become Katie's burial ground – I'd already dragged the fucking suitcase for almost a mile to get to my flat. Had I been able to go the direct route, I'd have shaved half a mile off. But I couldn't risk the busier parts of town – or any CCTV cameras. I had my backstory ready if required – I was simply transporting Katie's suitcase to mine, where she was staying the night prior to her flight to India – but I didn't want to be observed during this critical moment. I couldn't have people recalling seeing some sweaty bloke wheeling a heavy suitcase behind him. Too much chance of a link being made.

I'd gone to my place because I needed to be in my own surroundings to figure out the next part of the plan. I went in the back entrance and took the lift; there was no way I'd have managed to get her up the stairs without someone coming to see what the noise was. As it happened, my luck was in – no sign of Paul from the ground floor or Maxine and Joy from the second.

I'd been able to recover for an hour, and in that time I'd arranged a hire car. While that wasn't without further risk of leaving a trail, the hope was no one would ever find her, so my actions wouldn't come under scrutiny. If it came to it, I could say I'd hired it to take Katie to the airport anyway. In fact, I'll probably drive it to City Airport afterwards to maintain my story. I figure the car will be professionally valeted on its return, so any evidence of the suitcase will be wiped clean.

As I finally reach the little patch of woodland accessed from the back of my mother's place, I stop to take a breather. The house is deserted; Mother has been in a home for the past two years. Not from old age – she's only fifty – but because of dementia. Early onset, they'd said. I'm more inclined to think it's from the stress of all the lies she held inside. Maybe, after all this, I'll share the same fate.

Perhaps it's best. For her at least.

I haven't the strength to lift the suitcase over the fence, so I pull some of the wooden panels away instead. I go first, then I turn around to drag the suitcase through. I'll replace the panelling when I'm done so it doesn't draw attention to the location. With my energy at its lowest now, I don't go far into the woods. Just far enough that none of the neighbours will see me, or any suspicious mound of earth. As far as I'm aware, this land isn't used by the public. It's not an area where walkers frequent, so I think it's a relatively safe place to bury her.

Getting her inside the suitcase was problematic – it's as well she's petite, or I may have had to dismember her. That would've been a messy process and one I wouldn't have relished. I prefer to think of her as whole – her beauty intact. It was like packing away a large marionette. I'd considered having sex with her one last time before her body cooled, but I realised as I positioned her ready for me to enter that I wasn't aroused enough by her lifeless body. There was no excitement in seeing her waxy face, her inert limbs. No thrashing, no bucking. No need for control.

No. I enjoyed the fight and I enjoyed watching her die – but once that was done, she was redundant. Her body was a shell. I had no interest in her.

Of course, I loved her when she was alive. Obsessed over her. Wanted her to myself. That's why she was special. It's why I'd asked her to marry me. I'm not sure, exactly, why I gave her my mother's engagement ring – a unique single diamond-set ring made especially for her by my paternal grandfather. There was no inscription, just two initials and hallmarks. I hadn't told Katie it was my mother's, for some reason – I thought perhaps she might find it too much. I hadn't wanted to give her a reason to hesitate. But she seemed delighted to have an antique ring. She'd said she felt it had a story: a proper history.

Given my upbringing – how my mother had humiliated me, let my father abuse me and done nothing to stop him

– you'd think it would be too much to bear to see this symbol of apparent love on my fiancée's finger. But for whatever reason, I want Katie to have it. I've left it on her finger to remember me by, in whatever afterlife awaits her now.

It's only when I finish the job – stumble away, exhausted – that I realise I left Katie's mobile phone in the suitcase. *Dammit*. I was going to destroy it and leave it at the airport so that if someone was to report her missing – which they shouldn't do, bearing in mind how I've planned things – the last place it pinged would've been there. Not the back of my mother's house.

I have nothing left – all my energy, physical and emotional, is depleted. I simply couldn't dig the suitcase back up now to retrieve it. It's getting light, too.

No, it's fine. If I keep my head, send the emails to her father and friends as I plan to, there will be no reason for them to search for her.

No one will ever find her here.

Chapter 83

BETH

Now

Maxwell's call gives me the relief I so desperately need.

'It's done, Adam,' I say, once I hang up.

'They found her?'

'Yes. With what I told them and the equipment they have, they detected variations in the ground's surface in only three areas. Katie Williams was found on the second attempt.' My hand, holding the mobile, drops in my lap – every ounce of energy seems to have just been zapped from me. 'It's over.' I slump back into the sofa. My entire body feels like it's wilting.

'It's not though, is it?' Adam says, gently. 'I don't mean to sound negative, Beth. But they still have to link him to the body – it still has to be enough for a jury to return a guilty verdict at his trial.'

His trial.

Before he hung up, Maxwell said the date had been

set. Four months from now. I'm dreading it and want *that* over too as soon as possible. I need to move on. I know Adam's right – of course it's not over until then. But this part is. *My* part in it is done.

'Maxwell said that Imogen had sounded optimistic there's enough evidence to secure a conviction,' I say. 'Not good news for him and Tom, obviously. He sounded pretty devastated. He says they think they have vital forensic evidence from the crime scene as well as from Katie's remains and the burial ground. Let's face it, Tom took her to the back of his old family home. That's pretty damning; it all ties in.'

'I hope you're right,' Adam says. 'I want this to be over for you and Poppy, I really do. If everyone realises you've done what you can to help, and that you were lucky not to be one of his victims, then they should leave you alone – the bloody journalists and the idiots who are targeting you.'

I manage a smile and shift up the sofa to be closer to him. His arm drapes around me and he pulls me in to him. It's the first time we've allowed ourselves to be close like this. We sit in silence and I relish the warmth of his body.

'Oh, I meant to say.' Adam pulls away and faces me. 'I emailed the photo I took of that car to the police and they got back to me earlier to say they've traced the owner.'

'Good. And what are they going to do about it? I hope they charge him with—'

'It wasn't a him.'

'It was a bloke who spat at me!'

'Yes, but the car wasn't registered to him. The sergeant

334

I spoke to said he couldn't divulge any more to me as it was an ongoing investigation, but they did ask me to make sure you called them "at your earliest convenience".'

'Hmmm. Okay, then. Sounds intriguing.'

'Maybe they are also to blame for the gallows.'

'I hope so, then that can be cleared up too.'

'Things are looking up, finally.' Adam jumps up and heads towards the kitchen. 'I feel we should celebrate,' he calls.

I want to shout after him; remind him that he didn't think it was over yet – that it's too premature for celebration. But he appears as relieved as I am that I've told Imogen all that I know now, and I don't want to spoil the moment. Plus, I could really do with a drink.

'Here you go,' he says, handing me a champagne flute. 'It's not champers yet – it's just Prosecco. We'll save the good stuff for the final verdict.'

'Thanks, Adam. I really appreciate your support.'

'It's my pleasure. Thank you, too. Despite the stress and . . . well, *weirdness*, I'm so glad you came into my life.'

We clink glasses and settle back on the sofa again. 'You calling *me* weird?'

He doesn't give a comeback. Instead, without uttering a word, he takes my glass from my hand and puts it, together with his, on the table. Then, with no hesitation, he leans in and kisses me. Tiny electric shocks fire through me. I'm surprised at his swift move. Maybe it's the certainty that Tom will be going to prison that's allowed him to let go. Enabled him to let us take our friendship that one step further. All I know is it feels right.

We don't break away from each other until Poppy and

Jess run into the room. I'm not sure if Poppy caught us in the act, but she gives me a cautious look.

'When is it picnic time?' Jess asks.

Adam checks his watch. 'Ooh, right about . . . now!' And he leaps up and away from me and pretends to chase them. As I listen to their excited squeals, I realise I might have got away with the kiss, but I will still have to tell Poppy soon. There's no getting away from it.

Her father is not going to be part of her future, and I need to let her know in a way that she'll understand. She can't think he's abandoned her.

Chapter 84

BETH

Now

The smell of freshly baked muffins fills my cottage and I breathe it in greedily. I've missed this. While it's been wonderful to spend three days at Adam's – *with* Adam – I am happy back here in my kitchen doing what I do best.

Lucy has managed the café well in my absence. She even thought to increase the order from my usual suppliers so that my lack of baking didn't impact the business. She's been a great asset, and reading between the lines of her texts, she's actually quite enjoyed me not being there. This is unsurprising, given the drama surrounding me.

There's a heavy knock on the front door. I instantly feel fear; I've become conditioned, like Pavlov's dogs. I rinse my hands and cautiously check who it is.

It's Imogen. My heart falters.

'Hi, Imogen. Is everything okay?'

'Morning, Beth. I wanted to update you.' She walks in, and as usual, walks right through to the kitchen.

'Been baking?' she asks as she sits down.

'Yes, I needed to get some done for the café.'

I suck in a lungful of air and hold it, waiting for what I hope is good news. I'm not prepared for anything bad.

'You know the trial is set for August?'

'Yes, Maxwell informed me.'

'You'll inevitably be called to testify for the prosecution. Are you okay with that?'

'I'll have to be.'

'Good. Right, anyway – the evidence is strong, thanks to your information.'

Oh, shit. Is this visit to finally tell me I'm going to be charged with perverting the course of justice or something like that? Panic swells inside me. *Please, not now.* My hands tremble – I keep them occupied by transferring cooled muffins to boxes as I wait for her to continue.

'Has everything been all right since you've been back here? Any trouble with the mob?' Imogen says, gesturing towards the front of the house.

'I only got back this morning, but no one was outside when I arrived. Strange, actually, not having to bow my head and push through. I wonder how long the peace will last?'

'Until the trial, probably,' Imogen says, flippantly.

'I'll look forward to that then.' I attempt humour, but it falls flat. Imogen looks at me, holding my gaze with her intense steel-grey eyes. I suspect this chit-chat is a precursor to her real reason for being here. I wish she'd come right out and say it – tell me I'm being charged. I'm waiting for the inevitable line: 'Bethany Hardcastle, I'm

338

arresting you for failure to provide evidence of which you were in possession . . . You do not have to say anything . . .'
I faff about with the used baking trays, filling the sink with hot water to soak them.

'You seem a bit nervous, Beth,' she says.

'My nerves are constantly shredded. Have been for weeks. Hardly surprising, really, is it? I was scared of coming home this morning to find I'd been left further "gifts". Thank God there weren't any,' I say.

'Good. One of my updates was about that, actually.'

'Oh? I thought local police were dealing with it?'

'They were, but as it turns out, it's linked to our investigation.'

I sit down opposite Imogen ready to hear what's coming. 'So not just some random who wanted to scare me?'

'We searched CCTV footage. A Jeep with a trailer was picked up close to here and it fitted with the timeframe of you hearing a commotion in your garden. The officers were able to see the trailer had something in it covered in tarp on the way here, but it was empty on the way back, so it seemed a good bet that whoever was in the Jeep was the culprit.'

'And it links to the investigation how?'

'The registered owner of the vehicle was interviewed. It transpired that he was not alone in carrying out this act – his sister had asked him to help her.'

My brow knits together; this is so confusing. I'm about to say so, but Imogen continues.

'The sister was a good friend of Natalia's, the woman found murdered in her London flat.'

I let this sink in for a moment. 'How on earth would

she have known it was Tom who'd killed her? Or where I lived?'

'She told us she'd made plans with Natalia but she'd had a last-minute text cancelling. She didn't think too much of it, but she went around early Wednesday to check on her as she was aware of her line of work. She was the one who found her.'

'That still doesn't explain—'

'Natalia had told the friend about one of her clients. Mentioned details about his visits and apparently, in the days prior to her murder, Natalia had confided that she was becoming afraid of him and his taste for strangling her.'

My heart feels as though someone is crushing it.

'She saw the news about Tom being charged with Katie's murder and assumed he was the same person Natalia had told her about?' I ask.

'Yep. At the time of Natalia's death, she'd reported her concerns about this man and how Natalia had been afraid of him, but she'd had nothing solid. Couldn't even remember a name, until she saw the news and it sparked her memory. She didn't think it was enough to go on – she'd no proof, just a hunch, having never even seen him before his arrest. But she did see you, and she could get at you, even if she couldn't get at Tom.'

'Bloody journalists.'

'Once she knew your location, she felt she needed to do something to show you that she blamed *you* for her friend's death. She was angry – she needed to hit out at someone.'

I'm about to attempt the 'how is it my fault?' argument, but I realise it's futile. It *is* my fault. Had I informed the police of my husband's confession to me, Natalia's death would've been avoided.

'What'll happen to her?'

'Depends whether you want to bring charges.'

'No,' I say quickly. 'I don't. I understand her need to lash out. I deserve it.'

A solemn silence falls.

It's a while before Imogen speaks again.

'I need to ask, Beth – is there anything else you haven't told me? Any bit of Tom's past that might now ring alarm bells?'

'I don't think so. Why, do you believe he's killed others?'

'Do *you*?'

The question throws me. I shake my head. 'No . . . I – I . . .' How can I answer that? I hadn't been aware of Katie and Phoebe until last year. And Natalia's death was certainly not something I'd seen coming. 'Tom's behaviour, up until the night he was late home and lied the next day, hasn't ever given me cause for concern, really. Not that I can remember.' I add the last bit, just in case.

'Okay, Beth.' Imogen gets up. 'I'll leave you to your baking. I just wanted to give you the news.'

'Thank you.' Then I remember Adam saying they'd traced the car owner from the spitting incident. 'It didn't turn out to be the same person, then? The bloke who spat at me and the ones who left the gallows?'

'I guess not, but I'm afraid I don't know the details – I left that one to the local force. You need to call Banbury station.'

'Yes. I should've already called them – I've just not got around to it,' I say, as I walk with Imogen to the front door.

341

It's a huge relief she only came here to update me, not to arrest me.

Have I got away with that, then?

'I really appreciate you coming over,' I add.

Imogen stops and looks back at me. 'One more thing.'

My pulse skips. 'Yes?'

'Thank you for being brave enough to start the ball rolling.' Her lips form a half-smile as she gives a curt nod.

I'm not sure exactly what she means by that, but I return the gesture and say goodbye.

Chapter 85

BETH

Now

Julia rushes up to me as soon as I reach nursery at three. 'I thought you'd come with Adam to pick up the girls?'

'Why?' I narrow my eyes into a question.

'Well, you know – seeing as you two are a thing now.' I half expect her to give me a nudge and a wink, but her gaze remains stony.

'We're not "a thing", Julia,' I say, tutting. Her posse are all looking over at us. I suspect Julia is asking the questions all of them want the answers to; they've just made her do the asking.

'But you're staying with him at his place, aren't you?'

'I was there for a couple of nights, yes – but I'm home again now. He was being a good friend and helping us out because I was afraid of being on my own. You know, with the threats and the journalists.' I'm angry at myself for over-explaining.

'You could've stayed with me,' she says.

'Really? Having two extra people in your house would've been a real challenge. Remember how frantic you were when you had Poppy over?'

She bristles. 'Well, yes. But still. I wouldn't have turned you away now, would I?'

'Thank you, that's very kind of you, Julia. I'll remember that in future. Although I'm rather hoping I won't be run out of my own house again.'

'Hmm,' she says, her eyebrows rising. 'The trial is coming up. I don't think it's over yet.'

'The trial will prove Tom guilty. He'll be in prison and I'll be free to carry on my life with Poppy, here in Lower Tew, doing what I love.' It's a pretty sickly speech, I think, once I've finished. But I wanted to make it clear.

Julia leans in closer, whispering in my ear, 'Don't worry, your secret is safe with me.'

'What secret?'

'Don't you remember telling me?' Her eyes shine with what I assume to be mischievousness. Or is that a flash of malice? I didn't tell Julia anything even slightly secretive. Why would I? I frown, and silently shake my head.

'You had consumed rather a lot of alcohol,' she says. Her stare is fixed. My insides quiver. What is she saying? She was the one who drank the most, not me.

'Not really, Julia. You polished off the second bottle, if I remember rightly.'

She shoots me a curious look. 'You really don't remember, do you?'

'Obviously not, Julia, or we wouldn't be having this conversation,' I say, annoyance tipping my tone into sarcasm.

'Oh, Beth,' she says. '*I* didn't have the second bottle. *You* did. Not that it matters – don't worry.' She lays a hand on my arm. 'We both shared a lot that night.'

My mind whirls. Is she right? Did I really have the bottle of Prosecco? Not her, like I thought? My mother's face swims into my mind. Shit.

I decide I'd best play it cautiously. 'Well, if I told you a secret, then I assume it'll stay that way?'

Julia smiles and turns her back, walking back to the yummy mummies without answering me.

What the hell did I say to her that night?

Chapter 86

BETH

Now

My body feels heavy but restless today, like my internal organs are itching and the only way to alleviate it is to keep moving. The awful events are taking their toll physically as well as mentally. And I can't get Julia's words out of my mind. They're especially menacing now I know who the car in the spitting incident was registered to. I've kept the knowledge it was registered to one Julia Bennington to myself and informed the police officer from Banbury I don't wish to press charges. I've never seen Julia's car, so I hadn't even dreamt she could be behind it when Adam told me the owner was female. I've no idea who the man was – it most definitely wasn't her husband. I think it might have been her brother, but I'm not going to ask her.

Right now, it's the news which holds my attention. The remains of a woman's body have been found. The grim discovery is already being linked with Tom. They haven't released the victim's name; they only say that her identity has been confirmed and her family have been informed.

But I know.

More will follow, they say.

My phone rings and I immediately expect it to be reporters. I nearly hit the decline button, but it's Maxwell. I let it ring a few more times, debating whether to let it go to voicemail. He was very off with me during the previous two calls – abrupt and business-like. Likely due to my part in all this. I don't suppose he imagined that the wife of the accused would help the police secure such damning proof.

I answer it. It's to tell me the latest updates, he says, about the evidence against Tom. He is downbeat; his tone is flat, which leads me to mirror it. It's a depressing conversation.

'Alongside the evidence you were aware of, *Beth*,' he says, in such a way as to leave me in no doubt he's angry with me, 'I need to inform you of what else the police have in order to adequately prepare us all for the trial.'

'Before you go on, Maxwell, I want to say something.'

He gives an audible sigh. 'Right, go on,' he says.

I haven't prepared for this conversation, so my speech is scattered with pauses and *umm*ing and *ah*ing. But he seems to get my point, that I hadn't *meant* to sabotage Tom's chances of getting off – it wasn't intentional, it was just that I'd become so stressed and confused, and the police backed me into a corner which I'd struggled to get out of again. 'I crumbled, Maxwell. It was all too much,' I say through my tears.

He mumbles a bit, then carries on as though I've not

spoken. But his words seem softer; his hard edges are smoothed. I settle back on the sofa and listen to his monotone voice as he explains the evidence. He would make a great hypnotherapist.

'The forensics found blood stains at Katie Williams' flat—'

'Really? After all this time?'

'Yes, Beth,' he says. 'Even when someone attempts to wash blood away, traces can be found. And originally the hallway floor wasn't carpeted – once they lifted it, they found it.'

'That's where Tom threw the paperweight that killed her,' I say.

'Yes, *that* appears to corroborate what you say Tom told you. But there's more.'

'What do you mean?' I'm suddenly nervous. Tom said he'd thrown it to prevent Katie leaving; that she'd died there and he'd left her, afraid of what he'd done.

'The blood trailed from the hallway to another room, which is likely to have been Katie's bedroom at the time. But there wasn't enough blood, they reckon, for them to believe it was a life-threatening injury.'

This information barrels at me. It isn't how Tom described what happened. 'So, what you're saying is, Tom hadn't killed her? He'd just injured her and she managed to crawl to her room?'

'Not quite.'

'What, then?'

'Initial post-mortem results show a fractured hyoid bone. Indicative of strangulation.'

My hand unconsciously goes to my own throat. Christ, Tom strangled her too.

It was no accident.

For a moment I'm shocked, and then I'm angry. Angry he lied. Again. But then my emotions settle. I have to be honest with myself, if nobody else: this is what I expected. Deep down, I had always known it was no accident. Nor Phoebe's death. And Natalia's death wasn't a sex game gone too far either. He'd strangled her to kill her. He'd meant to murder them all.

I really have had a lucky escape.

Strangely detached, I ask Maxwell how Tom is bearing up. I don't know why.

'As you'd expect, given the circumstances. And although he hasn't been told you were the one to divulge the where-abouts of the body, he will of course know it was you, Beth.'

'Yes. I'm aware of that. Tell him I'm sorry, but I did what I had to do. What any good mother would.'

Chapter 87

BETH

Four months later

With the huge amount of circumstantial evidence, the forensic files and the DNA profile secured from Katie Williams' burial site, together with her mobile phone – complete with Tom's fingerprints – the jury only took three hours to deliberate. It'd felt more like three days. They returned a unanimous guilty verdict.

To say I was relieved didn't come close.

But seeing Tom in the dock was much more traumatic than I'd anticipated.

The way he looked at me had made me shudder.

Hatred. Those beautiful peacock-blue eyes were dark, and completely void of love. I've betrayed him more than anyone else in his life; even his parents. And that's the message he asked Maxwell to convey.

I'll have to live with that.

* * *

'Well done, Beth. I'm so proud of you. You're the strongest person I know.' Adam envelops me in his arms, and I stay there for a moment, cocooned in this safe, comfortable embrace. Having Adam here today has meant the world to me. At the beginning, he'd been cautious about us being seen together, about people gossiping, and so we'd conducted our relationship in private; we didn't want to rock the boat by flaunting it. But here he is, openly at my side. He couldn't bear to think of me alone in the court-room, he'd said. His need to support me outweighed his concern about wagging tongues. Although, of course, we're still being careful because we have the girls to think about.

Raised voices bring me back to the here and now. There are crowds of people outside the Crown Court waiting for me to walk out, and to bombard me with more questions.

'We'd better get this over with,' I say, giving him a squeeze, and then I release myself from his grasp. We leave the reception area of the court and walk outside. We don't hold hands. The noise surges as I open the door, and grows as I make my way down the steps through the archway towards the waiting cameras.

'How does it feel to be the one to put your own husband behind bars?'

Flashes. Groping. Pushing.

'What is it like being the wife of a serial killer, Beth?'

Hands too close. Lenses in my face.

'What are you going to do now?'

I almost look up.

This final question is the easiest to answer – and as much as I'd like to respond, I know I can't tell them. I

351

chew on my lip, tuck my chin down onto my chest, and allow Adam to drag me by the arm to the waiting cab.

'If this is how people react every time you step outside, Beth, I'm going to have to rethink being your boyfriend,' Adam jokes, as the car makes its way through the throng of people.

'I think a quieter life is preferable, don't you?' I say.

'Plan A still a go, then?' He smiles at me.

I nod, then when we're far enough away from photographers and film crews, I slide up to him and we kiss.

'Thanks so much for having the girls, Constance.'

'Oh, you're welcome, Adam. Always a delight to have Jess. And Poppy kept me entertained with her animal stories,' Constance says, laughing. 'She is quite the little storyteller, isn't she?'

I refrain from saying she takes after her father. 'She is! I see a future in writing for her,' I say, instead.

'I'm going to miss Jess. And you, of course, Adam.' Her eyes glisten with tears.

'I promise we'll visit, Constance. And anyway, we'll both be back to sort out house sales. And Beth will be checking in on Poppy's Place.' Adam puts his arm over Constance's shoulders and gives a gentle squeeze. 'We will miss you, though, won't we Jess?'

Jess wraps her arms around Constance's legs and says she will. 'But I really want to see the sea!' she beams.

Adam's parents retired to Devon, and after much discussion we're convinced that the only way of being together, happily, with no interference, is to move out of Lower Tew. Away from the stares and gossip – free from the constraints of Tom's notoriety and Camilla's ghost. Not

352

that she was in any way haunting us – it was more that other people were reluctant to let her go; to let Adam move on without putting in their two-penn'orth.

Particularly as he was choosing to move on with the wife of a serial killer.

Adam showed me the photos of his parents' house in its wonderful seaside location and it immediately felt right. Their place isn't huge, Adam had said, but they would accommodate us on a short-term basis until we found something else. In some ways everything had happened quickly between us – some might say we rushed – but in other ways, time had slowed, and each step we made felt precise and planned.

When he'd suggested Devon, I didn't hesitate. It made perfect sense.

'I can work from home, but I don't know what you'll do about the café, though?' he'd said.

I did.

Lucy will make the perfect manager.

So, we're doing what we have to do in order to be together.

'How do you feel now it's properly over?' Adam says, handing me a champagne flute – this time filled with the real thing.

'Cheers,' I say. 'Here's to new beginnings.' We clink glasses. 'I'm feeling relieved. I'm feeling lucky. But it's at a price, isn't it? Those poor women.' I lower my gaze.

'You must never blame yourself – do you hear me? You didn't know in time to save them. And when you did find out, you had to keep quiet to save yourself. You were really brave to tell the detective about the sweatshirt. We all make choices, Beth – we don't always like all of them. Some things are for survival.'

'Yeah, you're right. Thank you.' I note he doesn't mention my knowledge of the whereabouts of Katie's body. I know he understands my having been reluctant to take that information to the police, and even though I'd explained how it was more of a hunch than certain knowledge, I do think he feels awkward about me keeping it quiet once Tom was already in custody. I'm hoping now we won't ever need to discuss it.

'Now, drink up – we've a whole bottle to get through.'

'A couple of glasses is fine, thanks. Let Constance have the rest.' Another thing I need to change in my life is my alcohol consumption. It can get me into trouble. I've come to the uncomfortable conclusion I'm going down a similar path to my mother. Julia's comments about me having necked the second bottle of Prosecco the night she came over made me panic. And I'd clearly said more than I should've. I must've let something slip. Hopefully nothing too damning . . .

I need to make a fresh start for me and Poppy with Adam and Jess. I need to distance myself from everything that's happened.

Chapter 88

TOM

Now

Who the hell did she think she was? Sitting there, holier than thou – confidently eyeing the jury as she spouted lie after lie.

Never once did I control her. And manipulation? Bull. *She* is the master manipulator, not me. For a year after I told her about everything, she pretended to stand by me – promised she'd stay with me and get rid of that sweat-shirt – and all the while she was planning to send me down. I can't believe it.

'All I want is a secure family, to be good parents to Poppy,' she'd said. How does me getting sent to prison fit with that? Stupid bitch. I did everything for her and Poppy. I put them first every time.

The cell clanks shut behind me. I'm no longer on remand. I'm now a convicted criminal.

A serial killer.

There's some kudos in that label, I guess. It might go some way to ensuring I'm not messed with in this place.

But for life? My mind can't comprehend it yet. The judge – a bloody woman of course – gave me a whole life order.

Here until I die.

All because of Beth.

The betrayal cuts deep: I feel it in the pit of my stomach; I feel it in my heart. Every limb is heavy with it.

I sit on the bed and look at each of the four walls in turn. My life now is destined to be as dull and empty as they are.

I couldn't care less about Beth – she's hurt me too much. But as I lie down and stare at the ceiling, I wonder about Poppy. Will Beth tell her where I am? And eventually what I did? I suppose when she's old enough, Poppy will be able to Google me and learn the truth anyway. Technology has a lot to answer for.

I still don't get it, though. Why would Beth split our family up? She believed me that the deaths of Phoebe and Katie were accidental. And she was adamant we had to keep being a normal, happy family to ensure Poppy never grew up without a father, like she had. Or an abusive one, like I'd had.

What changed her mind?

Chapter 89

BETH

Now

It's been three weeks since the trial and we're due to leave for Teignmouth later. I just need to do one last thing before we go.

It's 8.30 a.m. and I'm at the visitors' centre for the second and final time. I'm here a full forty-five minutes beforehand to ensure I can go through all the security palaver, get my visit done and get back to Lower Tew for around lunchtime. We're planning to leave at two. Adam is currently loading his car with the first lot of luggage. He'll be hiring a van for the second trip, then once we're settled in our own house, which we're going to rent short-term, we'll organise for the rest to be brought and put into storage. I'm excited and terrified at the same time. It seems to have taken an age to have reached this point.

I don't want anything to get in the way now.

Once I'm through the processing stage along with the other visitors, I'm patted down and checked for drugs and other contraband. The female officer makes no effort to converse with me, which suits me fine. She sighs a lot, and even huffs loudly. She doesn't appear to want to be here any more than I do.

This isn't something I *want* to do. I need to. It's about closing the book on my previous life before I can begin another.

The door is unlocked by an officer and I walk forward into the visiting hall, my heart thumping hard.

I'm about to visit a convicted murderer.

My husband, the serial killer.

'I wasn't going to leave my cell,' he says as he sits in front of me.

'So, why did you?'

'I wanted to see you one last time. Assuming that's the reason for your visit. To say goodbye.'

My eyes narrow in confusion. I wasn't expecting him to realise that was my intention, but maybe it was obvious, given I have only come here once before.

'We've been married for seven years, Beth. I do know you.' He smiles. It doesn't reach his eyes. For now, I refrain from telling him I've already seen a solicitor to begin divorce proceedings.

With my head bowed, I fiddle with the edge of my t-shirt, rolling it up and letting it unravel, then rolling it again.

'Now you're here, aren't you going to speak?' Tom asks, his head lowering to catch my eye. 'Aren't you going to tell me how sorry you are for fucking me over?' His voice is a harsh whisper. I imagine his eyes are filled with hatred, but I can't meet his gaze. I feel like a scolded child. In some ways I do want to apologise, but I bite the inside of my cheek to stop me saying it. He's here because of his actions, not mine.

'You didn't really give me a choice, Tom,' I finally say.

'Oh? Really? I rather think I did. I told you about Phoebe and Katie. You knew, and you promised to stand by me. You could've left then. Gone to the police, anything. But you stayed. And we carried on as normal. For a whole year, Beth. You were the perfect wife and mother for that entire time. Why suddenly change your mind?'

'I didn't want that life. I was afraid of what might come next. We had no security – it might have all blown up in our faces at any time. I was continually looking over my shoulder, wondering when it'd all come out. Because I knew it would. It had to. Nothing stays buried forever.'

'Especially if you give them the fucking *location*.' Hurt and anger combine in his tone and his facial expression contorts as his words are propelled through his clenched teeth.

'I was right, though, wasn't I? You and that . . . *whore*! You killed again, Tom. And no doubt you'd have continued to act out your . . . your awful, twisted urges, until you murdered another innocent woman. Maybe even me!'

'I did that *for you*, Beth. To keep you safe.'

'No. Don't you dare,' I say. Spittle lands on the table between us. 'You can't blame me for what you did.'

'You said you loved me. You took an oath: for better, for worse. I trusted you.'

'And I trusted you, too. Once. But not any longer. How can I?'

359

'I would never have hurt you. But you've really hurt me.'

There's nothing I can say to make my betrayal easier on him, I realise. 'What's done is done,' I say instead. Silence falls as we both cast our eyes around the room rather than focus on each other. I want to leave now. I swivel in my chair, about to get up, but his words cause me to freeze.

'Nice and cosy with the widower, I see.' He gives a false, mocking laugh. 'I saw him in the court. You might've been trying to make it look like you weren't together, but I could tell, Beth.'

I don't like talking about Adam. 'Well, as you always told me, you have to keep looking forward. So that's what I did. What I'm doing now.' I give him a sarcastic smile and add, 'I needed a replacement.'

'Let's hope you made the right decisions, then. For Poppy's sake.'

'She can't have a worse father than you,' I say, to hurt him.

'Strange how things work out. Isn't it? I mean . . . my actions may well have benefited you, in the end.'

'Really? I don't see how you can look at it that way. Women have died, Tom. You took them away from their families, their friends. Destroyed lives.'

He doesn't say anything for a while, seemingly taking in my statement.

'Yes, true. And it was a shame about Camilla's *accidental* death, eh?' He smirks, giving a knowing nod of his head. He turns and raises his arm to the closest officer.

'I'm finished here,' he says. 'Goodbye, Beth.'

I'm left open-mouthed as he walks away.

Chapter 90

BETH

Now

We sing songs on the long drive down, the car laden with as much as we could fit in. Excitement exudes from the kids, and it's contagious.

'Oh my God, I can't wait to be able to open the curtains every morning to a sea view,' I say, laying a hand on Adam's thigh as he drives.

We're heading towards mine and Poppy's future. It's so important to me to ensure Poppy doesn't have to go through anything like I did; that she has a safe and secure upbringing. With luck, she won't have memories of the earlier blip: a few memories of Tom, but she won't recall that her father, who she loved, was a serial killer. I'll do my utmost to prevent her ever finding out.

A shiver runs down my back. It's been a challenging time. But, I remind myself, it *had* to come to this – Tom had to go to prison so that I was free to rebuild our lives.

Adam will be a better father to Poppy in the long term. And she has Jess now, too – and who knows, maybe another child is on the way. I lay a hand over my belly.

The sun is high over Teignmouth Pier. We're skimming pebbles and building sandcastles while the girls squeal with delight. I've finally found perfection. It does exist. And it's right here, with my Poppy, Adam and Jess.

I knew I had chosen right – I was sure from the moment I set eyes on Adam that he was the one. I was confident he would make the perfect husband and father. There'd been a lightning bolt when he looked at me as I served Camilla at the café that first time. I believe in sparks, and we definitely had those in abundance. But of course, Camilla was the perfect wife and mother. I knew it wouldn't be easy.

But it wasn't impossible, either. Nothing is, if you're determined enough.

What was it that Alexander, Tom's boss, had said? 'I had a feeling a determined woman like yourself wouldn't take any of this lying down.' And he was quite right. Once Tom opened up and told me what he'd done, it was just a matter of time. I had to act quickly to begin planning a new life – there was much to be done before I could leave him. I was careful to slot in each bit in just the right place; it had to be done in the correct order. If I didn't proceed with care, my plan wouldn't work out and I'd be left alone.

Or become one of his victims.

Now, though, I realise Tom wouldn't have killed me. That's why he'd been seeing the sex worker – so he could release the pent-up tension and act out the fantasies I was unwilling to allow. Still, even if I'd known that, I would've carried on plotting my escape. Being Tom's wife was too risky.

When I'd found Katie's email account on Tom's iPad, I'd taken the opportunity to read everything Tom had sent pretending to be her. Why were her father and friends falling for it? The tone was so off – and the excuses for why she wasn't coming home, why she hadn't kept in regular contact, were flimsy.

Tom was shocked when the police came looking for him that Monday evening – he'd looked so fearful as the detective asked for his help relating to a murder. But he didn't ever suspect me. I'd sent an email to Katie's father under the guise of being a worried friend. I'd gone to an internet café and used a new email address so it wouldn't be traced back to me. After I told him her emails seemed wrong, somehow, like they weren't even from Katie, he finally did some digging. He emailed Katie several times, but I deleted them before Tom could send a reply. It was enough to allow his suspicions to grow, and that's what led him to the police.

DC Imogen Cooper's parting comment the day she left my cottage made me realise she knew. 'Thanks for being brave enough to start the ball rolling,' she'd said. I am grateful she didn't make a thing of it. Grateful she didn't dig too deeply.

Now, I only hope that no one else does, either. With me out of the picture, maybe Julia will get on with her life; find a new best friend and forget all about me, and the secret I shared. My drunken confession to Julia came to me in the early hours of this morning, as I lay next to Adam, staring at him, thrilled to be finally at peace. How

I'd told her I thought Adam was a wonderful father, how I'd had a connection with him the very first time we'd met. That it was a shame we weren't both single. I'd told her how lucky I thought Camilla was. And how jealous I was of her perfect life.

'Jealous enough to do something about it?' she'd asked.

'Of course not,' I'd lied. 'But I think I always secretly hoped an opportunity would arise in the future. Now it looks as though that time might have come. Good things come to those who wait.'

I feel absolutely sure I wouldn't have told her anything more; but then I never imagined telling her that much. And maybe what I said was enough to make her question everything. I can only pray her memory is blurry; dulled by the Prosecco. Even if that wasn't the case, what can she do? There's no evidence of foul play.

Chapter 91

BETH

Fifteen months ago

It takes a lot of courage to do something as awful as I'm about to do.

I lay out the fresh cookies and other baked goods along the glass counter at Poppy's Place, ready to open at bang on nine a.m. I pop the special butterscotch and oatmeal cookie on a plate and place it underneath the counter until she comes in. Then I'll slip it into a paper bag and ask her to try it when she gets home. It's made from the recipe we chatted about last week, along with one more ingredient that means I would usually display this type of cookie with a label: *contains nuts*.

Camilla comes in at ten thirty. She's been running, by the looks of her – her hair is swept up in a ponytail, a sheen of sweat covers her face and arms. She's wearing Lycra running shorts and a t-shirt, so tight they show off her every curve. I note the bumbag attached around her waist. She's ever so slightly out of breath as she approaches me.

'Morning, Beth,' she says as she unclips her bumbag and takes a seat at the table closest to the counter. She plonks the bag to one side on the table. Bubbles of apprehension begin rising inside me. Will I really be able to go through with this?

'Hi, Camilla – good run?' I catch the wobble of my voice and clear my throat to hide it.

'Usual. I loathe running,' she says, 'but needs must. Can't keep eating your fabulous cookies if I don't put in some hard work!' She flashes me a wide grin.

'True,' I say, forcing my lips to turn upwards. 'No gain without a little pain, eh? Can I get you a latte?'

'Yes, please. No cookies today, though. I'm trying to be good.' Camilla taps her belly. It's as flat as a pancake, but I don't say so.

I make sure no one is within earshot when I speak again. 'Perhaps one for the road then? I've baked some butterscotch ones especially for you to try.'

'Oh, using the recipe I mentioned?'

'The very one.'

'Well I'll definitely take a few to go – I'm glad you've tried the new recipe. You'll have to write down the exact ingredients for me so I can have a go at making them, too. Not to try and do you out of business, of course,' she gives me a coy smile. 'But Adam adores cookies, and I'm sure Jess will have a nibble too. And it's safer all round if I bake the nut-free ones.'

The knot inside my stomach intensifies.

'Let's see if you like it first! I've only got the one today – I'm afraid we liked them a little too much and Tom and

366

Poppy devoured the rest. But of course, if you enjoy it, I'll be baking them regularly. And no doubt you will be too.' I hope the reason I only have the one sounds believable. I can't have her taking more than one and there being evidence left over.

We chat, in between me serving the odd customer, about the girls. About our husbands. It's a little awkward talking about Tom – I'm still feeling blindsided by his confession – but I try to be as natural as possible. I don't want to raise any red flags with Camilla; not when I'm so close. When she talks so warmly about Adam, my heart rate increases; a hard lump presses against my throat. I'm nervous for the future. There was a spark when Adam and I first met in here, but that doesn't mean he'll find solace in my arms once his beloved wife is dead. I could be doing this for nothing.

On the other hand, I could get exactly what I want, if I'm patient. It's not a quick fix by any means, but it does give me a way out eventually. That's the best I can hope for in this hideous situation.

In addition to her latte, I ply Camilla with a freshly squeezed glass of orange juice – a large one, on the house – and sit down beside her again. I need her to visit the bathroom. While her attention is taken by a noise outside, I surreptitiously take the bumbag from the table and place it on the chair beside me. I don't want her to take it to the bathroom with her if she goes.

This part is out of my control. If she doesn't leave me alone with her bag, I won't be able to take her EpiPen out of it. Then, even if she does get a reaction at home alone, she'll just give herself a shot and everything will be fine.

'Jess is with your friend today, isn't she?' I need to

check – as much as I need Camilla out of the way, I don't want a two-year-old put in danger through my actions.

'Yes, I've got a bit of time to myself today, thanks to Constance. Thought I'd do some reading. I have to catch up on the book, seeing as it was my choice for book club. Wouldn't look good if I couldn't discuss it at my own club, would it? Are you still good with me holding it here next week?'

'Sure. I'll be here on hand as always, to wait on you all.' There's a hint of bitterness in my voice, which I quickly rectify by adding how much I enjoy listening to them talk books.

'You should join us,' she says, brightly. 'Properly, I mean. I don't know why I haven't asked you before. The next book after this one is *To Kill A Mockingbird*. So many of us read it for school, but never since.'

I gulp the growing lump a bit further down my throat. The book title gives me a chill. Nerves and my guilty conscience mix. All this time I'd been trying to infiltrate her group, and now she invites me in, on the day I'm trying to kill her. Maybe I should back out; try another time. It's not working, anyway.

'And with that in mind, I'd best be going.' Camilla jumps up, and I see her gaze move fleetingly over the table.

Shit. She's looking for her bag.

'Might pop to the loo before I head off,' she says, and heads towards the back of the café.

Oh. My. God. This is my moment.

I'm strangely reluctant, now it's come to it.

You're doing this for Poppy. For her future, I remind myself.

There are two customers – one is attentively painting

a plate, the other is gazing out the front window, watching the street.

Must do it now.

I take the bag, unzip it, and pull out the EpiPen. I quickly get up and walk behind the counter to hide it. A noise to my left makes me jump, and I fumble and drop it on the ground at my feet.

Fuck. She's back.

With the side of my foot, I scoot it forwards, underneath the counter.

'I'll take a chocolate chip cookie too, please, Beth,' Camilla says.

My legs feel shaky; I'm light-headed – that was so close. What on earth would I have said to get out of that if she'd caught me?

'Sure,' I say, my voice sounding as though I'm being strangled.

'You okay?'

'Frog in my throat,' I say, putting my fingers up to my neck. 'Right – one choc-chip and one special butterscotch and oatmeal coming up.' I watch as she moves to the table to attach her bumbag around her waist, and then slip the cookie from the plate beneath the counter. I put it in a separate bag to the chocolate one.

'Thanks so much, Beth. I'm looking forward to this.' She flashes me a perfect grin before turning away.

My stomach twists as I watch her walk out.

What happens now is out of my hands. But that might well be the last time I see Camilla Knight.

When I'm closing up, I duck down to retrieve the EpiPen. I'm not sure what to do with it. Bin it? Leave it somewhere obvious and say she left it behind? I walk to the table we were at and get on my hands and knees. If Camilla had dropped the pen when sitting here, it could conceivably have rolled under the counter-front – there's a small gap running along the bottom. The counter is built-in – it doesn't get moved, just cleaned around – so no one would find it. But if they did, it would look like she'd accidentally dropped it.

Perfect.

Just an accident.

With Camilla out of the picture, I knew I'd have a little time to wait before I could put the rest of my plan into play. I had to ensure Tom was out of my life so that Adam and I were free to make a life together.

A new family unit.

Loving, safe and secure.

As I had told Maxwell, I did what I had to do. Just like any good mother would.

Epilogue

I've made my peace with God. I'm in here for the long haul, so no point licking my wounds like an injured bird forever – I must get on with prison life. There's no outlet for my fantasies in here, mind. Unless I fancy sexual encounters with one of the lads. I guess I can't rule that out. Life is an awfully long time.

The visiting order came as a shock. I was amazed when I saw the name on the paper. Curiosity has led me to the visits hall today. It's humid, the air thick as I walk towards the table, eyes narrowed.

'This is a surprise,' I say, as I take a seat opposite her.

'I can imagine.' She sips from a bottle of water, her full, luscious lips curled around it. I close my eyes a second to picture those lips elsewhere.

I snap them open – now isn't the time. I'll save those images for later. 'What do you want?'

She shifts awkwardly in the plastic chair. Her hot, bare legs against it cause a squeaking sound. Her hair is shiny;

silky smooth. I have an urge to reach out and run my fingertips through it.

She lets out a shuddering sigh. 'I'm . . . not sure I should be here, really.' She casts a wary glance around at the other visitors.

'Don't be nervous. You've obviously got something important to say.'

'I think there's something you should know,' she says, her voice no more than a husky whisper. She lays her hands flat on the table, her perfectly manicured, red nails splaying out in front of me. For a moment, I'm mesmerised by them. I imagine them clawing at my own hands, trying to fend me off; trying to stop me from strangling the life from her.

'Go on,' I say, my intrigue heightened.

'Okay. You need to hear me out. I know this will sound . . . well, far-fetched.'

'You'd be surprised,' I say. 'Just tell me.'

'I believe that Beth planned to get together with Adam Knight. When you were first in custody, she told me how she felt about him.'

'She told me, too,' I say.

'Did she? Did she mention Camilla?'

I have a feeling where this is going, but for now, I don't respond.

'I think she may have had something to do with Camilla's death.'

I raise my eyebrows and let her continue.

'The way Beth acted so devastated when you were arrested, but then began seeing more of Adam almost immediately – I get the feeling she was seeking more than a shoulder . . . and in hindsight, well – it's all very suspicious.'

I nod slowly. It's something I'd considered too – and from the look on Beth's face when I brought up Camilla's *accidental* death, I'd felt more certain. Now, hearing this, my suspicions are confirmed. I'd thought Beth was cutting off her nose to spite her face by handing over evidence. I couldn't understand why she'd put Poppy's future happiness in jeopardy. But she wasn't, was she? She'd already figured out how to get rid of me and set up with Adam. She obviously saw me as too risky. She believed he was better than me. He was someone who could offer lifelong security for her and Poppy.

The perfect man.

Only he was married.

'Thank you for coming here to tell me,' I say, smiling.

'The problem is, I don't have any evidence.'

I swallow hard, then sit forward, ensuring I have Julia's eye contact. She blushes. I still have that power. 'We can work on that.'

Acknowledgements

Thanks to my agent, Anne Williams, and the team at Avon, HarperCollins for making the writing of *The Serial Killer's Wife* possible. Huge thanks to my editor, Katie Loughnane, for her fabulous input, unwavering support, encouragement, and expert editing skills. I have thoroughly enjoyed working with her on this book. My thanks also to Phoebe Morgan and Sabah Khan for their input, Felicity Radford for her keen eye and helping with the timeline and aspects of police procedural, and all those people behind the scenes who work tirelessly to get books into the hands of readers.

The publishing industry and booksellers have had to adapt to new ways of working since the onset of the COVID-19 pandemic and I would like to thank them for continuing to ensure books find readership during such challenging times. The planning of this book took place prior to the pandemic, with much of the writing being done in the early months, therefore I do not refer to it, nor do any of the COVID-safe practices we have now become accustomed to, feature.

Thank you, as ever, to my family and friends for their ongoing support and to reviewers and book bloggers for their enthusiasm and the time they give to help promote new books. Most of all, thank you to those who read *The Serial Killer's Wife* – I hope you enjoy it and that it offers some escapism.